YOUNG SHERLOCK HOLMES: BLACK ICE

YOUNG SHERLOCK HOLMES: BLACK ICE

Andrew Lane

First published in Great Britain in 2011
by Macmillan Children's Books
This Large Print edition published 2012
by AudioGO Ltd
by arrangement with
Macmillan Children's Books

ISBN: 978 1445 886824

British Library Cataloguing in Publication Data available

Printed and bound in Great Britain by
MPG Books Group Limited

Dedicated to David Richardson, Justin Richards and Jac Farrow for enduring my temper tantrums while this book was being written; Ruth Alltimes and Katharine Smales for looking after me in Bologna, and to Louis Alcock, who was born at about the same time as this book was finished.

And with grateful acknowledgements to Philip Ardagh for asking penetrating questions about Jeremy Brett, and the students on the Lancaster University MA course on Children's Literature for not asking penetrating questions about Jeremy Brett.

CHAPTER ONE

Sunlight sparkled on the surface of the water, sending daggers of light flashing towards Sherlock's eyes. He blinked repeatedly, and tried to keep his eyelids half-closed to minimize the glare.

The tiny rowing boat rocked gently in the middle of the lake. Around it, just past the shoreline, the grassy ground rose in all directions, covered in a smattering of bushes and trees. It was as if it were located in the middle of a green bowl, with the cloudless blue of the sky forming a lid across the top.

Sherlock was sitting in the bows of the boat, facing backwards. Amyus Crowe was sitting in the stern, his weight causing his end of the boat to sink lower into the water and Sherlock's to rise higher out of it. Crowe held a split-cane fishing rod out over the lake's surface. A thin line connected the tip of the rod with a small clump of feathers which floated on the surface of the water: a lure that, to a hungry fish, might look like a fly.

Between them, in the bottom of the rowing boat, sat an empty wicker basket.

'Why did you only bring one rod?' Sherlock asked, disgruntled.

'This ain't a day's fishin',' Crowe replied genially, eyes fixed on the floating lure, 'much as it may look like it. No, this is a lesson in life skills.'

'I should have guessed,' Sherlock muttered.

'Although it's also a way to get some dinner for me an' Virginia tonight,' Crowe conceded. 'Ah always, if possible, try to arrange that what ah do

1

serves several purposes.'

'So I just sit here?' Sherlock said. 'Watching you fish for your dinner?'

'That's about the size of it.' Crowe smiled.

'And is it going to take long?'

'Well, that depends.'

'On what?'

'On whether ah'm a good fisherman or not.'

'And what makes you a good fisherman?' Sherlock asked, knowing that he was playing into Crowe's hands but unable to stop himself.

Instead of answering Crowe wound the bone-handled brass reel at his end of the rod, expertly pulling the line in. The feathered lure jumped out of the water and hung suspended in the air, glittering droplets of water falling from it and striking the lake. He jerked the rod back. The line flew above his head, the lure blurring as it moved. He whipped the rod forward again, and the lure made a figure-of-eight shape against the blue sky as it flew over his head and hit the surface of the lake in a different location, making a small splash. He watched, smiling slightly as it drifted.

'Any good fisherman knows,' Crowe said, 'that fish react differently dependin' on the temperature and the time of year. Early mornin' in spring, for instance, fish won't bite at all. The water is cold and it don't heat up much, because the sun is low and its rays bounce off the water, so the fish are sluggish. Their blood, bein' cold and influenced by the surrounding environment, is flowing slowly. Wait 'til late mornin' or early afternoon an' things start to change. The fish will bite intermittently because the sun is shinin' on the water, warmin' it up and makin' them more lively. Of course, the wind will push the warmer surface water and the little midges an' stuff they feed on around, an' as a fisherman you got to follow that movement. No point in fishin' where the water is still cold or where there ain't any food. An' all that can change dependin' on the time of year.'

'Should I be taking notes?' Sherlock asked.

'You've got a head on your shoulders—use it. Memorize the facts.' He snorted, and continued: 'In winter, to take an example, the water's cold, maybe even iced up, an' the fish ain't movin' too fast. They're livin' off the reserves they built up in the autumn, by an' large. No good fishin' in the wintertime. Now—what have you learned so far?'

'All right.' Sherlock quickly went over the facts in his mind. 'In spring your best bet is early morning or late afternoon, and in winter you are better off heading for the market and buying something from the costermonger.'

Crowe laughed. 'A good summary of the facts, but think about what's *behind* the facts. What's the rule that *explains* the facts?'

Sherlock considered for a moment. 'The important thing is the temperature of the water, and the thing that drives the temperature of the water is how hot the sun is and whether it's shining straight down on the water or at an angle. Think about where the sun is, work out where the water is warm but not hot, and that's where you'll find the fish.'

'Quite right.'

The lure jerked slightly, and Crowe leaned forward, washed-out blue eyes unblinking beneath bushy grey eyebrows.

'Each fish has a different temperature which it

prefers,' he continued quietly. 'A good fisherman will combine his knowledge of the fish's preferred water temperature with his knowledge of the time of year, time of day and lake turnover conditions to work out which fish will be in a particular part of a lake at a particular time of the year.'

'This is all very interesting,' Sherlock said cautiously, 'but I'm not likely to take up fishing as a hobby. It seems to consist of a whole lot of sitting around waiting for something to happen. If I'm going to sit around for a long period of time, I'd rather have a good book in my hands than a fishing rod.'

'The point ah'm tryin' to make,' Crowe responded patiently, 'in my own countrified, homespun way is that, if you're tryin' to catch somethin', you need to go about it in a structured way. You need to know about the habits of your prey, and you need to know how those habits change dependin' on the local environment and circumstances. The lesson applies equally well to men as it does to fish. Men have their preferences, their preferred locations, at different times of day, and those preferences might be different if the sun's shinin' compared with when it's rainin', or if they're hungry compared with when they're full. You got to get to know your prey so you can anticipate where they will be. Then you can use a lure—just like this pretty collection of feathers ah tied together with cotton—somethin' they can't resist takin' a bite at.'

'I understand the lesson,' Sherlock said. 'Can we go back now?'

'Not yet. Ah still ain't got my dinner.' Crowe's gaze was moving around the surface of the lake,

4

looking for something. 'Once you know your prey and his habits, you got to look for the signs of his presence. He ain't just goin' to pop up an' announce himself. No, he's goin' to skulk around, bein' careful, and you gotta look for the subtle signs that he's there.' His eyes fixed on a patch of water some twelve feet away from the boat. 'For instance, look over there,' he said, nodding his head. 'What do you see?'

Sherlock stared. 'Water?'

'What else?'

He narrowed his eyes against the glare, trying to see whatever it was that Crowe had seen. For a moment, a small area of water seemed to dip slightly, like a wave in reverse. Just for a moment, though, and then it returned to normal. And once he knew what he was looking for, Sherlock saw more dips, more sudden and momentary occasions when the surface of the lake seemed to flex slightly.

'What *is* it?'

'It's called "suckin'",' Crowe replied. 'It happens when the fish—trout, in this case—hang nose-up just below the surface of the water, waitin' for insect nymphs to float by. Once they see one, they take a gulp of water, suckin' the nymph down with it. All you see on the surface is that little dip as the water is pulled down and the nymph is sucked below. And that, my friend, tells us where a trout is located.'

He tugged on his fishing rod so that the lure drifted across the surface of the lake, pulled by the line, until it passed through the area where Sherlock had seen the trout sucking nymphs down. Nothing happened for a moment, and then the lure suddenly jerked below the surface of the lake.

5

Crowe hauled on the rod, simultaneously winding the reel in as fast as he could. The water exploded upward in silvery droplets, in the centre of which writhed a fish. Its mouth was caught up in the hook which had been hidden inside the lure and its scales were mottled in brown. Crowe flicked his rod expertly upward and the fish virtually flew into the boat, where it flapped frantically. Holding on to the rod with one hand so that it didn't fall into the water, Crowe reached behind him with the other and pulled a wooden club from beneath his seat. One quick blow and the fish was still.

'So what have we covered today?' he asked genially as he detached the hook from the trout's mouth. 'Know the habits of your prey, know what bait he's likely to go for, and know what the signs are that he's in the vicinity. Do all that, and you've maximized your chances of a successful hunt.'

'But when am I ever likely to be hunting someone or something?' Sherlock asked, understanding the basics of the lesson but unsure how they applied to him. 'I know you used to be a bounty hunter, back in America, but I doubt I'll ever go into that profession. I'm more likely to end up as a banker or something.' Even as he said the words he felt his heart sink. The last thing in the world he wanted to do with his life was a boring desk job, but he wasn't sure what else there was for him.

'Oh, life's full of things you might want to catch,' Crowe said, throwing the fish into the basket and placing the wicker lid over the top. 'You might want to flush out investors for some moneymakin' scheme you've come up with. You might consider findin' yourself a wife at some stage. You might be trackin' down a man who owes you money. All kinds of reasons a soul might want to hunt someone down. The basic principles remain the same.' Glancing over at Sherlock from beneath his bushy eyebrows, he added: 'Based on previous experience, there's always the murderers and criminals you might come across during the course of your life.' He took hold of the fishing rod and flicked the lure back over his head in a figure-of-eight and into the water. 'And then, when all's said and done, there's always deer, boar and fish.'

With that he settled back with eyes half-closed and devoted himself to fishing for the next hour while Sherlock watched.

After two more fish had been caught, dispatched and thrown into the basket, Amyus Crowe set his rod down in the bows of the boat and stretched. 'Time to head back, ah think,' he announced. 'Unless you want to try it yourself?'

'What would I do with a fish?' Sherlock asked. 'There's a cook at my aunt and uncle's house. Breakfast and luncheon and dinner just arrive on the table without me having to worry about it.'

'Someone has to catch the animals to make the food,' Crowe said. 'And one day you might actually find yourself having to worry about where the next meal comes from.' He smiled. 'Or maybe you might want to surprise the lovely Mrs Eglantine with a nice plump trout for dinner.'

'I could slip it into her bed,' Sherlock muttered. 'Would that do?'

'Tempting,' Crowe laughed, 'but no, I don't think so.'

Crowe took the oars and rowed the boat back to the shore. After tying it to a post that had been set into the ground, he and Sherlock set off back to his cottage.

Their path led up the steep side of the bowl containing the lake. Crowe pushed on ahead, carrying the wicker basket. His large body made surprisingly little noise as he moved. Sherlock followed, tired now as well as bored.

They got to the ridge at the top of the slope, where the ground fell away steeply behind them and levelled out in front, and Crowe stopped to let Sherlock catch up.

'A point to note,' he said, gesturing down at the blue surface of the lake. 'If you're ever out huntin', don't be tempted to stop at a place like this, either to take in the view or to get a better look at the surroundin' terrain. Imagine what we look like to any animal in the forest, silhouetted here on the ridge. We can be seen for miles.'

Before Sherlock could say anything, Crowe started off again, pushing through the undergrowth. Sherlock wondered briefly how the man knew which way to go without a compass. He was about to ask, but instead tried to work it out himself. All Crowe had to go on was their surroundings. The sun rose in the east and set in the west, but that wasn't much help at lunchtime when the sun would be directly overhead. Or would it? A moment's thought and Sherlock realized that the sun would only be truly overhead at noon for places actually on the equator. For a country in the northern hemisphere, like England, the nearest point on the equator would be located directly south, and so the sun at noon would be south of a point directly overhead. That was probably how Crowe was doing it.

'And moss tends to grow better on the northern side of trees,' Crowe called over his shoulder. 'It's more shaded there, and so it's damper.'

'How do you do that?' Sherlock shouted.

'Do what?'

'Tell what people are thinking, and interrupt them just at the right moment?'

'Ah,' Crowe laughed. 'That's a trick ah'll explain some other time.'

Sherlock lost track of time as they walked on through the forest, but at one point Crowe stopped and crouched down, putting the basket down.

'What do you deduce?' he asked.

Sherlock crouched beside him. In the soft ground beneath a tree he saw a hoof print, small and heart-shaped.

'A deer went this way?' he ventured, trying to jump from what he saw to what he could work out based on what he saw.

'Indeed, but which way did it go and how old was it?'

Sherlock examined the print more closely, trying to picture a deer's hoof and failing.

'That way?' he said, pointing in the direction of the rounded part of the print.

'Other direction,' Crowe corrected. 'You're thinking of a horse's hoof, where the round bit is at the front. The sharp bit of a deer's hoof always points in the direction it is heading. And this one's a young 'un. You can tell by the small oval shapes behind the print. Those are made by the dewclaws.'

He looked around. 'See over there,' he said, nodding his head to one side. 'Can you make out a straight trail through the bushes and grass?'

Sherlock looked, and Crowe was right—there

was a trail, very faint, marked by the bushes and grasses being pushed to either side. It was about five inches across, he estimated.

'Deer move all day between the area they bed down in and their favourite watering hole, trying to find food,' Crowe said, still crouching. 'Once they find a safe route they keep usin' it until they get spooked by somethin'. And what does that tell you?'

'Prey tends to stick to the same habits unless disturbed?' Sherlock replied cautiously.

'Quite right. Remember that. If you're lookin' for a man who likes a drink, check the taverns. If you're lookin' for a man who likes a bet, check the racin' tracks. And everyone has to travel around somehow, so talk to cabbies and ticket inspectors— see if they remember your man.'

He straightened, picking the basket up again, and started off through the trees. Sherlock followed, glancing around. Now that Crowe had pointed out what to look for, he could see sets of different tracks on the ground: some deer, of various sizes, and some obviously something else— maybe wild boar, maybe badgers, maybe foxes. He could also see trails through the underbrush, where the bushes and grasses had been pushed to one side by moving bodies. What had previously been invisible was suddenly obvious to him. The same scene now had so much more in it to look at.

It took another half an hour to reach the gates of Holmes Manor.

'Ah'll take my leave of you here,' Crowe said. 'Let's pick up again tomorrow. Ah've got some more to teach you about trackin' and huntin'.'

'Do you want to come in for a time?' Sherlock

asked. 'I could get Cook to make a pot of tea, and one of the maids could gut and bone those fish for you.'

'Mighty accomodatin' of you,' Crowe rumbled. 'Ah believe ah will take advantage of that offer.'

Together they walked up the gravelled drive towards the impressive frontage of Holmes Manor. This time Sherlock was in the lead.

Without knocking, he pushed open the front door.

'Mrs Eglantine!' he called boldly.

A black shape detached itself from the shadows at the base of the stairs and slid forward.

'Young Master Sherlock,' the housekeeper answered in her dry-as-autumn-leaves voice. 'You seem to treat this house more like a hotel than the residence of your family.'

'And you seem to treat it as if you are a member of that family rather than a servant,' he retorted, voice cold but heart trembling. 'Mr Crowe will be taking afternoon tea with me. Please arrange it.' He stood waiting, uncertain whether she would take his orders or dismiss him with a cutting word. He had a feeling that she wasn't sure either, but after a moment she turned and moved towards the kitchens without saying anything.

He felt a sudden and irresistible urge to push things a bit, to needle the woman who had done so much to make his life uncomfortable over the past year.

'Oh,' he added, gesturing towards the wicker basket at Amyus Crowe's feet, 'and Mr Crowe has caught some fish. Be so good as to have someone gut them and bone them for him.'

Mrs Eglantine turned back, and the expression

on her face could have curdled milk and caused sheep to give birth prematurely. Her lips twisted as she attempted to force back something she was going to say. 'Of course,' she said finally, through gritted teeth. 'I will send someone up for the basket. Perhaps you would be so good as to leave it here and repair to the reception room.'

She seemed to melt back into the shadows.

'You should watch that woman,' Amyus Crowe said quietly. 'When she looks at you there is violence in her eyes.'

'I don't understand why my aunt and uncle tolerate her presence,' Sherlock replied. 'It's not as if she's a particularly good housekeeper. The other staff are so terrified by her that they can barely do their jobs properly. The scullery maids keep dropping dishes when she's around, their hands shake so much.'

'The subject would benefit from some further investigation,' Crowe mused. 'If, as you say, she's not a particularly good housekeeper then there must be some other compellin' reason why she's kept on, despite her vinegary personality. Perhaps your aunt and uncle are indebted to her, or to her family, in some manner, and this is a way of repayin' a debt. Or perhaps she's privy to some fact that your family would rather keep secret, and is blackmailin' herself into a cosy job.'

'I think Mycroft knows,' Sherlock said, remembering the letter his brother had sent him when he first arrived at Holmes Manor. 'I think he warned me about her.'

'Your brother knows a lot of things,' Crowe said with a smile. 'And the things he don't know generally ain't worth knowin' anyway.'

12

'You taught him once, didn't you?' Sherlock asked.

Crowe nodded.

'Did you take him out fishing as well?'

A laugh burst through Crowe's usually calm expression. 'Only the once,' he admitted, through chuckles. 'Your brother an' the great outdoors ain't exactly on speakin' terms. It's the first time and the last time ah've seen a man try and catch a fish by chasin' it into its natural environment.'

'He dived in after a fish?' Sherlock said, trying to imagine the scene.

'He fell in, tryin' to reel it in. He told me, as ah was haulin' him out, that he would never leave the safety of dry ground again, and if that dry ground was a paved city street then so much the better.' He paused. 'But if you ask him, he can still tell you the feedin' an' swimmin' habits of all the fish in Europe. He may have a dim view of physical exertion, but his mind is as sharp as a seamstress's bag of pins.'

Sherlock laughed. 'Let's go into the reception room,' he said. 'Tea will be on its way.'

The reception room was just off the main hall, at the front of the house. Sherlock threw himself into a comfortable chair while Crowe settled himself on a sofa large enough to take his considerable bulk. It creaked beneath his weight. Amyus Crowe was, Sherlock estimated, probably as heavy as Mycroft Holmes, but in Crowe's case it was solid bone and muscle.

A soft knock on the door heralded the appearance of a maid carrying a silver tray. On the tray were a pot of tea, two cups and saucers, a small jug of milk and a plate of cakes. Either Mrs

Eglantine was being unusually generous or one of the staff had decided to make the guest feel welcome.

There was also an envelope, white and narrow.

'A letter for you, sir,' the maid said without making eye contact with Sherlock. She set the tray down on a table. 'Will there be anything else?'

'No, thank you.'

As she left he reached out eagerly to take the envelope. He didn't get many letters at Holmes Manor, and when he did they were almost always from—

'Mycroft!'

'Is that a fact or a deduction?' Crowe asked.

Sherlock waved the envelope at him. 'I recognize the handwriting, and the postmark is Westminster, where he has his office, his lodgings and his club.'

He ripped the envelope open, pulling the flap from the grip of the blob of wax that held it firm.

'Look!' he said, holding the paper up. 'The letter is written on the headed stationery of the Diogenes Club.'

'Check the postmark on the envelope,' Crowe murmured. 'What time does it show?'

'Three thirty yesterday afternoon,' Sherlock said, puzzled. 'Why?'

Crowe gazed imperturbably at Sherlock. 'Mid-afternoon on a weekday, and he's at his club, writing letters, rather than at his office? Does that strike you as unusual behaviour for your brother?'

Sherlock thought for a moment. 'He once told me that he often walks across to his club for lunch,' he said after a moment. 'He must have written the letter over lunch and got the footman to post

14

it for him. The post would have been collected in the early afternoon, and the letter would have got to the sorting office for around three o'clock, then been stamped half an hour later. That's not suspicious, is it?'

Crowe smiled. 'Not in the slightest. Ah was merely tryin' to indicate that there's a whole lot of facts that can be deduced from a simple letter. If the postmark had been Salisbury rather than Westminster it would have been unusual, and would have prompted further questions. If we knew your brother never left his desk durin' the day, not even for lunch—an unlikely occurrence, ah have to admit—and yet the letterheaded stationery was from his club then that would have been unusual as well. You might have surmised that your brother had lost his job, or was sufficiently disturbed that he had not gone into work, or left early.'

'Or maybe he'd just taken some stationery from the Diogenes Club and was using it in his office,' Sherlock pointed out.

Crowe looked discomfited. 'Ah guess there's always an alternative explanation,' he growled.

Sherlock scanned the letter quickly, excitement growing as he read the words until he was almost at fever pitch.

My dear Sherlock,

I write in haste, as I am awaiting the arrival of a steak and kidney pudding and I wish to do it full justice before I return to my office.

I trust you are well, and that the various scars from your recent adventures have healed. I trust also that our aunt and uncle are well, and that our Mrs Eglantine is not proving too unpleasant.

You will be pleased to hear, I am sure, that arrangements have been satisfactorily concluded to allow your education to continue at Holmes Manor. The news that you will never have to return to Deepdene School will, I presume, not come as too much of a shock.

Amyus Crowe will continue to school you in the more practical and sporting aspects of life and Uncle Sherrinford has agreed to become responsible for your religious and literary education, which only leaves mathematics. I will ponder on that, and let you know when I have reached a decision. The aim, of course, will be to prepare you for university in a few years' time. We can discuss at some stage whether you have a preference for Oxford or Cambridge.

This morning, by the way, a letter arrived from our father. He must have posted it in India the moment he arrived, as it summarizes everything that happened to him on the voyage. I am sure that you would rather read the letter than have me tell you about it, and so I invite you to dine with me (at my club, naturally) tomorrow.

Please pass the invitation on to Mr Crowe: I have some details I wish to discuss with him about your education. The 9.30 a.m. train from Farnham will bring you to Waterloo in good time to meet me at 12 sharp.

I look forward to seeing you tomorrow, and to hearing all about the events that have befallen you since we last met.

Your loving brother,

Mycroft.

'Anything interestin'?' Amyus Crowe asked.

'We're going to London,' Sherlock replied, grinning.

CHAPTER TWO

Sherlock rode into Farnham that afternoon, through a light rain that left puddles on the roads and trickled down the back of his neck no matter how much he turned his collar up or tucked it in. He was riding the horse he had 'liberated' from Baron Maupertuis—the horse he still had to find a name for, if he ever did.

He just couldn't understand why people gave names to animals. The animals didn't care if they had names, or numbers, or nothing, and it implied a level of empathy and equality that shouldn't exist. Animals were animals and humans were humans.

As his horse splashed its way towards the market town, Sherlock found himself thinking about the strange difference between pets and animals. If you could eat a cow, in the form of beef, then why couldn't you eat a horse? There seemed to be no logical reason why not—as far as he knew, horse flesh wasn't poisonous or anything. Alternatively, if cats and dogs were off the menu then why weren't rabbits safe from being put in the stewpot? It didn't make any sense. Someone had drawn an arbitrary line through the animal kingdom, saying, 'All right, the ones over here you can eat to your heart's content, but the ones over there you take for walks, and stroke, and care for, and bury when they die.'

He wondered, as the water found its way through every gap in his clothes, whether other countries had the same illogical rules. Were there countries somewhere where the inhabitants ate horses and dogs, but maybe considered cows sacred? If there were, it indicated that the whole thing was just subjective, if not random, but if all countries made the same distinctions then maybe there was something about humans that meant they all considered cows as food and horses as friends.

He absently patted the neck of the horse he was riding. *Could* he ever eat it? Could he sit down to a juicy steak, knowing that a few hours earlier he'd been riding the animal it had come from? Logically, he didn't see why not, but in practice he could detect a little squeamishness in his mind. Maybe if he was starving. Maybe if the two of them were caught in a blizzard, and the only way to survive was for him to cook and eat his horse. That would make sense.

As the horse clopped through the outskirts of Farnham, a disturbing thought occurred to Sherlock. If he was willing, in principle, to eat his horse, then why not his friends? If he and *Matty* were caught in a blizzard . . .

Even the thought made him feel sick, and he quickly squashed it, but a lingering doubt remained. Logically, there was a sliding scale between, say, insects and humans in terms of intelligence and general development. Fish and frogs were closer to the insects, arguably, and dogs and cats were closer to humans. Wasn't that what Mister Charles Darwin had recently written in his book *On the Origins of Species*—a book he'd heard his Uncle Sherrinford complaining about over the dinner table some weeks before? Humans were just

19

another type of animal, according to Darwin, with nothing special or God-given about them. But if you factored religion out of the discussion, if you accepted that humans were just animals who could make tools and talk, then why weren't you allowed to eat people the way you were allowed to eat cows?

Too many questions, and logic did not seem to be any help. Logic was telling him that if *this* was all right then *that* was all right as well, but instinctively he knew that there was a difference. There were limits. The trouble was, he didn't know where they had come from or how to think about them properly.

And all this because he hadn't given his horse a name.

'I'll call you Philadelphia,' he murmured, patting its neck again.

He smiled. As names went, it had a whole lot of meaning attached to it. Virginia—Amyus Crowe's daughter—had named her horse Sandia after a range of mountains in America, after all, so he should be able to name his horse after an American city. The train that he, Virginia and Matty had been trapped on months ago, after Matty had been kidnapped by the agents of Duke Balthassar, had belonged to the Philadelphia Line, and the name would always remind him of what they had been through. And the short form of Philadelphia was Philly, and 'filly' was another name for a young female horse, so it was also a kind of joke. It worked on all kinds of levels.

'Philadelphia it is,' he said. The horse made a whickering noise, as if it understood and approved. That, of course, really was just his imagination.

They were in the centre of town by now, and Sherlock left his horse—left *Philadelphia*—tied up next to the grain market and walked along under the brick colonnades, looking for Matty. He knew Matty's habits by now—where to find him at any time of day or night. The boy seemed to have fallen into a routine. Rather than move on in his narrowboat, looking for new towns and new opportunities, he had settled in Farnham, at least for a while. Sherlock secretly hoped it was because of him—because of their friendship. He liked Matty, and he would miss him when—if—he left.

Matty was sitting by the river, apparently watching nothing in particular, although Sherlock knew he was waiting for a barge to show up that usually delivered boxes of fish from the coast, laid out on crushed ice. Matty had found that if one of the boxes was dropped and smashed then he could steal a fish or two from the wreckage before anyone stopped him. Sherlock sometimes wondered if Matty occasionally got in the way of the men unloading the boat, making them slip and drop the boxes they were carrying, but he never asked. Best not to know.

'Hi,' Matty said. 'I was wondering if you were going to show up.'

'I'm going to London tomorrow,' Sherlock responded. He had meant to make conversation first, find out where Matty had been and what he had done recently, but he couldn't help himself. He wasn't good with conversation. 'I've got to go to the station and get the tickets.'

'Good luck with that,' Matty muttered.

'You could come,' Sherlock said, defensively, but

he wasn't sure whether the invitation from Mycroft extended that far.

'To the station? Thanks, but I've already seen it.'

'To London!' Sherlock said in exasperation.

'You won't get me back up in the Smoke.' Matty shook his head. 'I still remember what happened last time. After you an' Ginnie were kidnapped by that Baron Maupertuis bloke, I had to travel all the way back here to Farnham with her father. He tried to teach me to read!' His voice rose aggrievedly. 'I told him I didn't *want* to read, but he kept trying to tell me about "*a* before *e* except after *c*" and stuff. An' then we had to sail to France to try and find the two of you, an' he just kept at it. Wouldn't stop.'

'I think he just likes to teach,' Sherlock said. 'And you were the only audience.'

'Well, I'm not making that mistake again.'

'Have you seen Virginia?' Sherlock asked.

'Not for a few days now.'

'You want to go and look for her?'

Matty shook his head, eyes still fixed on the canal. 'No, I'd rather eat.'

'I could buy you a pork pie,' Sherlock offered.

Matty looked tempted, but he shook his head. 'You won't always be around,' he said. 'I can't rely on anyone else to feed me. I got to do it myself, an' that means I got to keep my skills sharp. I got to make sure I can snaffle a cauliflower or a ham hock without anyone noticing.'

'It's all right,' Sherlock said quietly. 'It's not charity, it's friendship.'

'Feels like charity,' Matty mumbled. 'And I don't accept charity. Not ever.'

Sherlock nodded. 'I understand.' He looked

around. 'I'm going to head across to the station. See you later?'

'Depends on when lunch turns up,' Matty said gloomily.

Sherlock walked off, not sure where exactly he was going. He felt edgy. He wanted to be on his way to London, but he knew that he had to wait until the next day for that. Mycroft had been very specific.

He wandered along the High Street for a while, past taverns that were already doing a roaring trade, even though it was barely after midday, past baker's shops with windows piled high with breads twisted into knots and covered with seeds, past shops selling vegetables and fruit, or tools and seeds, or clothing ranging from the rough to the exquisite, pressing through crowds of locals who were buying, or selling, or just standing around idly, gossiping.

'Sherlock!' a voice called.

He turned, surprised. For a moment he didn't recognize the tall, slim man with long black hair who was smiling at him from the other side of the road. Or rather, he knew that he *knew* him, but he wasn't sure where from. His gaze scanned the man's clothes and hands in the way that Amyus Crowe had taught him, looking for signs of his profession, but apart from a worn area on the left shoulder of the man's patched corduroy jacket and the smattering of orange dust beneath his fingernails, there were no clues.

Except . . .

'Mister Stone!' he shouted, at the same moment that his brain supplied the information that the man was a violinist down on his luck, based on the signs on his clothing.

Rufus Stone's smile stretched wider, revealing the gold tooth that Sherlock remembered from their voyages out to and back from New York, where the man had been teaching him the violin to help pass the time.

'I keep telling you,' Stone shouted as he started to cross the road, dodging the carts that clattered past and avoiding the piles of manure that had been left by the horses that pulled them. 'Only employers call me "Mister Stone", and there have been fewer of those over the past months than there are teeth in a chicken's beak.'

'What happened to you after we docked in Southampton?' Sherlock tried to keep a petty tone out of his voice, tried to make it just an ordinary question, but he had thought that the violinist was going to head for Farnham after they docked and set himself up as a tutor.

Stone winced. 'Ah, there I have a confession to make. I was all ready to move my life down to this area of the world, but I got sidetracked and went to Salisbury for a few weeks instead. Suffice to say there was an actress, and a vacancy in the Salisbury Playhouse pit orchestra, and the chance to gaze up at her beautiful face all evening as I played and she acted her little heart out.'

'What happened?' Sherlock asked.

'She parcelled that same heart up and gave it to the leading man, of course,' he replied, wincing. 'As they always do, of course, buoyed up by the admiring glances of their followers in the pit. I later found that we'd all joined because of her, and we were all receiving less than standard rates just for the privilege of being there.' He sighed theatrically.

'Ah well. We live and learn. So—do you think that this part of Hampshire is still looking for a good violin tutor?'

'I think so,' Sherlock replied. 'There're a couple of good schools around, and quite a few big houses in the vicinity.'

'And what about you?' Stone asked. 'Have you been keeping up with your lessons?'

'I've been looking around for a cheap violin,' Sherlock admitted. 'Which reminds me—where's yours?'

'I have secured lodgings nearby. My possessions—such as they are—and my violin are in my room. Which reminds *me*—I'm on an errand for my landlady, and I need to stay in her good books. If I don't bring back a chicken within the next hour then I suspect I'll be out on the street—again. Tell me, where can I find you, so we can continue our lessons?'

'Holmes Manor,' Sherlock said. 'Give me a day or two to broach the subject with my brother and my uncle, but I think they'll be fine about it.'

Stone smiled, and extended a hand. 'It's a pleasure to renew our acquaintance, Mister Holmes,' he said as Sherlock took it. His hand was warm and dry, and Sherlock noticed that he didn't press hard when he shook. Perhaps he was worried about damaging his fingers. 'I will see you soon.'

He turned, and within moments was swallowed up by the crowd.

Absurdly pleased to see Rufus Stone again, Sherlock turned and moved off to get his horse.

The station was on the outskirts of the town. No trains were scheduled for that time in the early afternoon, so the place was deserted as he dismounted and approached the ticket office.

'Two tickets to London,' he said to the elderly man behind the counter. 'Leaving on the train at nine thirty tomorrow morning. One adult and one child, second class.'

The ticket seller raised an eyebrow. 'Afford two second-class tickets, can you?' he grunted. 'Or are you going to tell me you'll pay me tomorrow, after your pocket money comes in?'

Sherlock slid a handful of coins across the counter. Mycroft had been keeping him supplied with postal orders and, as he didn't spend very much, he'd built up quite a large balance. His brother hadn't indicated how he should pay for the tickets, or included any additional money in his letter, so Sherlock presumed that Mycroft wanted him to pay out of his own money. Another small step towards adult responsibilities.

'Two tickets,' the ticket seller grunted. 'One adult and one child. Second class.' He passed two small slips of cardboard across the counter, along with a smaller pile of coins. 'And change.'

'Thank you.' Sherlock dropped the tickets into one pocket and the coins into another, and turned round. He was just in time to see a figure in dark clothes step into an alley that ran alongside the station. He thought it was a woman.

A chill ran down his back. Was Mrs Eglantine following him, checking up on him? Had he humiliated her so much that she was looking to take some kind of revenge? He moved quickly down the slope to the hotel, stepping out into the road before he got to the alley, just in case whoever it was was waiting there for him, but when he got past the corner of the building the alley was empty.

He checked the walls, but there were no doors the figure could have gone through. It had apparently vanished.

Had he imagined it? Had his brain conjured up a figure out of thin air? Or was there a simpler explanation—a local woman who had decided to take a short cut around the hotel to wherever she was going?

Sherlock moved into the alley, and bent down to check the ground. There were footprints, leading away. The toes were pointed and the heels small, judging by the impressions left in the mud. And there were no traces of patches or holes in the soles, indicating that they were either new or well cared for, or both.

He checked over the ground again, and walked a few yards further down the alley, but there was nothing else to see.

Thoughtfully, he mounted Philadelphia and set off for Amyus Crowe's cottage to give him his ticket.

There was activity inside the cottage when he arrived, and Virginia's horse was in the paddock, cropping the grass. He felt his mood lighten as he dismounted and approached the open door.

Virginia wasn't in the main room, but Amyus Crowe was sitting in an armchair, looking through a book. He glanced up as Sherlock came in, gazing at the boy over the top of his half-glasses. 'Did you get the tickets?'

'I did.' Sherlock paused. 'I met Rufus Stone,' he added. 'He was in Farnham.'

'Obviously.' Crowe pursed his lips. 'Strange that he should turn up here, just where you happen to be living.'

'I'd told him where I live. I'd said he might want to come to Farnham to teach the violin.'

'Very charitable of you,' Crowe conceded, his faded blue eyes studying Sherlock. 'Ah can see what *you* get out of that, but ah fail to see the advantage to Mister Stone.'

'He has to live somewhere,' Sherlock pointed out, uneasy at Crowe's obvious lack of pleasure at the news that Rufus Stone was in the area. 'And he's better off living where there are people who want to play the violin.'

'As you do.'

'As I do.'

Crowe put his book on his lap and removed his spectacles. 'Music is a distraction, Sherlock,' he said, not unkindly. 'It ain't a fit pastime for a man who is tryin' to fill his brain with things of use. Just think how much space in your brain would be taken up by learnin' all the notes for some fancy piece of music. That space could better be used for memorizin' the marks left by animals, or the shapes of people's ears, or the traces left on their hands and their clothes by whatever it is that they do to get through the day. Not music, son. Music ain't no use to anyone.'

'I don't agree,' Sherlock said, feeling strangely disappointed by Amyus Crowe's dismissal of something he was finding himself more and more interested in. He remembered his thoughts while riding into town, about the difference between animals and humans—or the lack of difference. 'Yes, I could memorize all those things—I could learn all about edible fungi, and telling about the state of a man's marriage by the stains on his hat, but why? What's the point? That just turns me into

28

some kind of super-predator, able to track its prey through nearly invisible signs. Surely it has to *mean* something? Surely there has to be more to life than just being a better kind of animal?'

'And music is the thing that separates us from animals?' Crowe asked, eyes guarded.

'One of them.'

Crowe shrugged. 'Can't say ah've ever had much time for it. For me, bein' human means lookin' after my kin, lookin' after myself an' tryin' to ensure that the people around me look after each other. If that makes me just another animal, then that's what ah am.'

'But what's it all for?' Sherlock found himself asking. 'If there's nothing that makes us feel . . .' he struggled for the right word, *'uplifted*, then what's the point in doing anything at all.'

'Survival,' Crowe said simply. 'We live to survive.'

'And that's it?' Sherlock asked, disappointed. 'We keep going so that we can keep going? We live to survive and survive to live?'

'That's about it,' Crowe confirmed. 'As philosophies go it ain't pretty, but it has the advantage of bein' succinct and largely undeniable. Now, you stayin' here for food or you goin' back to *your* kin?'

Sherlock suppressed the arguments he had been marshalling, disappointed that Crowe had changed the subject so abruptly but also glad that the two of them weren't going to have a confrontation. He liked Amyus Crowe, and he didn't want them to fall out over something as simple as music lessons. 'Is Virginia around?'

'She's out back, gettin' water for Sandia. Go

lookin' for her, if you want.'

As Sherlock turned towards the door, Crowe's voice rumbled: 'Might interest you to know that Rufus Stone is also the name of a village near Southampton. Maybe it's a coincidence . . . or maybe he was short of a name at some point, and settled on one that was floatin' around his mind cos he'd seen it on a road sign somewhere. Just a thought.'

A thought that Sherlock found unsettling. He also thought it was rather petty of Amyus Crowe to have raised it.

He found Virginia outside. She had bought a bucket of water around, and Sandia was drinking from it enthusiastically.

'What has your father got against Rufus Stone?' he asked.

'And hello to you as well.' She glanced sideways at him. 'You really telling me you don't know?'

'I really don't,' he admitted.

She shook her head. 'I've said it before and I'll say it again: for a clever lad you can be really stupid sometimes.'

'But it doesn't make any sense!' he protested. 'I thought your father would be *glad* that I was making new friends and finding new interests.'

Virginia turned full on to him and stood, hands on hips. 'Let me ask you a question. If your father were still in this country, instead of being in India, what would he make of my father? Would they get on?'

Sherlock frowned, thinking. 'I doubt it,' he said finally. 'They come from different social strata, for one, and . . .'

He trailed off, unsure how to put the thought

into words.

'And what?' she prompted.

'And in a way, your father is doing what my father would be doing if he were here.' Sherlock felt awkward just voicing the words. 'Teaching me stuff. Taking me out for walks. Giving me advice.'

'Right. He's acting like a father to you.'

He smiled at her uncertainly. 'You don't mind?'

She smiled too. 'It's nice having you around.' She looked away, then back again. 'An' you're right—your pa would be jealous that you were spending time with someone who was treatin' you like their son. Especially if that person was teachin' you things that *he* couldn't teach you.'

A bright light of understanding seemed to explode like a star in Sherlock's head. 'And *your* father is jealous of Rufus Stone because he thinks Rufus is acting like a father to me?' The thought was so big, so momentous, that it seemed to fill his entire mind. 'But that's *stupid*!'

'Why?'

'Because Rufus is nothing like a father. He's more like a much older brother, or a young uncle, or something. And besides, me learning the violin from Rufus doesn't mean I don't value your father's lessons any the less. The two things are completely separate. It's just . . . illogical!'

She gazed at him, and shook her head. 'Emotions ain't logical, Sherlock. They don't follow rules.'

'Then I don't like emotions,' he said rebelliously. 'They don't do anything but cause confusion and hurt.'

The words hung between them for a long moment, vibrating like a struck bell.

31

'Some emotions are worth having,' she said softly, turning away. She bent down and picked the bucket up. 'At least *I* think so, even if you don't.'

She walked off, towards the rear of the house. Sherlock stared after her until she vanished around the corner. He felt like something big had just happened, but he wasn't sure what it was.

After a while, he walked over to his horse. He hadn't even told Virginia that he'd named it Philadelphia, he brooded. Maybe he didn't know very much about emotions, but he knew enough to suspect that this wasn't the time to go back and tell her.

He headed back to Holmes Manor, his head spinning with conjectures about Amyus Crowe, Virginia, Rufus Stone and his father, now so far away. He didn't like these conjectures. They were complicated, grown up and illogical. Emotional.

When he got back he sought out his Uncle Sherrinford, and told him about Mycroft's letter. He didn't exactly ask permission to go to London, but he didn't exactly tell Sherrinford that he was going regardless of what was said. He just left the impression that it was a fait accompli. Fortunately, his uncle was in the middle of drafting another of the religious sermons which he sold to vicars all around the country for a few shillings apiece, and his distraction meant that he was more than happy to accept what Sherlock wanted to do, as long as it was what Mycroft wanted as well.

The next morning, when he awoke, the sun was just clearing the trees and the sky was blue from horizon to horizon. The worries of the night before seemed trivial in the bright sunshine. He quickly dressed and, after a rushed breakfast of porridge and toast, asked if one of the carts could run him to the station. It was better than leaving his horse tied up there for hours while he was in London.

Amyus Crowe was waiting for him on the platform, impressive and almost monumental in his white suit and white hat. He nodded to Sherlock.

'Think we got off on the wrong tack last afternoon,' he rumbled. 'Ah regret if ah sounded a mite terse an' unreasonable.'

'It's all right,' Sherlock said reassuringly. 'If you believe something, you ought to say it. Not doing so is hypocritical.'

Crowe made a sound deep in his throat. 'Ginnie's mother liked opera,' he said quietly. 'Big on a German named Wagner, she was. After she died, ah could never stand the sound of an orchestra, nor the sound of a singer.'

'I understand,' Sherlock said quietly.

'Then you're a wiser man than ah am.'

Fortunately, the train arrived before the conversation could get any more awkward.

The two of them sat in a decent compartment by themselves. The seats were upholstered and comfortable. Steam from the engine rushed like low cloud past the window, and Sherlock watched through gaps as the countryside unfolded before them.

A ticket collector checked their tickets just past Woking. As he left the compartment, sliding the door shut as he went, Crowe said: 'What did you make of the man that just left?'

Knowing the way Crowe's mind worked, Sherlock had been expecting a question like that.

'His shoes were freshly shined,' he said, 'and his shirt had been ironed. Either he's got a maid or he's married, and as I don't expect a ticket collector to be able to afford a maid to iron his shirts then I assume it's more likely that he's married.'

'Good so far,' Crowe rumbled.

'His wife is older than him,' Sherlock ventured.

'How can you tell?'

'He's in his thirties, but his collars are of an old-fashioned design. They're like my uncle's. They aren't worn, so it's not as if he's been wearing them for years. It must be that whoever is responsible for his clothes prefers the older style of collar, so if it's his wife then she must be older than him.'

'You forget the possibility that he may have a younger wife who hails from an old-fashioned family, but yours *is* the most likely explanation,' Crowe conceded.

'And he is slightly blind in his right eye,' Sherlock finished triumphantly.

Crowe nodded. 'Indeed. What gave it away?'

'He has shaved the left side of his face and neck carefully, but the right side still has stubble visible. I deduce that he has difficulty in seeing out of his right eye.'

'Excellent. You are picking up the skill of observation very nicely.'

'Did I miss anything?' Sherlock asked, smiling.

Crowe shrugged. 'Several points, in fact. The man has been married before, but his wife died. His current marriage is childless, which causes his wife some distress. Oh, and I believe he is pilfering money from the railway company, but that is a stretch.'

Sherlock couldn't help laughing. 'How can you tell all that?'

'Practice,' Crowe said, smiling. 'That and natural

talent. One day you'll be able to do it too.'

Sherlock shook his head. 'I doubt it,' he said with a laugh. 'I really doubt it.'

CHAPTER THREE

The journey to Waterloo seemed shorter than Sherlock remembered. Crowe was on good form all the way, making deductions about the various people who came and went in their carriage and on the stations they passed. Sometimes, just to tease Sherlock, he engaged the people in conversation and got them to talk about the things he'd already told Sherlock. The earlier discomfort between them over the subject of Rufus Stone seemed to have vanished.

When the train had heaved its way into Waterloo and slowed to a halt at the platform, the two of them descended and walked through the station to find a hansom cab.

Sherlock had experienced the bustle of Waterloo Station before, but as he and Amyus Crowe made their way through a particularly dense crowd of men in top hats he found himself imagining that he was moving through a grim landscape of industrial chimneys rising up from dark factories. The steam from the trains that drifted around the station just made the comparison worse. Irritated, he tried to put the image to one side. He didn't often get flashes of imagination like that, and he didn't like it when he did. There was no logical way to get from top hats to smoky industrial landscapes. That was a poetic comparison, not an analytical one. Amyus

Crowe would not approve.

Although Rufus Stone probably would. The thought made him pause uncomfortably.

Crowe hailed a hansom cab outside the station. They had no luggage, as they were just up for the day, so they climbed inside and set off.

The cab was little more than a box on two wheels, with the driver sitting on top and the horse attached to the front with a leather harness and reins. It jerked and rattled terribly on London's bumpy roads.

'The Diogenes Club,' Crowe called up to the driver.

'Where's that, guv?' the man called back.

'Head for the Admiralty,' Crowe shouted. 'Ah'll direct you from there.' Settling back down in his seat as the cab started off, he said conversationally: 'The club's only been in existence for a year or so. Seems your brother was one of the founders, or so he tells me. Named after the Greek philosopher Diogenes of Sinope. Diogenes was one of the founders of the Cynic philosophy, or Cynicism, as it has become known.'

'I've heard the word "cynics",' Sherlock said, 'but I'm not exactly sure what it means.'

'Cynics suggested that the purpose of life was to live a life of virtue in agreement with nature, which meant in practice rejecting all conventional desires for wealth, power, health and fame, and living a simple life free from all possessions. Can't fault them for that, although it does more or less rule out any industrial progress in a society. The Cynics also believed that the world belonged equally to everyone, and that suffering was caused by false judgements of what was valuable and by the worthless customs and conventions which surrounded society.' He paused. 'Not sure how that applies to your brother, or the club, but you ought to know that the Diogenes Club has one very strict rule. Nobody is allowed to talk on the premises. Not one word. The only exception is the Strangers Room, which is where ah assume your brother will be meetin' us. If not, we're in for an uncomfortable day.'

The cab clattered across Westminister Bridge, and Sherlock's attention was caught by the various boats being rowed along or across the dirty brown mass of the water. 'Were Diogenes and Plato alive at the same time?' he asked, remembering the book that his brother had given him as a gift when he sailed to America—Plato's *The Republic*.

'They were,' Crowe answered, 'and they didn't get on. Ah'll tell you the story sometime.'

At the north side of the river the cab turned left, then right on to a broad, tree-lined avenue. At the top of the avenue, Sherlock recognized Trafalgar Square, with its memorial to Lord Nelson. He'd seen that the last time he'd come to London.

A few seconds later, the carriage stopped. The two of them descended to the pavement, and Crowe paid the driver the few pence fare.

They were still on the broad, tree-lined avenue, but at the top, where it curved round to form another road. A small door was set into a wall ahead of them. A brass plaque by the side of the door read *The Diogenes Club* in copperplate script.

Crowe rapped on the door with the head of his cane. A few moments later, it swung open. He led the way in, ducking his head to miss the low lintel. Sherlock followed.

They were standing in a narrow hall with oak-panelled walls and a marble floor. A stairway led up to the first floor, and an open door to one side gave access to what looked like a large room full of green leather armchairs. The silence was so oppressive that Sherlock could almost feel it pressing on his ears. The ticking of a clock somewhere in the shadows echoed around the hall.

The man who had opened the door was small and weaselly. He was dressed immaculately in a blue footman's uniform and had the look of a former soldier. Sherlock was no expert, but the man held himself rigidly upright, and his boots were shined to a degree where Sherlock could probably have seen his face in them. Crowe handed him a card. He glanced at it, nodded, and then gestured to Crowe and Sherlock to follow him through the room that led off the hall, the room full of green armchairs. The armchairs were occupied by men reading newspapers, and the footman led a winding course to a door on the far side of the room. He knocked on the door.

A few people lifted their heads from their newspapers and glared at the source of the noise.

Sherlock listened, but heard no response. He mentally kicked himself: if nobody was allowed to speak in the club then he could hardly expect anyone to call 'Enter!' The footman was obviously waiting for the door to be opened.

Nothing happened. The footman knocked again.

This time there was a scuffle from inside the room. Something thudded against the door. A bolt was thrown, and the door opened.

Mycroft Holmes stood in the doorway, blocking the room beyond with his large body. He looked confused.

He brought his hand up, as if to touch his forehead, and he seemed just as surprised as Sherlock, Crowe and the footman to find that he was holding a knife.

Mycroft stared at the knife as if he had never seen it before. He turned his head to look back into the room. As he did so, he stepped sideways, and Sherlock could see past him.

The room was lined with wood panelling, like the rest of the club, but it had no windows. In the centre of the room was a large table. Upholstered chairs were arranged symmetrically around it.

A man sat in one of the chairs. Judging by the spreading bloodstain on his shirt, and the way his sightless eyes stared at the chandelier hanging from the high ceiling, he was dead.

'Mycroft?' Sherlock said.

A ripple of surprise ran round the club room, followed by hisses of disapproval at his flagrant breaking of the rules, but he didn't care. He just wanted to know what had happened.

The footman backed away, eyes wide. Crowe snapped his fingers at the man, then mimed blowing a whistle. The footman nodded, turned, and ran off.

Crowe grabbed Sherlock's arm and pulled him into the Strangers Room, shutting the door behind them. Sherlock noticed that the back of the door was heavily padded, presumably to keep the noise of conversation from drifting into the club room. Mycroft backed away, his eyes still confused, his hand still holding the knife.

'I don't . . . understand,' he said hesitantly.

'Mister Holmes,' Crowe snapped, 'you need to

concentrate. What happened? Tell us everything.'

'I was . . . waiting for you,' Mycroft replied. His voice gained strength as he spoke. 'I had predicted your time of arrival based on the train timetable and the usual traffic between Waterloo Station and the club at this time of day. There was a knock on the door. The footman—Brinnell—delivered a card on a tray. Apparently a man wanted to see me. I didn't know who he was, and I was about to send him away when I noticed that some words had been scrawled on the back of the card. They were words that . . . that I had come into contact with during the course of my employment. Words of significance. I indicated to Brinnell that he should bring the man here, to the Strangers Room.'

He paused, frowning, as if he was attempting to remember something difficult.

'I waited here,' he continued. 'There was a knock on the door. Rather than call out, I went to the door to open it. That is the custom, here in the Diogenes Club. It avoids undue speech, which most members find unpleasant. A man was standing outside—'

'That man?' Crowe asked, indicating the body slumped in the chair.

'Yes,' Mycroft said, wincing. 'That is the man. I gestured to him to come in. He did so. I shut the door behind him, and . . .'

He trailed off. His hand—the one not holding the knife—rose as if he wanted to touch something on his head. 'That's all I remember until I heard another knock on the door. I thought I was having one of those moments that the French call déjà vu, where you believe that something is happening to you that has happened before. I opened the door, expecting to find Brinnell and the visitor outside, but it was you. Both of you. I was confused. I turned round, expecting to find the visitor behind me.' Mycroft indicated the dead body in the chair. 'I did,' he continued, a touch of the dryness with which Sherlock was so familiar creeping back into his tone, 'but not in the manner I expected.'

'Mister Holmes,' Crowe said, 'for the sake of completeness, and because it is undoubtedly a question the police will ask, did you kill that man?'

'I have no recollection of killing that man,' Mycroft said carefully.

'Ah would suggest that you give a simple "no" next time the question is asked. Not that it will do you much good.' Crowe sighed. 'Do you know a good solicitor?'

'The Diogenes retains one,' Mycroft replied. 'Brinnell can give you the man's details.'

'Then whatever happens in the near future, rest assured that we will engage the Diogenes' solicitor and we will work to get you released.'

Mycroft turned to look at the body. 'That may be difficult,' he said painfully. 'There is precious little evidence, and what little there is seems to implicate me.'

'You did not kill him,' Sherlock said firmly. 'I don't know much about what happened in here, but I know that.'

Mycroft smiled slightly, and patted Sherlock on the shoulder. 'Thank you,' he said. 'I think I needed to hear that.'

A commotion outside alerted them to the arrival of the police.

'Ah suggest you put the knife on the table,' Crowe said. 'It never looks good to be holdin' a

41

weapon when the police arrive.'

Mycroft stepped towards the table and set the knife down on it just as the door burst open, and a group of blue-uniformed men entered. Crowe stepped forward, covering Mycroft's movement.

'There's been a murder,' he said. 'The body is over by the table, as is the knife that was probably used in the execution of the crime.'

'And who are you?' the lead constable asked.

'My name is Amyus Crowe. Who are you?'

'A foreign gentleman,' the policeman remarked, looking pointedly at his companions. 'Were you here when the crime was committed?'

'Ah asked you for your name,' Crowe said, voice civil but with an edge of iron.

'I am Sergeant Coleman,' the policeman said, drawing himself up. 'Now perhaps you could answer *my* question.' He paused. 'Sir.'

'Ah was outside the door,' Crowe said, 'with the young man there. The footman can bear that out.'

'And what is the young man's name?'

'Sherlock Holmes,' Sherlock replied.

'Then who was *in* the room?' the sergeant pressed.

Crowe hesitated, wincing slightly. 'Ah believe this gentleman was in the room.' He indicated Mycroft with a nod of his head.

The sergeant stepped forward. 'Is this true, sir?' he asked Mycroft.

Mycroft nodded. 'I was in the room,' he said clearly.

'What is your name?'

'Mycroft Siger Holmes.'

'And did you kill this man, sir?'

'I did not kill this man.'

42

Sherlock noticed Crowe's lips twitch slightly at the firmness in Mycroft's voice. The sergeant looked taken aback.

'I'm afraid, sir, that I must place you under arrest. You will be taken to Scotland Yard, where you will be questioned under oath.' He glanced over at the corpse, then towards one of the constables. 'Send someone for the pathologist. Old Murdoch is on duty today. Get him to come and fetch the body. And bring that knife. We'll be showing it to the judge, all right.'

The words were like the tolling of some huge, discordant bell to Sherlock's ears. He watched in horror as Mycroft was taken by the shoulder and manoeuvred out of the Strangers Room, through the club room and into the hall. One of the constables took the knife gingerly by the handle and carried it away.

'Mister Crowe . . .' Sherlock started.

'No time,' Crowe snapped. 'Ah understand you're emotional. That's to be expected. Trouble is, if we're to clear your brother's name and save him from jail then we need to move fast, and we need to move with complete precision and accuracy. Emotion, right now, will slow us down an' cloud our judgement. Do you understand what I'm saying?'

'Yes,' Sherlock breathed.

'Suppress whatever grief and shock you're feelin'. Imagine that you're wrappin' it up in a blanket, tyin' it tight and stowin' it in the back of your mind. Ah ain't askin' you to forget about it forever, just for now. You can retrieve those emotions later, when it's safe, an' wrap yourself in them for as long as you want. Just not *now*.'

43

'Yes. All right.' Sherlock closed his eyes and tried to do what Crowe was suggesting. He tried picturing his roiling mixture of emotions as a fiery ball hanging inside his mind, and then he tried to imagine a fireproof cloth as black as night wrapping itself round that fiery ball. Ropes and chains emerged from the darkness and looped around the cloth, drawing tight until the ball was completely swaddled. And then he imagined it sinking down through the shadows until it sat on the floor, in a dusty cupboard, at the back of his mind. And then he closed the door.

He opened his eyes and took a breath. He felt better. Less panicky. He knew the feelings were there, in the cupboard, but he didn't *feel* them. He could get them out whenever he wanted to, but right now he wasn't sure if he *would* ever want to.

'You all right?'

'I'm fine. What do we need to do?'

'We need to search the body, and we need to search the room. A'll do the first thing, you do the second.'

'All right.' He thought for a moment. 'Why did the police leave us alone in here with the . . . the body?'

Crowe glowered. 'Trouble with the crime-fightin' profession is that they like nice simple answers. They got two people in a locked room, one of them dead an' the other one not. To them, the answer is simple, an' ah must admit if I didn't know your brother like I do then it would look just as simple to me. So as far as they're concerned, they've got their man. The knife is more like a trophy to them—they can wave it around at the trial an' scare the jury. The corpse—well, he's dead, an' he ain't

44

goin' nowhere until the pathologist arrives to cart him away. An' that should give us enough time to see what they might have picked up, if they'd bothered lookin'. Now, enough talkin'. Get to work!'

While Crowe busied himself at the table, Sherlock started in one corner of the room and methodically examined every inch. He didn't know what he was looking for, so he looked for anything out of the ordinary. He checked the panelled walls and the pictures hanging from them, and he even pulled one of the chairs away from the table and moved it over to the wall so that he could climb on it and inspect the picture rails that ran along the top just underneath the ceiling. Then he threw himself to the ground and checked the carpet for things that might have dropped from someone's hand or pocket and got caught between the fibres.

'Anythin'?' Crowe called after a while.

'Not so far,' he said dejectedly.

He kept moving around the room, letting his eyes rove everywhere. As he got to the corner of the table he noticed something on the floor beneath it: a small leather case, left in the shadow of the table leg as if someone wanted to put it quickly out of the way.

'I've got something,' he announced, pulling the case out and putting it on the table.

Crowe crossed from the body to see what had been found. He examined it critically.

'Basic wooden construction, leather facing, brass hinges, brass lock and brass feet,' he murmured. 'Nothin' special or out of the ordinary. No scuff marks on the feet an' no wear on the handle, indicatin' that it's new. Ah, look at the handle

45

there—can you see that thread tied around it? Probably where the price label was attached. This man, or someone else, pulled the price off but forgot about the thread. That was a mistake.' He reached for the case and clicked the locks. 'Unlocked, which is good for us.' He opened it so that he and Sherlock could see inside.

The case was lined with a red material, probably silk or satin. The material was heavily padded so that anything in the case would have been pressed between the two sides when the case was closed.

'Two depressions in the padding, see?' Crowe pointed to two areas where the padding was pressed in, suggesting that the case had contained two objects, but Sherlock had already noticed them. 'Too diffuse to tell us what the shapes were, although they appear to be different.'

'The padding around one of the depressions is a different colour,' Sherlock pointed out. 'It's slightly darker.'

'Could just be wear,' Crowe muttered.

'But the case is new—just bought.'

'Good point.' Crowe reached out to touch the surface of the material. 'It's slightly damp. That's odd. Something wet was in here—maybe a bottle containing a liquid that partially leaked out.'

Sherlock looked around the room. 'A bottle of what?'

'Not sure yet. Let's just file the information away for later.' He closed the lid of the case and looked around the room. 'What about those panels on the wall—any hidden doors? Any sign that there might be a window under there? Someone had to get in and out of this room without being seen.'

'I thought of that, but there's no sign of hinges

46

or seams. I knocked on the walls, but none of them sound hollow.'

'All right.'

'Do you want to check?'

'Why should ah?' Crowe sounded surprised. 'You've got a good set of eyes, an' a good mind behind them. What about the carpet?'

'Looks like it gets cleaned every day, and I can't see anything that might have dropped on it today.'

'So,' Crowe said grimly, 'there's nothin'.'

'Except . . .' Sherlock started.

'Except what?'

'Except there's a damp patch on the carpet just here. And it's cold.'

Crowe turned and stared at Sherlock. 'A what?'

'A damp patch. Maybe someone spilt a glass of water.'

Crowe raised his eyebrows. 'Interestin'. We have a case that might have contained a bottle of somethin', and we have a damp patch where that bottle might have spilt, but what we don't have is the bottle itself, an' whatever else was in there with the bottle. It's an anomaly, and anomalies are what we need right now. Things that just don't fit.'

Sherlock wasn't sure. 'So what does it mean?'

The big man shrugged. 'Ah don't know yet, but ah'm filing it away for later consideration, an' ah suggest you do the same. Now, keep lookin'. Just cos you found one thing, don't mean there ain't more things to find.'

Sherlock spent the next ten minutes searching the rest of the room, but when he got back to the corner where he had started, he stopped. Amyus Crowe appeared to have finished with the corpse as well: he was standing back and looking around the

47

room.

'Did you find anything?' Sherlock asked.

Crowe shrugged. 'Some minor points of interest. This man wasn't well, for a start. He'd lost a lot of weight recently, an' he was under the care of a physician. I found this—' he said, holding up a small glass bottle with what looked like a spring-loaded button on the top. 'I think it's a medicine of some kind, although I'll need to get it checked out.'

'May I look?' Sherlock asked. Crowe handed the bottle across. It was about the size of Sherlock's thumb. The sprung button on the top looked as if it might be used to pump something out of the bottle in a fine spray through a small nozzle on the side. Sherlock sniffed at the nozzle, and recoiled. There was something familiar about that bitter smell, but he couldn't quite remember what.

'His clothes make him look like a gentleman,' Crowe continued, 'but the tattoos on his arms suggest he was anything but.'

Sherlock slipped the glass vial into his pocket and crossed to stand beside Crowe. The man was thin, and tiny thread veins were noticeable in his cheeks. His head was thrown back, and he was staring at the ceiling with bulging and bloodshot eyes. His skin was white, but Sherlock wasn't sure if it was naturally like that or if it was a result of his recent death.

The white front of his shirt was now completely maroon with drying blood. A tear had been made around the level of his heart: the point where the blade had penetrated, Sherlock thought grimly.

But who had wielded the blade?

He leaned closer. There was something about

48

that tear that had caught his attention, but he wasn't sure what it was.

'Spotted something?' Crowe asked.

Sherlock hesitated. 'I was just trying to remember what the knife looked like—the one in Mycroft's hand.'

'Got to confess, I never got a clear look at it,' Crowe admitted.

'I did,' Sherlock said. 'It was thin, like a letter opener, but the tear in this shirt is quite big. Bigger than the knife that I remember seeing.'

'Interestin',' Crowe mused. 'I took a quick look at the wound as well. That's quite a size. Suggested to me that the knife had a broad blade, but if you're sayin' the knife that was taken away had a narrow blade . . . well, that's another anomaly that needs explainin'.'

'Could the man have struggled?' Sherlock asked. 'Could that have caused the blade to tear a larger hole in his shirt and . . . and his skin?'

'Possible.' Crowe thought for a moment. 'That's the kind of thing we might need to conduct an experiment to verify.'

'What?' Sherlock exclaimed. 'You mean stab someone else, and hope they struggle?'

Crowe laughed. 'No, I mean we get a slaughtered pig from somewhere, dress it in a shirt, an' then one of us stabs it with a paperknife while the other one wiggles it about a bit. See if we can replicate the tear and the wound on this poor guy. Guessin' only takes us so far—we need evidence more than anythin'.' He gestured towards the door. 'Go an' see if you can find that footman—Brinnell. Bring him back here. I've got some questions I want to put to him.'

Sherlock made his way out to the club room. The occupants glanced up at him with irritation as he passed—they'd seen the police, and they obviously knew that something out of the ordinary was happening, but they seemed determined to pretend that everything was as calm as usual within the club's precincts. Sherlock tried to make himself as small and as quiet as possible. He had to admit, as he wound his way through the plush green armchairs, he couldn't work out what it was his brother saw in this club. It was the most boring place he'd ever been in—murder excepted, and he presumed that the Diogenes Club was not in the habit of playing host to murder.

He found Brinnell in the hall. The footman was looking worried. Sherlock was about to ask him to come back to the Strangers Room when Brinnell raised a finger to his lips and shushed him. Sherlock pointed at Brinnell, then back towards the Strangers Room. Brinnell nodded. He walked past Sherlock, past the stairs to a door that probably led back to the servants' area. Within a few moments he was back with another liveried footman, this one older and balder. Leaving the man in the hall presumably to stand guard and prevent strangers from wandering in and making a noise, Brinnell followed Sherlock back through the club room.

Crowe was standing exactly where Sherlock had left him.

'Appreciate you makin' time to talk to us,' he said to the footman as Sherlock closed the door. 'I understand you've got a lot on right now, what with the murder and all.'

'It's a shocking thing,' Brinnell said. 'Shocking it is.' He glanced over at the corpse. 'And it's us that's got to clear it up, as well.'

'You escorted the gentleman here to the Strangers Room, didn't you?'

'I did, sir. That I did.'

'How did he approach you?'

Brinnell thought for a moment. 'He came in through the front door, just like you gentlemen did. He handed me a card. On the back of the card he'd written the name of Mister Holmes, and another few words that I didn't rightly recognize.'

'What were those words?'

Brinnell frowned, struggling to remember. 'I think it was the name of another club,' he said, 'but I can't say I remember which one it was. I thought for a moment the gentleman had come to the wrong place, until I saw Mr Holmes's name written on the back.'

Another club. For some reason the man's words grabbed Sherlock's attention. Another club . . . He filed the thought away until he could consider it in more detail.

'So he obviously knew the workings of the Diogenes Club,' Crowe pointed out. 'He knew enough not to speak.'

'I suppose he did, sir. I suppose so.'

'What did you do then?'

'I put the card on a tray and took it to Mister Holmes. He was waiting in here already. He looked irritable, like he wasn't expecting this man, but someone else. Irritable, that's how he looked. I think he was about to send the bloke away, but he turned the card over and read what was on the back. He seemed to change his mind and he said: "Bring the fellow in, Brinnell."' So I came back, fetched the bloke and brought him through.'

'How long was that before we turned up?'

The footman thought for a moment. Couldn't have been no longer than five minutes,' he said eventually. 'Or maybe ten.'

'Any noise or disturbance?'

'Not a thing, sir.'

Crowe nodded. 'And what did you think of this visitor, then? What was your opinion?'

Brinnell grimaced. 'Not my place to say, sir,' he muttered.

Crowe held his hand up. A bright half-crown flashed between his fingers. 'I value your opinion,' he said. 'Nobody else will know—just us.'

Brinnell considered for a moment. 'No need for that,' he said finally. 'I like Mister Holmes. He's always been good to me. Been good to me, he has. If you're trying to help him, then that's all right with me.'

'Good man,' Crowe said. The half-crown vanished in his large hand.

'I thought the bloke who came visiting was a little overdressed for his station in life, if you know what I mean,' he said.

'Ah know exactly what you mean, and ah 'ppreciate your honesty.'

'Was the man carrying anything?' Sherlock asked suddenly.

Amyus Crowe nodded. 'Good question,' he rumbled.

Brinnell frowned, trying to remember. 'I believe he did have a small case. I recall trying to take it off him to put in the cloakroom, but he clutched it to him as if it were valuable. I presumed he needed it for the meeting with Mister Holmes.'

'Very instructive,' Crowe said.

The door burst back open, and one of the constables who had been there before entered. 'Sergeant Coleman wants you to come down to Scotland Yard and give a statement,' he said.

'Glad to,' Crowe replied. 'I'd be interested to see how his investigation is gettin' on.'

'Investigation?' the constable repeated, smiling. 'No need of that. Got our man bang to rights, we did.'

The constable ushered them out of the Strangers Room and through the club room. As they left, Brinnell looked as if he wanted to say something, but instead he marched across and handed Sherlock a scrap of paper. When he looked at it Sherlock saw the words: *Orville Jenkinson, Solicitor* and an address. This must be the solicitor that Mycroft had mentioned—the one retained by the Diogenes Club. He smiled at Brinnell, and nodded his thanks.

Out in the open air, as the constable struck out along the pavement, Sherlock turned to Amyus Crowe and asked the question that had been burning in his brain for the past hour. 'Mister Crowe—if we can't prove my brother innocent, what happens?'

'There's a trial,' Crowe said grimly, 'an' then, if he's found guilty, ah'm afraid they hang him by the neck until he is dead.'

CHAPTER FOUR

Bow Street Police Station and Magistrates' Court was a monolithic building of white stone set on a corner just off Covent Garden. As they approached, Sherlock let his gaze wander over the building, committing its details to memory. He had the strangest feeling that this building was going to become important to him, although he hoped it wasn't because it was the building in which his brother would be sentenced to hang.

The walls were ridged with jutting rows of stone, while the roof was set with crenellations which made it look more like a medieval castle than a place of law enforcement. Looking at those stones, Sherlock smiled. If Matty Arnatt was here, he could have scooted up them like a ladder to the roof.

The doors on the corner were set at street level, with no steps leading up to them. White lamps hung outside. Amyus Crowe frowned up at the lamps, and turned to the constable.

'Are you sure you've brought us to the right place?' he asked. 'Ah was led to believe that all police stations in this country had blue lamps outside, not white.'

'That was the rule,' the constable confided. 'Happened about seven years ago, but Her Majesty the Queen objected about the blue lamps they put on this building. Apparently the Prince Regent died in a blue room, God bless his soul, and ever since then she couldn't stand the sight of the colour. She used to come to the Opera House just down the road quite a bit, and driving past the blue

54

lamps gave her a funny turn every time. So she asked for them to be replaced. Well, I say "asked" but I think she more or less told the Commissioner of Police to replace them, or she would replace him.'

'Interestin',' Crowe rumbled, 'that a woman has so much power in a country that denies its women the vote an' the opportunity to own property.'

The constable led them inside, past the large desk in the front hall and into the depths of the building. Uniformed and suited men scurried past, each on some important piece of business. He took them down a corridor, round a corner and up a set of stairs, then gestured towards a room that had a table with three seats set around it: two on one side and one on the other. The walls were brick, painted a depressing shade of green.

'Wait here,' he said. 'The sergeant will be along in a moment. Don't leave the room.'

As he left, Crowe dropped heavily into a chair. It creaked beneath his weight. 'May as well make yourself comfortable,' he said. 'We could be here for a while. He'll probably leave us to stew, hope we get uncomfortable and more willing to answer his questions.' He snorted. ''Course, if ah were him ah would have separated us and questioned us individually.'

'Why?' Sherlock asked, sitting next to Crowe.

'If he questions us separately then he can check to see if we give the same answers to his questions. If we don't, he knows that there's areas where we might be lyin'. If he questions us together then you can hear my answers an' change your story accordingly, an' vice versa.'

He leaned back in the chair and closed his eyes,

reaching up to pull his hat forward to block out the light.

Sherlock glanced around, but there was nothing in the room that was of any interest. It was deliberately bare of decoration and ornamentation.

He found his thoughts turning to Mycroft. His brother might be nearby at the moment, but wherever he was it was probably even less comfortable than the room where Sherlock and Amyus Crowe were being kept.

After about a quarter of an hour the door was flung open and the sergeant they had met before, Coleman, bustled in. He was carrying a notebook and a pencil.

'Just some details to clear up,' he said before he even sat down. 'I don't think this is a particularly difficult case. Quite clear to me.'

Amyus Crowe removed his hat and raised an eyebrow. 'You might be surprised,' he said.

'The facts seem undeniable,' the sergeant said. 'Stop me if I'm wrong, but the room was locked and there was only one way in and out—the door. Two men were inside. When the room was unlocked, one man was found to be dead and the other was holding a knife. Have I missed anything?'

'No blood on the knife,' Sherlock pointed out.

'The blood was wiped off on the dead man's shirt as the knife was pulled out.'

'Have you checked the shirt for signs of wiping, or is that just an assumption?' Crowe asked.

'You can't deny there's blood on the shirt,' the sergeant protested.

'Pumped out of the wound, yes, but are there any signs that the blade was deliberately or accidentally *wiped* against the material? Wipin' and pumpin' leave very different traces.'

'Irrelevant,' Coleman snapped. 'Blood is blood, and there was only one knife in the room. Now, what I need you gentlemen to tell me is what you were doing visiting the accused.'

'He's my brother,' Sherlock said quietly. 'Mister Crowe is a family friend. We were meeting Mycroft for lunch.'

'Which tells me that the murder was not premeditated,' Coleman said, pencilling a note in the notebook. 'You don't kill a man knowing you've got someone turning up for lunch any moment. It was a spur-of-the-moment thing.'

'For what motive?' Crowe asked.

The sergeant looked up from his notebook. 'Business deal gone wrong, argument over a woman—could be a whole set of reasons. In the end, that's just a detail. The important thing is that we've got a murder and a murderer. That's all the magistrate will be interested in.' He paused. 'Now, if I could have your full names and addresses, I'll make a note for the file.'

Crowe gave the information, and Coleman dutifully wrote it down. Judging by the way he put his hands on the desk, ready to push himself to his feet, Sherlock realized that the interrogation was already at an end. He felt as if they were on a train, already hurtling down a preordained set of tracks, and there was no way to turn off and choose another direction.

'Could we see Mycroft?' he blurted. 'Just for a few minutes?'

Coleman looked dubious.

'What harm could it do?' Crowe asked gently. 'They are brothers, after all. And maybe seeing young Sherlock here will make your prisoner more amenable. More likely to confess.'

Sherlock glanced sideways at Crowe, shocked, but the big American winked at him with the eye that was facing away from Coleman.

The policeman thought for a moment, obviously reluctant. 'Oh, very well,' he said eventually, with bad grace. 'I don't suppose it will do any harm.'

He went to the door and opened it. A constable—the one who had escorted them from the Diogenes Club—was standing guard outside.

'Take these two down to see the accused,' Coleman said. 'Give them ten minutes with him, then escort them to the front door.' He turned back to Crowe and Sherlock. 'I appreciate your time, gentlemen. An unfortunate business, of course, but please remember—if nobody committed any crimes then you wouldn't need us, and I could go and join my father in the family haberdashery business.'

Coleman bustled out, and the constable gestured to them to follow him. He led them back through the maze-like interior of the building, down several flights of stairs to a basement level where the walls were lined with unpainted brick and pools of water glittered blackly on the tiled floor. A row of closed metal doors extended along the length of the corridor. The constable led them to a door about a third of the way along, then took a key ring from his belt and used one of the keys to unlock it. He gestured them in. 'Ten minutes, and not a second more. I'll be out here if there's any trouble.'

Crowe gestured to Sherlock to go in first and followed him in.

Mycroft was sitting upright on a bench that ran

along one side of the room, hands neatly clasped on his lap. His eyes were closed, but he opened them and looked up as Sherlock entered. Light was provided by a narrow barred and glassed slit at the top of the far wall that presumably gave on to the road. The cell was so small the three men nearly filled it. There was nowhere for Sherlock and Crowe to sit, so they stood.

'Nice of you to visit,' Mycroft said. 'I apologize for my surroundings.'

Crowe looked around. 'Cosy,' he said. 'Ah had worse when ah first sailed from America to England.'

'Yes,' Mycroft pointed out, 'but you had the chance to leave when the ship docked.'

'A good point,' Crowe conceded, 'but at least you get this accommodation for free. Ah had to pay for mine.'

'Will you two stop!' Sherlock snapped. 'This is serious.'

Mycroft nodded. 'I understand. I was merely trying to find some levity in the situation.'

'How are you feeling?' Sherlock asked.

'My head is pounding, and I feel woozy. That may just be the stress of being hurried through the streets by a group of burly policemen.' He shuddered. 'I rarely travel more than a hundred yards away from the Diogenes Club. My office and my lodgings are both within that ambit.' He glanced at Crowe. 'Have you made any progress in establishing how the murder was committed? I have come up with seven separate theories, but I lack the evidence to distinguish between them.'

Sherlock frowned. Seven possible theories? He couldn't even think of one.

'The man who visited you had a case,' Crowe pointed out.

'I remember it.'

'The inside was padded. Two objects had been stored inside. At least one of them was damp—or at least it left traces of a liquid behind.'

Mycroft frowned. 'Did this liquid smell of anything in particular? Was it sticky to the touch?'

Crowe shook his head. 'Felt an' smelt just like water.'

'And was there a pool of liquid anywhere in the room?'

'There was. Sherlock found it.'

'Instructive.' Mycroft nodded. 'That narrows the solution to one possibility.'

'Indeed,' Crowe said, nodding, 'but the evidence has vanished.'

Sherlock felt his fists clench. 'What on earth are you both talking about? What solution?'

The two men looked at each other. Mycroft gestured to Crowe to explain.

'Let's agree that there was no way for another man to be in the room,' Crowe started. 'There were no windows, no places to hide, and we would have seen anyone when your brother opened the door.'

'Agreed,' Sherlock said.

'And your brother didn't kill the dead man.'

'Of course not.'

'Therefore he killed himself.'

Sherlock felt as if the ground had suddenly dropped out from underneath him. 'He *what*?'

'He killed himself. Two men in a room, one is murdered, and we know that the other one didn't kill him. Ergo, he killed himself.'

'But . . .' Sherlock's voice failed him for a

moment. 'But Mycroft was holding the knife.'

'He was holding *a* knife,' Crowe corrected. 'The victim entered the room with a case containing two objects. One of them was the knife that we found your brother holding. There was no blood on the knife because it was not the knife that killed the dead man.'

'But there was no other knife!' Sherlock protested.

'But,' Mycroft interrupted, 'there was a damp patch in the case and a damp patch on the carpet.'

Crowe glanced at Mycroft, who shrugged.

'I apologize,' Mycroft added. 'I couldn't resist joining in.' He glanced back at Sherlock. 'Tell me, did the damp patch on the carpet feel cold at all?'

'It did,' Sherlock recalled, and then he realized. *'Ice?'* he exclaimed. 'The knife was made of *ice*?'

'Indubitably,' Crowe said. 'The second object in the case was a knife made of ice. The padding prevented it from melting, although some water did soak into the satin. The case had probably been kept cold before being used, to ensure that the knife did not melt.'

'The visitor incapacitated me,' Mycroft said grimly. *'How,* we will leave for a moment. After rendering me insensible, he placed the real knife in my hand. He then sat down and stabbed himself with the ice knife. With his last ounce of strength he pulled the ice knife from his chest and threw it to the floor, where it melted in the warmth of the room.'

'There was a risk that he would have died too quickly to pull the knife out,' Crowe pointed out, 'but in that case the residual warmth of his cooling corpse would have melted it anyway.'

61

'But why use two knives?' Sherlock protested. 'Why not just stab himself with the real knife and leave it in the wound?'

Crowe glanced sympathetically at Mycroft. 'Whoever arranged this little charade wanted to leave your brother with no room for manoeuvre. If he had been found in a room with a dead body which had a knife in its chest, he might have been able to claim that he'd found it there and was about to call for help. But if he was found with a knife in his hand, and no knife in the wound, he would not have been able to think of a convincing explanation.'

'A neat touch,' Mycroft admitted. 'I am quite in awe of whoever created this scenario.'

'Then why did the man kill himself?' Sherlock asked, exasperated. 'What were his reasons?'

'There,' Crowe said, 'we can only speculate, but remember that I thought the man looked ill. He was thin and pale, an' he'd been seeing a doctor. Let us suppose that he was poor an' he was dyin' of something like consumption, or a cancer. Let us suppose that someone currently unknown to us approached him an' offered him a deal. This unknown person would pay his family a large sum of money if the man would anticipate his own death by a few weeks, kill himself in service of this unknown man. This dyin' fellow agrees, an' is kitted out with a decent suit, a case containin' a real knife an' an ice knife, an' instructions as to what to do.'

'Which does raise the question,' Mycroft interrupted, 'as to how he rendered me temporarily insensible so that he could place the knife into my hand.'

'What do you remember?' Crowe asked.

Mycroft closed his eyes to recall. 'The man came in, and put his case on the table. He was coughing. I asked whether there was anything I could do to help. He said no, and added that he had some medicine that would help him breathe more easily. He reached into his jacket and took out a small bottle. The top was oddly shaped, more like a button than a cap. He asked me to give him a hand. I walked over to him, and . . . nothing. The next thing I remember is hearing you knocking on the door.' He paused, then went on, 'And a smell. I remember a smell. Heavy, and very bitter.'

'Ah venture,' Crowe said, 'that the medicine bottle was actually a pump spray of an alcoholic tincture of opium. He sprayed it in your face, rendering you insensible for a few moments. Your loss of memory would be consistent with being drugged in this way. This gave him enough time to set the scene.'

An alcoholic tincture of opium, otherwise known as laudanum—the same thing that Baron Maupertuis had drugged Sherlock with in order to take him from England to France. Sherlock still remembered the deep unconsciousness, the dreams and the loss of memory that accompanied his drugging. And the strange, almost pleasant, feeling of lassitude. He shook the memories away. This was no time to reminisce.

Crowe continued: 'If found, by the police or the pathologist, it would be assumed that he carried it around for his own purposes. Perhaps even to dull the pain of the disease that was killing him.'

'What happened to it?' Mycroft asked.

'Sherlock took it.' Crowe shrugged. 'Better that

than the police losing it.'

Mycroft nodded. He thought for a moment. 'A spray that can render people momentarily insensible. How very interesting. I can think of several official and semi-official uses for that.'

'All right.' Sherlock paused, trying to arrange his thoughts. 'We know how it might have been done. We have a theory that fits all the facts. The question is: *why*? *Why* was it done?'

Mycroft shrugged. 'As to that, I am engaged with several difficult negotiations with foreign governments. Perhaps one of them wishes to get me out of the way for a while so that they can gain some advantage. Alternatively, work I have been engaged in previously has several times led to treaties being signed with one country rather than another. Perhaps those other countries have taken exception to my actions, and have decided to extract some form of revenge.' A thought occurred to him. A serious thought, judging by the expression on his face. 'Except . . .'

'Except what?' Crowe asked.

Instead of answering, Mycroft reached inside his jacket. 'I still have the card the dead man gave to Brinnell. There was something written on it. Something that made me interested in seeing him.'

He pulled a slip of cardboard from his inside pocket. 'John Robertshaw,' he read, 'along with an address in Chelsea—Glassblowers' Road. Probably false, just created to add veracity to the card.'

'But worth checking anyway,' Crowe pointed out.

'Indeed. I would not want to let a clue get away from us because we dismissed it from our minds.' He turned the card over. 'My name, handwritten,

64

so that Brinnell would know who he wanted to see. And three words.'

He glanced up. His eyes met Sherlock's.

'The Paradol Chamber,' he said grimly.

Shocked, Sherlock's mind flashed back to the time he had spent in the clutches of Baron Maupertuis. The Baron had mentioned the Paradol Chamber. He hadn't said what it was, but he had referred to it as if he worked for it, or reported to it. As if it was something important, and secret.

'I remember now,' Mycroft continued. 'I saw the words, and I remembered what you had said about hearing Baron Maupertuis use the same phrase. I had Brinnell bring the man in so that I could question him. But this card was the bait in a trap.'

'And you took it,' Crowe observed mildly.

'In my own defence,' Mycroft protested, 'I was on familiar territory, and not expecting an attack.'

'And yet it came.' Crowe waved a large hand. 'No matter. We must move on. Ah will secure a solicitor for you. Sherlock, do you still have the name and address of the solicitor given to you by the footman at the Diogenes?'

Sherlock nodded, and passed across the slip of paper which he had kept in his shirt pocket.

'And you, Sherlock,' Crowe continued, 'will investigate this calling card.' Crowe handed over the card that Mycroft had retrieved from his jacket. Sherlock turned it over, and read the ominous words *The Paradol Chamber* with a shiver.

'How do I do that?' Sherlock asked.

'Smell the card,' Crowe instructed.

Sherlock raised it to his nose. There was a slight but noticeably sharp odour. 'What is it?' he asked.

'Printer's ink,' Crowe replied. 'The card has been

65

freshly made, probably as a one-off, just to get the man into the club. No respectable club would admit a man without a card, after all. He wouldn't have any cards himself, given his station in life, and his mysterious employer would hardly have given him one of his own. No, it was made recently, which means it was made locally.' He turned to Sherlock's brother. 'Mister Holmes, how many printers are located in the vicinity?'

Mycroft thought for a moment. 'I can think of four, all of them in the Chancery Lane area. I will give you the addresses.' He took a scrap of paper and a pen from his pocket and began to write.

'Check each of the printers,' Crowe instructed Sherlock. 'See if they recognize the card. See what they can tell you about the man who had it printed.'

'All right.'

'And meet me back, oh, outside the Sarbonnier Hotel in two hours. You remember where that is?'

'The place we stayed the last time we came to London? Yes, I remember.'

'Good.'

The door swung open as Crowe was speaking. 'Time's up,' the constable said. 'You gentlemen have to go.'

'Don't worry, Mycroft,' Crowe said. 'We will get you out of here.'

'I just hope that happens before dinner time,' Mycoft replied with a wan smile. 'I have missed luncheon, but I am not sure that the food here will be up to my usual standards.'

He extended a hand to Sherlock. 'Try not to think of me like this,' he said.

'Here, or in the club, or anywhere else,' Sherlock said, taking Mycroft's hand, 'you are my brother.

You take care of me. Now it's my turn to take care of you—if I can.'

'You can,' Mycroft said. 'And you will. I know that once you set your mind to something, it gets done. That is a trait we both inherit from our father.'

The constable coughed, and Sherlock reluctantly followed Amyus Crowe from the cell.

The clanging of the door behind him made him flinch. He hated to think what the sound did to Mycroft.

'Where now?' he asked as they emerged into the fresh air of Covent Garden.

'You to Chancery Lane, which is in that direction.' Crowe waved a hand vaguely. 'Me to—' he checked the card, 'Glassblowers' Road, Chelsea. We will meet later.'

He turned and strode off without a backwards glance, leaving Sherlock to stare after him uneasily. He was alone in London—again. He couldn't help remembering what had happened last time.

Eventually he turned away and started to walk in the direction Crowe had indicated. He passed taverns and shops, market stalls and people standing on street corners with trays of goods. And people—all kinds of people, from toffs in fine clothes to urchins in rags. London was indeed a melting pot for all humanity.

He was about to ask someone the way to Chancery Lane when he noticed a sign on the side of a road he was passing. He turned in. It was a more salubrious area than the one he'd passed through: judging by the brass plates on the buildings it was comprised mainly of firms of solicitors, augmented by the occasional doctor's practice.

After five minutes or so he came across the first printer's shop. The location made sense to him now: the solicitors and barristers in the area would no doubt have need of a lot of printing services. Nervously, he pushed the door open.

The smell inside was an intensified version of what he had smelt on the card: dry, musty and sharp. What he hadn't counted on was the noise. The clatter of several printing presses in the back of the shop made it almost impossible to hear his own voice when he said: 'Excuse me!'

A man turned to look at Sherlock. He was in shirtsleeves, but he wore a bowler hat. His moustache was luxuriant, covering not only his mouth but most of his chin as well.

'No jobs 'ere,' he said. 'Got all the printer's devils I need. Shove off!'

'I need to ask a question,' Sherlock said.

The man stared suspiciously. 'What?'

Sherlock passed the calling card across. 'Did you print this?'

He examined it critically. 'No. Now shove off.'

Sherlock backed away as the man turned back to his work. If each of the printers was that rude then he'd be finished within a few minutes, and at a loss to know what to do until he had to meet up with Amyus Crowe again.

The second printer was friendlier. This time Sherlock could see into the back of his shop, where metal drums covered in tiny metal letters were being rotated by boys younger than him, who were pushing all of their weight against great metal handles. The drums were pressed against long ribbons of paper that were pulled past them, leaving inked letters on the paper. The boys were covered in patches of ink as well, marking their skin in black and white.

He asked the same question, proffered the same card, but despite the fact that the printer smiled and tried to be helpful, he hadn't printed the card either.

Sherlock struck gold with the third printer.

This man was tall and thin, with whiskers that hung like ribbons down his gaunt cheeks. Looking at him, and remembering what Amyus Crowe had told him on the train about each man bearing the marks of his profession, Sherlock began to see the typical marks of a printer: the ink ingrained under the fingernails and in the creases in the fingers, the ridges along the fingertips left by years of prising metal type out of the printers, the long, straight cuts along the palms of the hands left by the ribbons of paper as the rollers whisked them past. All the marks were there for the person who wanted to see.

'Oh yes,' the man said, nodding. 'I remember this. Odd request. Normally people want four, five hundred cards, cos they're for leaving behind, right? I mean, you don't show someone your card and then take it back, do you? But this cove just wanted the one. Handed me a scrap of paper with the details written on it.' He shrugged. 'So I set the machine up and just printed the one card. Told him he could have a hundred for just a shilling more, but he said no.' He thought for a moment. 'Actually, he didn't say no—he went outside to talk to some other cove and *then* he came back and said no.'

'This other man—can you describe him?'

'Funny old thing,' the printer said, 'but I recognized him. He didn't recognize me. Nobody recognizes the people who serve them.'

'I do,' Sherlock promised. 'I *will.*'

'Then you're a better man than the rest. No, I used to work in a printer's down Drury Lane way, before I got this place. Used to do a lot of work for the theatres: programmes, playbills, posters—you know the kind of thing. This bloke—the one who was outside—used to come in sometimes. He was associated with one of the taverns along there. Worked as a bouncer—throwing out people who were too drunk or too poor to pay, or those who started fights. The Shaftesbury, I think it was. We used to print up menus and posters and suchlike for them.'

'Can you describe him?' Sherlock asked, holding his breath.

The printer shrugged. 'Small, like a whippet. Hair was long and stringy. Black beard. Wore a fuzzy coat. Asktrakhan, I think they call 'em. Don't remember his name.'

'Thanks,' Sherlock said. 'If I ever need a printer, I'll remember you.'

He left, triumphant. He checked his watch: still an hour and a half before he had to meet Amyus Crowe. Time enough to check out the Shaftesbury Tavern perhaps? That way, at least he could tell Crowe not only that he'd identified the man who had hired the dead man, but that he'd tracked him down as well.

He asked a passing woman where Drury Lane was, and then headed off in that direction. It only took him ten minutes.

Drury Lane was lined with theatres and taverns.

Some of the theatres were obviously music halls, showing numerous variety acts like jugglers and singers and escape artists. Some were more high-class, offering performances of classic plays. A few were playing host to musical recitals, and Sherlock found himself nostalgic for his violin playing when he saw that a woman named Wilma Norman-Neruda (a female violinist!) was playing at one of the theatres.

He found the Shaftesbury Tavern halfway down. It was next door to a theatre which was advertising a comic opera by F. C. Burnand and A. Sullivan called *Cox and Box*. It didn't sound appealing.

Sherlock sat on a doorstep outside a tavern across the road, and settled down to wait. He slumped sideways, and rested his head against the door frame, to make it look as if he was asleep, but he was watching out all the time for a small man with long stringy hair.

It was probably three-quarters of an hour later that a man fitting the description he'd been given left the Shaftesbury by the front door. He was dressed exactly as the printer had described him. He glanced up and down the street, then set off to his right.

Sherlock followed. Maybe the man would lead Sherlock to where he lived. That would be something to give to Amyus Crowe!

The man led Sherlock down Drury Lane, across a place called Seven Dials and then down towards Trafalgar Square. Sherlock was beginning to recognize bits of London now, and he was busy committing as much as he could to memory. The man turned left when he got to Trafalgar Square, walking past the ornate brown frontage of Charing

Cross Station and the Charing Cross Hotel. He walked fast, and Sherlock had to hurry to keep up.

At Aldwych he turned right, and Sherlock realized he was heading over the Thames, across Waterloo Bridge. He stopped at a booth at the end of the bridge and handed over some coins. Sherlock debated quickly with himself: should he follow, or should he just go back to see Amyus Crowe? But what was he going to tell Crowe? That he'd found the man and then lost him again? No, he had to go on—at least to the other side of the bridge to see which way the man went.

Sherlock scrabbled in his pockets for some coins. The toll was just a penny. He paid as he squeezed past the toll-collector and kept going, catching up with his quarry.

The small man just kept on walking, without looking backwards or to left or right.

At the other side of the bridge, he walked towards what Sherlock recognized as Waterloo Station, but instead of going into the station he turned left. Sherlock followed, trying to hide himself behind other people in case the man turned round.

He didn't turn round, but he did suddenly turn right, into an archway.

When Sherlock got to the archway, he paused, and peered round the edge of the crumbling brickwork. The interior of the arch was in shadow, and he couldn't see the man.

He took a step forward, then another, until he was half in and half out of the light. Still no sign of the man.

Sherlock turned round, ready to head back to meet Amyus Crowe.

The small man with the long, stringy hair was standing right behind him.

'You've been following me,' he said. 'I want to hear you tell me why. And then, just for giggles, I want to hear you scream.'

CHAPTER FIVE

'You got a penny, mister?' Sherlock whined, trying to look smaller than he was. 'I ain't eaten for days. Just a penny for a piece of bread.'

'Don't come the coney-catcher with me,' the man snarled. 'I ain't buyin' it.'

'All right,' Sherlock said in his normal voice, straightening up. 'So what *is* a coney-catcher, then?'

The man grinned. His teeth were black stubs. 'You want to know what a coney is? A coney is a rabbit that's been raised for the cooking pot, so it's tame and won't run away when you come to break its neck. A coney-*catcher* is a man who pretends to catch a coney—a man who makes something easy look difficult.'

'Oh, a con man,' Sherlock said.

'Exactly. Now we've got that out of the way, why *are* you following me?'

'I wasn't following you!' Sherlock protested.

The man raised a bushy eyebrow. 'Remember, I can see through every garment of pretence you care to put on, sonny. You started following me outside the theatre, and you've been with me ever since. What I want to know is, why?' He looked Sherlock up and down. 'You're not a flimp.' He

73

noticed Sherlock's expression. 'A pickpocket,' he clarified. 'So what is it you're after?'

'I'm not after anything.'

'You followed me through London, across Waterloo Bridge and down here, into the tunnels.'

'Coincidence,' Sherlock said.

'No such thing.' He shrugged. 'You don't have to tell me now, if you don't want to. I can just as easily beat it out of you. I'd enjoy that. It's been a while since I did some serious damage to a body. I've been following instructions, keeping my head down. I ain't seen the claret flow for a few weeks now, and I'm nostalgic.'

'The claret?' Sherlock asked, knowing that he wasn't going to like the answer.

'Blood, sonny. Blood.' He slipped his hand into his pocket. When it emerged, he was holding two metal objects that clinked together. 'Best as I can figure it, either you work for one of the local gangs and they want to know what's going on in the theatre, or you've spotted something odd at the theatre and you're hoping that you can sell a tale to the Peelers for a few coppers.' He slipped the fingers of his right hand through one of the metal objects. It looked to Sherlock like a collection of rings, fastened together and covered with spikes which pointed outward, rising up from his knuckles. 'Either way, your curiosity is going to cost you dearly.' He slipped the other metal object over the fingers of his left hand, and raised his fists so that Sherlock could see. The sparse light gleamed off the metal spikes. His hands had been transformed into deadly weapons that could slice Sherlock's face apart if they even came close. 'Now, let's make a start, shall we? I ain't got long. Things

74

to do, people to see.'

Sherlock started backing away, heart beating faster. The man was blocking the route out of the arches, but there was bound to be another way, somewhere behind him, in the darkness. Sherlock just had to find it.

The man smiled coldly. He slipped a hand inside his coat pocket, the spikes on his knuckledusters catching on the fabric as he did so. The hand came out again with a bunch of silvery coins held between the fingers.

'Half a crown for the first person to bring the kid to me!' he called out. 'You hear? You can live like a lord for a month on that, if you want. Half a crown, and I don't even care if anything's broken. Just as long as he can still answer my questions.'

The air around Sherlock seemed to rustle, as if it had a life of its own. He'd thought that he and the bearded man were alone in the arches underneath Waterloo Station, but the darkness moved, separating itself into five, six, ten small figures. They seemed to step out of the walls and pull themselves out of the squishy ground. They were small—smaller than Sherlock, smaller than his friend Matty—and their skin, where it could be seen through clothes that were more rips than rags, was grey with dirt and grease that had been ground in for so long that it had become a part of them. Children. Tunnel-dwellers, with no families and no way of surviving apart from scavenging in the dirt for things dropped by passing passengers. Their eyes were large and dark, like rats', and the nails on their fingers and what he could see of their toes were sharp and long and encrusted with dirt. Their mouths were ragged: blistered, split lips stretched tight over diseased gums. What few teeth remained in those mouths were blackened and jagged, like ancient mountains. The children couldn't even stand up straight: they spent so long scrabbling through narrow tunnels and searching through the mud and slime for dropped coins that they were hunched and bent. Their arms and legs were thin and twisted like branches, but their stomachs were strangely swollen. Straggly hair hung around their faces. He couldn't even tell which ones were boys and which ones girls: the dirt and the starvation made them look the same. And the smell: dear Lord, the sheer stench of rot and decay that poured off them, so intense that Sherlock could almost see the air rippling around them.

How could people *live* like this, he asked himself as he backed away. There was nothing in their eyes as they moved towards him apart from a voracious hunger. To them, he was nothing but a way to secure the next meal.

His perception kept shifting. For a second or two they were monsters, creatures of the night ready to swarm over him and take him down, and then suddenly they were children, driven to desperate things by hunger. He felt his emotions swing frantically between horror and sympathy. How could people—how could *children*—be allowed to live like this? It was *wrong*.

'You don't have to do this,' he said, still moving backwards. The feral children cocked their heads at the words, but he wasn't sure they'd understood. Or, if they'd understood, that they cared. All they knew was that the big man with the beard would pay riches for Sherlock to be bought to him, and if they had to break Sherlock's arms and legs to stop him getting away then that was just the way it had to be.

Sherlock had a feeling they'd done worse things, there in the darkness.

He turned to run, but there were four—no, *five*—of the children behind him. They had appeared noiselessly out of the shadows.

A hand caught at his sleeve. He recoiled, pulling the material from the thin fingers and hearing the fabric rip beneath the sharp nails.

He was surrounded.

In the light that spilt in from the street, Sherlock could see the bulky shadow of the bearded man. And he could hear him laughing.

Desperately he tried to suppress the panic that bubbled up within his chest. He had to think, and think quickly.

Another hand clutched at his elbow. He pushed it away. The skin that he touched felt *squishy*. Unconsciously, he wiped his hand on his jacket.

In seconds they would be swarming over him. He gazed around, looking for something, *anything* that he could use to get away.

The wall. His only hope was the arched wall to his left. The feral children were crowding him on all sides, but the way to the wall was clear.

He ran for it, jumping when he was just a few feet away. His feet scrabbled for gaps where the brick had crumbled away, and his fingers managed to get a grip between the bricks higher up. He hauled himself up, feeling the arch curve towards him above his head. He climbed as high as he could. Gravity was pulling at him. Beneath, the feral children were scampering up the wall after him, but the curve of the arch meant that he was now closer to the centre of the tunnel.

He pushed himself away from the wall, partly falling and partly leaping over their heads. He hit the spongy ground in the centre of the tunnel, stumbling but pushing himself back up to his feet. Before the children could work out what he had done, he turned and ran off into the darkness—the only direction he could go.

Within moments he had been swallowed up by shadows. In the distance behind him he could hear the *slap* of naked feet on moist earth. They were in pursuit.

He kept running, trusting to luck to keep him from hitting a tunnel wall. Either his eyes were growing accustomed to the darkness or there was some light spilling in from somewhere above, or perhaps some phosphorescent moss clinging to the tunnel walls, but he found that he could just make out the edges of the bricks as he ran.

He made out the curved shape of a second arch to one side—a tunnel, joining on to the one through which he was running. He swerved sideways, down this second tunnel. If he had any chance at all to escape his pursuers it was by confusing them, giving them too many options as to where he might have gone. If he just kept running in a straight line they would track him down for sure, and then . . . well, he wasn't entirely sure that the promise of a half-crown would overcome their immediate hunger, and their desire to search his pockets for whatever coins he might have on him.

The tunnel ended in a black wall and Sherlock nearly ran into it. Only a momentary change in the quality of the fetid air warned him that there was an obstruction ahead. He stopped abruptly and reached forward with a cautious hand. The wall was about two feet in front of him. If he hadn't realized in time then he would have collided with it, knocking himself out and leaving himself as easy prey for his feral pursuers.

Was he going to have to go back, try to find his way past them?

A breeze blew on his face, warm and stagnant, but definitely a breeze. Maybe this wasn't a dead end at all. Maybe it was a junction where one tunnel ended by joining up with another one.

He turned left and started to run, arm stretched ahead just in case he hit the wall. He didn't—the tunnel extended on towards whatever fresh hell was awaiting him.

A sudden thunderous noise overhead made him flinch. It seemed to go on forever. Rancid drops of water pattered on to his head from the roof of the tunnel. A train, maybe? He was probably beneath the tracks coming out of Waterloo Station.

Perhaps it was a train heading for Farnham, where his friends were. Would he ever see them again, or would he die here, in darkness, undiscovered forever?

He felt his breath catch in his throat. Somewhere up there was a calm, ordered world where well-dressed people walked purposefully back and forth. Up there were blue skies, solid brick walls, firm marble floors and gas lights. Up there was heaven. Down here there was crumbling brickwork trickling with water, ground that was somewhere between solid and liquid, a smell that combined the worst elements of tar, human filth and decaying plants, and despondent children who were little more than animals. This was definitely hell.

He felt as if he couldn't go on. He wanted to sit down, curl himself up into a ball and hope that he could force himself awake from this nightmare. Because it had to be a nightmare, didn't it? There couldn't really be places like this in the neatly ordered world in which he lived.

But it was real. He knew it was real. He couldn't give up. He had to find a way out.

Mycroft was depending on him.

Up ahead he could see a shaft of light crossing the tunnel diagonally, top to bottom. It was probably just a crack in the brickwork through which weak sunlight was filtering, but to his dark-attuned eyes it was like a pillar of gold. He stumbled towards it, hoping that maybe the crack was big enough for him to climb into, up towards the station. Up towards safety and sanity.

It wasn't. The crack was barely big enough for him to get his fingers into, and the light was a mere glimmer, refracted through a trickle of water that flowed down from above. Angrily he clawed at the brickwork, hoping against hope that he could widen the gap. For a moment it resisted him, but then it crumbled away, falling to the floor of the tunnel.

Beneath the brick, he caught a glimpse of something moving: something hard, black and glistening. He stared, wondering what on earth it was, and then recoiled in horror as he realized that he was looking at a mass of beetles, or maybe cockroaches, all scurrying away from the light and the air now that he had destroyed the walls of their hideaway, their lair. Within seconds they had vanished, leaving a rough hole behind. Sherlock glanced around, feeling his skin crawl. Was it the same behind every wall, every brick in the tunnel? Was there a second, hidden world of eyeless beetles living in cavities and channels, scavenging on what even the feral children left behind?

Listening carefully, he thought he could hear the quiet scurrying of the beetles everywhere around him. Surrounding him. Burying him.

With a meaningless cry of heartfelt fear, he started to run.

Ten steps down the tunnel, something dropped on him from the darkness above.

He screamed, clawing at whatever it was that was wrapping itself around his face. In his mind it was a mass of beetles, all working together, or perhaps just one gigantic cockroach the size of his head, but as his fingers clawed at the thing he found he was touching rags and slimy flesh. A hand tried to get a grip beneath his chin. It was a girl! One of the feral children who had been tracking him through the tunnels! Somehow she had managed to get ahead of him and waited, pressing herself tight to the brickwork before dropping on him as he passed beneath. His fingers closed on her neck, just as he felt her mouth, with whatever remnants of teeth she still possessed, try to fasten itself on his cheek. She was small and weak, and despite the way she squirmed away from him he managed to get a grip with his other hand on her leg, or perhaps her arm. He hesitated for a moment, aware that this was a *child*, a *girl*, and knowing that civilized people didn't hurt girls, but her fingernails were raking painfully against his skin. He didn't see that he had any choice. With a convulsive movement he pulled her off him and threw her across the tunnel. She hit the soft, marshy ground and rolled away. In the

81

meagre light that spilt into the tunnel he could see her eyes gleaming. She hissed, and scuttled back into the darkness, but he knew she hadn't gone far. She was still there, watching and waiting for her chance.

His emotions flickered again, and he thought with a desperate lurch of his stomach about Matty, living by his wits and always wondering where the next meal was coming from. How much would it take to push Matty into a life like this? Not much, he suspected. These were *children*, for Heaven's sake! They weren't vampires!

He moved on, hearing a scrabbling in the shadows as the girl paced him. Somewhere behind he could hear a wordless yelping as the other kids searched.

Children or vampires, it didn't matter. He was going to die. There was no way out. He could feel his heart thudding against his ribs, feel the desperation in his lungs as he tried to catch his breath, feel the burn within the muscles of his legs as he staggered on. He wasn't going to make it.

'A farthing for your life,' a voice hissed from beside him.

'All right,' he breathed. 'A farthing it is.'

'Got to see it now,' the voice insisted.

Sherlock slipped a hand in his pocket and pulled out a handful of loose change. 'You can have all this if you get me out of here alive.'

The child in the darkness drew in a breath. 'Never seen that much before!' it whispered. 'You must be rich!'

'Not that it's going to do me much good if I die down here,' Sherlock said urgently, aware of the sounds of searching in the darkness. 'Take me back to where I came in!'

'Can't do that. They're watching and waiting. Got to go another way.'

Sherlock swallowed. 'Which way?'

'Follow me.'

A shape appeared beside Sherlock, seeming to pull itself out of the wall. It—he?—barely came up to Sherlock's chest, but there was something in his eyes that made him much older. That child had seen things that Sherlock hoped he'd never have to see.

'What's your name?' Sherlock asked as the child slipped away like a fish through the darkness.

'Don't got a name,' the whisper floated back.

'Everyone's got a name,' Sherlock insisted.

'Not down here. Names don't help anything.'

Sherlock was dimly aware that the child had turned sideways, back into the curved wall from where he had come. He moved across to the brickwork. A gap extended from floor to head height: not a crack, but an artificial, regular space. Maybe something left for ventilation, or perhaps for some other purpose. Sherlock heard scrabbling inside. Taking a breath, he followed.

The next five minutes were the worst Sherlock had ever experienced. Pressed between two vertical cliffs of damp, crumbling brick and hearing, or perhaps just *sensing*, the blind insects crawling through their channels a few inches away from his face, he pushed his way deeper and deeper into the unknown. Rough brick scraped at his face and hands. Cobwebs, strung from side to side, caught in his hair. Things dropped, scuttling, from the webs into his collar, and he had to fight the almost overwhelming urge to hit at his clothes to kill them as they looked for somewhere to hide. Every now and then his questing hands would find a trickle of something damp coming down the walls. He supposed it was water, but in the dark he couldn't see what it looked like, and if it *was* water then it didn't smell like anything he'd ever smelt before. It was more like something sticky and alive, as if he was pushing himself deeper and deeper inside the throat of some vast, ancient dragon, and what he could feel was its corrosive saliva. He could feel the ground—if it was ground, and not a tongue— beneath his feet squishing as he walked, and he had the terrible feeling that if he were to stop then he would slowly sink into the mire, up to his knees, then his hips, then his neck and then, if his feet hadn't touched something solid, the soft mud would close over his head and he would suffocate.

The feral boy ahead of him seemed to be climbing rather than walking. Fingers and toes found cracks in the brickwork, and he moved above, rather than across, the yielding mud. Nails scraped against the bricks with a grating sound that made Sherlock want to scream. He'd obviously learned how to move around the tunnels and arches in a way that Sherlock couldn't.

Abruptly the brickwork narrowed to a point where Sherlock had to turn sideways to get through. The walls clutched at his chest and his back. He breathed out, making his chest as thin as he could. He squeezed himself forward as far as possible, but eventually a projecting brick caught against his ribs and he knew he couldn't go any further.

He couldn't breathe. Not properly, anyway. The gap was too small to allow him to take more than a small gulp of air.

Panic welled up within him, dark and acidic. He tried to move back, but something in the narrow cleft had changed. Maybe by moving through it he had shifted some of the bricks. Whatever it was, it was as if the gap behind him had actually narrowed after he'd passed through it. When he tried to push himself backwards he found that something hard was pressing into his spine. He couldn't move forward or back. He was trapped!

He wanted to cry out, but he couldn't take enough air into his lungs. A red mist seemed to spill across his vision. His heart stuttered, beating heavily and irregularly, apparently trying to break out of his ribcage as desperately as he was trying to break out of the cleft.

A hand grabbed his wrist and pulled, hard. Brick scraped skin from his back and his ribs, but then the brick crumbled away in a shower of gritty dust and desperately flailing insects and he popped out like a cork from a bottle into a wider area.

The feral boy was standing in front of him. It had been his hand that had pulled Sherlock free.

'You could have just left me,' Sherlock breathed through gulps of air. 'You could have just waited until I'd suffocated and just taken all the money from my pockets.'

'Oh,' the boy said, expression unreadable. 'Yeah. S'pose I could've at that.' He turned away, then looked over his shoulder at Sherlock. 'Got to keep going. They're not far behind.'

Just a few feet ahead, the gap ended in a narrow flight of steps. Sherlock followed the boy up and out into a cavernous space, and what he saw made him gasp in disbelief.

They had emerged into what appeared to be a massive warehouse, so full of stacked boxes that Sherlock couldn't see the walls. He could see the ceiling, however. It was made of grimy panes of glass held together in an iron framework, with blessed sunlight spilling through them, so bright to his dark-adapted eyes that he had to squint to see anything. Bigger iron girders crossed the space beneath them. Somewhere up there he could hear birds fluttering.

But it was the boxes that caught his attention. They were long—about seven feet from end to end—and narrow, but their sides weren't regular. They swelled out to their widest point about a quarter of the way along, then narrowed again. For a few seconds he stared at them blankly, trying to work out what they were, and then he realized. Actually, he had known from the first moment he saw them, but his mind just hadn't let him accept the horrible truth.

They were coffins.

'What *is* this place?' he gasped.

'It's where they store the bodies, ready to ship 'em to the Nekrops.'

'The Nekrops?' He'd not heard the word before.

'Yeah. You know. The place where dead people are taken.'

Sherlock's mind raced. 'You mean a cemetery?' And then it clicked. 'You mean a *Necropolis*.' The Greek he'd learned at Deepdene School came flooding back: a necropolis, a city of the dead.

'Yeah. Down at Brookwood. That's where the trains go.'

Brookwood? That was near Farnham, where his aunt and uncle lived. Where he was staying. And then he remembered something that Matty Arnatt had said when they first met, about not wanting to cycle to Brookwood. He hadn't wanted to say why, and Sherlock hadn't pursued the matter. Now he knew. There was obviously some kind of massive cemetery at Brookwood: a place where bodies were shipped from far away.

'Why don't they bury them in London?' he asked.

'No room,' his rescuer said succinctly. 'Graveyards here are all full. Bodies buried on top of other bodies. Come a decent rainstorm and coffins're bein' washed up an' exposed for everyone to see.'

Sherlock looked around at the piles of coffins, noticing that they all had a chalked number on the side. Presumably the numbers corresponded to entries on a list that somebody had written down somewhere, so that a particular coffin could be associated with a particular funeral. 'And all of these are . . . occupied?'

The boy nodded. 'Every one of them.' He paused. 'Good pickings.'

'What do you mean?'

'Boxes sometimes get dropped. Smashed. And people sometimes get buried with their possessions—watches, rings, all kinds of stuff. And there's the clothes as well. Some people'll pay well for a nice jacket. Don't matter who was wearing it before them.'

Sherlock felt sick. This was a whole new world, and one he didn't want any part of. But despite himself, he couldn't help but ask more questions. He needed to know. 'So how do they get to Brookwood?'

'Special railway.' The boy gestured into the distance. 'Nekrops Railway. Tracks are over there.'

'They run trains just for the dead?'

'And for the ones they left behind.' The kid smiled, revealing a mouth with one rotten tooth left in it. 'First, second and third class travel, just for the coffins. Travel in style when you're dead, you can.' He gestured around. 'Good thing people don't see how their loved ones're looked after before they get put on the train, ain't it?'

Sherlock looked around again, at the serried ranks of coffins, stacked up higher than his head. All with dead bodies inside. He was standing among enough dead bodies to populate a small town. Scary stuff.

'All right,' he said. 'Let's go.'

The boy shook his head. 'You're on your own from here, mate.'

'All right.' Sherlock handed across the fistful of change from his pocket. 'Thanks.'

The boy nodded. 'You're a gent.' He stepped back, put his fingers to his lips and let out a whistle so loud it hurt Sherlock's ears. ''E's over 'ere!' he yelled at the top of his voice. ''E's escapin'!'

'I thought you were helping me,' Sherlock protested.

'I was.' The boy shook the fist in which he was holding the coins. 'Deal's completed. Now I'm 'elpin' them. Maybe they'll let me 'ave your shoes.'

Sherlock could hear noises from the narrow gap he'd emerged from—the sound of long fingernails and toenails against brick. Looking into the darkness he could see the glitter of tiny eyes blinking in the light.

He stepped forward and caught the boy by the

wrist. Twisting him round, he pushed him into the gap. 'He's got my money!' he shouted. 'He's holding it!'

The boy stared back at Sherlock in horror for a moment before he was pulled into the shadows by a score of tiny hands. Sherlock heard him shout, and then there was nothing but the sounds of fighting and cloth tearing.

He ran. While they were distracted, he had a chance to get away.

Still feeling breathless, still feeling a burning in his lungs and his muscles, he moved as fast as he could through the stacks of coffins. Within a few moments he was clear and out in the open.

Ahead of him were three steam trains. They were on rails, but standing at the end of the line, nestled against barriers. They were like the one that had bought him and Amyus Crowe to London, except that they were painted black: engine and carriages. Each of the carriages had a white skull painted on it at the front and the back. The white skulls had crossed bones beneath them.

Sherlock assumed that the trains only ran after dark. Seeing one of those during the day would be a distressing experience for anyone.

Then again, having one appearing at night out of a cloud of smoke, boiler glowing red with the heat of the burning coals, would be a pretty terrifying experience as well.

He glanced back over his shoulder at the stacks of coffins. In the shadows around them he thought he could see the glimmer of eyes watching him, but he wasn't sure. The important thing was that they weren't pursuing him. They wouldn't come into the light, and he certainly wasn't going to go back into the darkness. It was over. For the moment.

He turned and took a step forward. Something crunched beneath his feet. He looked down, and saw a white section of bone protruding from the ground. He'd stepped on it, cracking it in two. *Boxes sometimes get dropped,* the feral boy had said. *Smashed.* It looked like the contents got left where they had fallen. All this pomp and circumstance for the dead—special trains, a massive city of the dead at Brookwood—and yet the remains were just left to rot where they fell if the coffins got broken. It was as if the spectacle was more important than the actuality. The mourners did not know, or maybe even did not care, whether the family member they had lost was in the coffin when it was buried.

Somewhere beyond the trains, the tracks would lead out into the open air. A breeze was blowing in, scouring away the smell of the catacombs through which Sherlock had been chased and in which he had so nearly lost his life. He trudged wearily towards the weak sunlight. Somewhere out there, back in the real world, Mycroft was still facing a murder charge, and Sherlock had to help clear his name. He was exhausted and in pain, but that didn't matter. Mycroft needed his help.

He was so tied up with his own thoughts that it took him a few seconds to register the fact that the man with the stringy hair had just stepped out from behind the engine of one of the trains.

'No escape for you, sonny,' he said. He raised his hands. The meagre light glinted off the metal spikes on his knuckledusters. 'And it looks like I saved myself a half-crown into the bargain.'

90

CHAPTER SIX

Sherlock felt his heart sink. All that effort, all that running, all that scraping of his skin against brick, and he still couldn't get clear. He was too tired to do anything more. He had run out of energy.

'How did you find me?' he wheezed.

'I couldn't get through those gaps, could I?' the man replied. 'But I knew most of them came out here in the bone yards, so I made my way around the outside and waited. I was about to give up when I heard you scraping through.' He paused. 'I still need you to tell me why you were following me,' he said darkly. 'And then you die.'

A bulky shape moved smoothly out from the space between engine and tender, behind the man with the beard and the knuckledusters. It was wearing a hat.

Sherlock recognized Amyus Crowe just as Crowe slipped his left arm round the thug's neck, grabbing the wrist with his right hand. The man's neck was caught in the crook of Crowe's elbow. Sherlock saw the fabric of Crowe's sleeve tighten as he tensed his muscles.

The man's eyes bulged. He brought his hands up to grab at Crowe's arm, but he couldn't budge it no matter how much he pulled. His face turned purple as Sherlock watched, too tired to be amazed. Crowe must have been exerting enough force to stop the man from breathing.

The man desperately kicked back with his booted right foot, but Crowe had braced his legs to either side and his captive couldn't reach. Next

91

he took his hands away from Crowe's arm and punched backwards, behind his head, hoping to catch Crowe with the spikes of his knuckledusters, but Crowe just moved his head out of the way and increased the pressure on the man's throat.

'Ah'm disappointed that you were careless enough to let this man see you following him,' he said mildly, looking at Sherlock over the man's shoulder.

Sherlock ran a grimy hand through his hair. 'Sorry,' he said. 'I thought I'd kept myself well out of sight.'

'Learn a lesson,' Crowe said amiably. 'Traps can be reversed. *That's* the difference between animals and humans—rabbits don't suddenly turn around and hunt foxes, but men can switch roles. Prey can become predator. Look out for the signs. If your prey is leadin' you somewhere isolated then just maybe they've spotted you and want to get you alone.'

'Don't you ever stop teaching?' Sherlock asked wearily, remembering the lesson on the lake while they were fishing.

'Life teaches us all the time, if we're alert enough to understand.' Crowe's gaze flickered sideways, to where the man's face was becoming increasingly congested and his eyes were bulging. 'Now,' he said conversationally, 'let's you and me have a little talk. Why are you threatening my friend and protégé here with violence? That ain't particularly civilized, friend.'

'He was following me,' the man wheezed.

Crowe looked over at Sherlock and raised his eyebrow. 'Ah presume you had a reason,' he said. 'You weren't just practisin' your trackin' skills—

although they obviously do need the practice.'

'I found the printer who made the visiting card,' Sherlock said. 'He said that this man was waiting out in the street for the man who had the visiting card printed. They went off together.'

Crowe nodded. 'I assumed it was something like that.' He turned his attention back to his captive. 'So, that leads us to the question of *why*? Why did you pay for a poor, sick man to have a single visiting card printed up, and why did you then send him in to visit Mister Mycroft Holmes in his club?'

The man tugged at Crowe's arm. 'You're *choking* me!' he protested.

'Neatly spotted. I *am* choking you.'

'You're breaking my *neck*!'

'Not yet. Another few ounces of pressure and your neck will snap like a rotten twig, yes, but not just yet. You'll suffocate first.'

'You're *killing* me!'

'Yes,' Crowe confirmed. 'Ah believe ah am. Talk fast.'

'I was paid!'

'Of course you were. Ah didn't think you were doin' this out of love of Queen and country. The question is: who was payin' you?'

'I don't know their name!' The man pounded on Crowe's rigid left arm. 'Just let me breathe! Please!'

Crowe released his grip by a fraction, and the man drew in a shuddering breath. His lank hair was plastered across his face. His face lost some of its beetroot colour.

'I was approached in the Shaftesbury Tavern one night,' he gasped. 'People know I'm a fixer. I can make deals, and find the right people for a blagging, or anything you want. I was told to find a man who was close to meeting his Maker and needed money for his family. I was told to persuade him to do one last thing, and if he did it properly he would secure his family's future comfort.'

'And you knew a man like that?'

'I knew hundreds of men like that! They're ten a penny around here. Consumption, alcoholism, gut-rot—there're many ways to die in London.'

'And what *was* this last task he had to complete?'

The man was silent.

Crowe tightened his grip. 'Just one more ounce of pressure,' he murmured, 'and the last sound you will hear is your neck breaking. Ah've done it to cougars, ah've done it to alligators, and ah've even done it to a bull in my time. You will not present much of a challenge, believe me.'

'He had to go to this club in Whitehall,' the man said hurriedly, 'and ask to see a man in private. Alone, like. A man named Mycroft Holmes. And then hand over a card which we had to have printed up. Just the one card. And when he was alone with this cove, he had to spray some stuff in the cove's face—stuff from this thing like a perfume bottle. The cove would look like he had fallen asleep on his feet. Then he had to put a real knife in the cove's hand and stab *himself* in the heart with another knife made of ice. Like a pantomime it was.'

'Where did the knives come from?'

'I was told that a boy would run up to us as we got to the club. He'd give us a case with the knives in it. We had to do it that way, otherwise the ice knife might melt, even though it was in the case.'

Crowe smiled. 'Didn't this all strike you as a bit

94

strange?'

'I've done stranger,' the man admitted, 'and I was being well paid.'

'This man who hired you—did you know his name? Can you describe him?'

'I didn't say it was a bloke, did I?'

Crowe's eyebrows lifted in surprise. 'Indeed you did not. My mistake. So—you were hired by a woman?'

He nodded, as much as he was able with Crowe's arms around his neck. 'A woman, yes.'

'Describe her.'

'Youngish. Slim. Well-dressed.'

Crowe snorted. 'The face, man—describe the face.'

'Couldn't see it. She was wearing a big hat and a veil.'

'Colour of hair?'

'Couldn't see under the hat.'

'But you followed her, didn't you? After she hired you?'

Sherlock saw the man's eyes flicker with surprise. 'How did you know?' he hissed.

'Ah know *you*, my friend. Or at least, ah know men *like* you. A woman with a large wad of cash— of course you followed her. You wanted to find out where she lived, in case you could break in later and steal the rest of the cash she obviously kept on the premises. Men like you are always looking for an openin', an opportunity. So—where did she go?'

The man shrugged, shifting Crowe's arms slightly. 'Didn't go to no house. She went to a museum in Bow. Called the Passmore Edwards, it is. Used to be a big manor house. I waited for a couple of hours, but she never came out again. I don't know if she lives there, or if there was a way out at the back, but I never saw her again.'

'Anything else? Any other facts you want to impart to us?'

'No—no, I swear!'

Crowe abruptly released the man, who fell to his knees, choking and holding his throat.

'Ah think we've gotten all we can from this fellow,' Crowe said to Sherlock. 'If you're feeling up to it, let's repair to a coffee house and get some refreshments.' He cast a critical eye over Sherlock's mud-stained trousers and boots, and his brick dust-splattered jacket. 'Maybe we can find a clothes shop first. You're not going to make a good impression looking like that.'

Before Sherlock could reply, the small man suddenly surged up from the ground, arm swinging round, spiked knuckleduster slicing towards Amyus Crowe's face. He was snarling; his face contorted in a mask of fury. 'Try to choke me, would you?' he shouted.

Crowe leaned back out of the way of the spikes. They slashed across in front of his eyes, just a few inches away. As they passed he stepped forward, twisted his body to the left and kicked out with his right foot. His boot made contact with the man's knee. Sherlock heard something snap. The man crumpled to the ground, screaming.

'Let's go,' Crowe said, gesturing to Sherlock. 'Ah feel there's a pot of coffee and a cream cake somewhere with my name on it, an' ah intend findin' it.'

He led the way out, with Sherlock following. They left the small thug curled up on the ground, holding his shattered knee.

'Shouldn't we notify the police?' Sherlock asked. 'Shouldn't they arrest him?'

Crowe shrugged. 'If it makes you feel better ah guess we could, but it's his word against ours, and the only permanent damage was done by me to him. Any self-respectin' policeman would prob'ly arrest me instead of him. Or arrest both of us until he sorted out what had actually happened.'

'But that's not fair!' Sherlock protested.

'Perhaps not, but it's justice. If you don't know the difference between the two, you need to learn.'

Crowe led the way back towards the streets and alleys and archways of the area around Waterloo Station.

'How did you find me?' Sherlock asked, walking alongside him.

'Simple answer: ah was followin' you.'

'I didn't see you,' Sherlock protested.

'That's what you can expect when ah follow you. Unlike you, ah can keep myself in the shadows, or in crowds, or around corners.'

'Why were you following me?'

'After ah'd checked out that address on the card—which was false, by the by—ah thought ah'd catch up with you. Ah checked the printers in reverse order—startin' at the last one on the list and workin' backwards. Ah saw you leavin' the second printer ah tried—the third one *you* tried. Ah was tryin' to catch up, but you were walkin' fast. An' then you stopped an' started watchin' a tavern. Ah guessed you were on a trail, an' ah didn't want to draw attention to you, so ah just hunkered down in a doorway to see what was goin' on. After a while you started followin' that bearded guy, so ah just tagged along for the ride. Saw him corner

97

you in the archway, but you ran off before ah could intervene. Ah spent the next hour workin' my way around the outside, tryin' to determine where you might emerge.'

'Oh,' Sherlock said, mollified. 'That makes sense.'

They were at the front of the station by now. Crowe spotted a small tailor's shop located a few doors away from a cobbler's. Within ten minutes they had a new pair of trousers, new jacket, new shirt and new boots for Sherlock. Crowe paid without any comment. Sherlock assumed that he would sort it out with Mycroft later—if Mycroft ever got released, that was.

Leaving the cobbler's shop, Crowe led the way to an Aerated Bread Company tearoom nearby. They sat at a table in the window. Sherlock felt oddly disconnected from reality. Less than an hour before he had been running for his life through dark tunnels, and now he was sitting in the sunshine waiting for a cake to arrive. Life could be strange, sometimes. Actually, he reflected, life could be strange a lot of the time.

'So, what next?' he asked once the tray of coffee and cakes had arrived.

'Let's take stock of what we know.' Crowe took a bite of his sponge cake. 'There's at least a double cut-out between the person givin' the orders and the people carryin' them out.'

Sherlock frowned. 'What do you mean, a "double cut-out"?'

'Ah mean that the man who killed himself in the Diogenes Club never met the woman in the veil. *She* hired the man with the beard, an' *he* hired the man who was prepared to kill himself so that his family's financial future could be assured.'

'Maybe the woman was hired by someone else. Maybe there's a triple cut-out.'

'It's possible,' Crowe mused. 'Whoever is organizin' this is very cautious. They're makin' sure that nobody can trace back to them. The only reason we got this far is thanks to two unplanned events—the first bein' that your printer recognized the man with the beard, an' the second bein' that the fellow with the beard was greedy and immoral enough to follow the woman who hired him to this museum he talked about. Never underestimate the value of an unplanned coincidence.'

'But to what end?' Sherlock asked. 'What exactly are they trying to achieve?'

Crowe shrugged. 'The immediate aim seems to be to discredit your brother, or otherwise get him out of the way. The long-term aim—not sure about that. We need more information.'

Sherlock sighed. He'd thought he was hungry, after all the running around, but the cakes just didn't appeal to him. 'What can we do?' he asked.

'As ah see it,' Crowe said, 'we have three options. First: we could tell the police what we know and return to Farnham, hopin' that the Diogenes Club solicitor can get Mycroft out of prison and clear his name.'

'What are the odds on that?' Sherlock asked.

'Slim. The police ain't goin' to be inclined to investigate a crime where they've got clear evidence against a man already in custody, an' with the best will in the world our story ain't exactly easy to believe. An' our evidence has melted away.'

'But we've got the laudanum spray!'

Crowe shrugged. 'Could be medicine, like your

brother said. An' we can't just produce it out of nowhere. We might have bought it at a pharmacist down the street.'

'What's the second option?'

'We stay in London an' talk to your brother's employers in the Foreign Office—get them to take action an' get him out.'

Sherlock winced. 'Even to me, that doesn't sound likely to succeed.'

'Indeed. There's a good chance that the Foreign Office will just leave your brother twistin' in the wind. Last thing they want is embarrassment an' publicity.'

'Then we follow the third option,' Sherlock said decisively.

Crowe smiled. 'You don't even know what it is yet.'

'I can guess.' Sherlock's gaze met Crowe's deceptively amiable stare. 'We amass enough evidence by ourselves to clear Mycroft's name. We go to this museum in Bow and try to find the woman in the veil.'

Crowe nodded. 'That's about the size of it. An' frankly, I don't hold out much of a hope for our chances. It's a long shot, it really is.'

'Why isn't there someone we can go to?' Sherlock exploded. 'Why isn't there someone who can investigate things that the police won't or can't investigate? Some kind of independent, consulting force of detectives who can set things straight, like the Pinkerton Agency in America that you told me about?'

'It would require someone with a whole set of interestin' qualities, that's for sure,' Crowe said with a strange expression on his face. 'But it's a career niche that's currently unoccupied here in England.' He seemed to pull himself back from wherever his thoughts had taken him. 'All right, I suggest we secure a hansom cab an' ask the driver to take us to the museum in Bow.'

They caught a cab straight away, although Sherlock noticed that Crowe deliberately let two empty cabs go past without hailing them, choosing the third at the last second as it was about to swing past the spot where they were standing.

'Why didn't you go for the first cab?' Sherlock asked as they climbed in.

'Because we're blunderin' around the edges of a web spun by someone,' Crowe answered, 'an' I wanted to make sure that the cab we got into was our choice, not someone else's.'

'What was wrong with the second cab, then?'

Crowe smiled. 'The horse was lame. Ah doubt it would have made it all the way to Bow. An' ah didn't like the driver's moustache.'

They settled themselves down in the seats, and the driver's face appeared in the hatch above them. 'Where to, gents?'

'Do you know the Passmore Edwards Museum?' Crowe asked.

The journey took half an hour or so, and Sherlock spent the time looking out at the slices of real life presented to him: washing lines full of clothes, strung between windows on opposite sides of the street; hard-faced men lounging around on street corners; street vendors with trays of sweets, fruits and flowers; knife grinders wheeling their barrows around and calling out to see if anyone wanted their knives sharpened on the pedal-operated whetstones they were pushing.

The museum was an orange-brown stone building with built-out corners and an ornately pillared porch. It was set back from the street, separated from the pavement by a strip of grass and a knee-high metal fence. A block of stone set into the wall next to the front door had been carved with the words *Passmore Edwards Museum of Natural Curiosities*.

'Drive on past,' Crowe called to the driver. 'Drop us off on the corner of the street.'

The cabbie brought his horse to a halt where Crowe had indicated. Crowe paid, and the two of them got down from the cab.

'Don't look directly at the building,' Crowe instructed. 'Just stand here and talk for a few seconds. Let's absorb any impressions we get.'

'Call me stupid,' Sherlock said, 'but I get the impression it *is* a museum. It doesn't look like it's a front for anything.'

'It might just have been a convenient meeting place,' Crowe mused. 'Something chosen almost at random, rather than the headquarters of a conspiracy. If so, we're not going to discover anything here, and we've pretty much run out of evidence to follow.'

'The least we can do is look around,' Sherlock pointed out. 'We might see something, or hear something, or someone might remember seeing a woman in a veil.'

'Good point, well made,' Crowe said.

Crowe led the way towards the front door, to all intents and purposes a father taking his son out for the day.

They entered an empty lobby from which a stairway led up and then split left and right. It could have been the entrance hall of any reasonably large town house, if not for the huge glass case that filled the centre of the tiled floor. Inside the case was a reasonably accurate representation of a section of woodland, and populating it were various stuffed animals: a fox, several stoats, numerous mice, rats and voles, and one rather tatty otter which looked as if it belonged somewhere else entirely. The animals were posed in positions of startled alertness, as if they had been caught in the middle of investigating an unexpected and loud noise. Their glassy black eyes seemed to be staring in all directions.

A man in a blue uniform and a blue peaked cap approached them. 'Would you like two tickets, sir?' he said. 'Just tuppence apiece, and you can stay as long as you want. Very quiet at the moment.'

'Thank you,' Crowe said, handing the man a couple of coins. 'What can you recommend in the way of exhibits?'

The man considered for a moment. 'The small mammal gallery, up and to your right, is often praised for its veracity. Alternatively, the amphibian gallery up and to your left has a number of unusual specimens which the kids seem to love.'

'We'll split up,' Crowe said as the man moved off. 'Ah'll do amphibians, you do mammals. Meet back here in half an hour and if we haven't discovered anything of interest then we can move on to another gallery.'

'What counts as something of interest?'

'Like ah said back at the Diogenes Club— anything that doesn't fit. Anything that stands out.'

'In a museum of stuffed animals?'

Crowe had the grace to smile. 'It's all to do

103

with context. In the street, a dog walking past isn't unusual. In a museum of stuffed animals, it is.'

'All right,' Sherlock said dubiously.

They climbed the first set of marble steps together, then separated where the stairs went left and right. Sherlock went right, Crowe left.

The stairs led to a balcony that ran around the upper space of the entrance hall. The balcony was edged with a waist-high balustrade of stone. Doors led off to what were presumably different halls of exhibits. A chandelier of cut-glass droplets and candles hung from the centre of the ceiling.

Sherlock headed through the first door. Beyond, he found himself in a long room which was broken up by a series of glass cabinets so that he couldn't get a view all the way down. A skylight in the roof let in bright sunlight. He could hear voices somewhere in the room, but he couldn't see anyone else.

He set off towards the far end, walking around the cases where he had to and briefly checking each of them out. As the attendant had said, this was the small mammal gallery. A ferret, poised perkily in an arrangement of dried grasses, was in a case next to a large, tan-coloured cat with tufted ears that was sitting on a flat stretch of desert sand. A badger, vividly striped in black and white, emerged tentatively from a burrow just a few feet away from a fox with absurdly large ears padding forever across a landscape of artificial ice and snow. Presumably it all made sense to someone.

Sherlock stopped beside the badger for a moment. The sight of the animal took him back to Farnham, and the dead badger he had used to distract Baron Maupertuis's guard dog. At the time that had seemed about as bad as life could get. If only he'd known . . .

He passed cases of various rats and mice, cats and miniature dogs before he got to the end. Their emotionless eyes seemed to track him as he passed. The doorway at the end led out into a smaller hall with two doors leading off it. He chose one at random, and went through.

A figure loomed over him, arms upraised, vicious spikes emerging from its hands. He jerked backwards, nearly falling, before he realized that the figure was in a case and the spikes on the hands were actually claws. It wasn't the bearded man from Waterloo Station. Straightening up, he brushed at his jacket self-consciously. It was a bear of some kind, with a tangled brown pelt and a muzzle that had been treated in some way to appear wet. It was bigger than Amyus Crowe, and that was saying something.

The room over which the bear stood guard contained a handful of larger cases. As well as the bear there was an elk with spreading, branch-like antlers, several wild boar with coarse bristles and tusks posed in a family group, and what seemed to be a cow so covered with long brown hair that Sherlock couldn't even make out its eyes.

The door at the end led into yet another room. Sherlock was beginning to feel as if he was in a maze of some kind. As well as glass cases along the walls, it had cases in the centre. Each held a bird of some kind, and from what Sherlock could see they were all birds of prey.

The nearest case contained a lone eagle, set into a noble pose. Its wooden backdrop had been painted to represent a cloudless blue sky and distant mountains.

Sherlock moved further into the room. He heard something moving—the scrape of a shoe against the floor. Someone was obviously in the room with him, although he couldn't hear any voices. Maybe it was a lone visitor.

He passed several cases containing owls of various types. They were sitting on branches—possibly real, possibly made of plaster of Paris; Sherlock couldn't tell. Their claws encircled the branches: sharp killing weapons wrapped in scaled skin, designed to punch into the body of their prey and lift it up so the birds could fly away to their nests and feast.

As he went by, he thought he caught a movement out of the corner of his eye. He quickly turned to look. The birds were all staring at him. Hadn't their heads been turned towards the door when he entered? Now they were facing into the centre of the room. Or was it something about owls that made it difficult to tell which way they were looking?

Something fluttered across the other side of the room. Was there a bird, a real bird, trapped in the room? A sparrow, or a pigeon, or something?

The next few cases contained an assortment of birds of prey. Sherlock spotted hawks, falcons, ospreys and several types of bird that he didn't even recognize.

Even though they were dead and stuffed, there was something eerie about the birds, more so than the small mammals or the larger animals. Maybe feathers just looked more realistic than fur when what was underneath was stuffing rather than flesh and bone. Or maybe there was something

106

about the shape of their skulls and the lack of body fat that meant the process of taxidermy left them looking as if they might at any moment just twist their heads and start preening, or stretch their wings to get the kinks out of their muscles. Even though their eyes were made of glass beads too, Sherlock thought he could detect a coldness in them, a dangerousness. The mice and the voles looked at passers-by as predators; the birds in this room looked at passers-by as prey.

He was imagining things again. It wasn't helping. *They're just stuffed birds!* he told himself. *They aren't real. They can't move.*

He heard another sudden movement in the far reaches of the room. Footsteps, perhaps. Cloth brushing against the wooden edge of a display case. It didn't matter: he was bound to come across other visitors at some stage.

And then he was startled by a loud *boom*! For a moment he was shocked, wondering what it was, and then it occurred to him that the door at the far end of the room had slammed shut. Perhaps it had been caught in a draught.

Sherlock moved around a case that was blocking his way. Ahead of him, a larger case contained a vulture—its head bereft of feathers, its beak cruelly curved down at the end; its wings stretched out as if to bar his progress.

He looked up. There was another bird: a falcon, he thought. This one wasn't behind glass, though. It was poised on top of the case as if it had just landed there.

A mournful whistle of three musical notes floated through the air.

As Sherlock watched, the falcon turned its head

107

so that it could see him clearly and leaned forward as if it was about to launch itself off the case and dive towards his face.

CHAPTER SEVEN

A gleam of light caught Sherlock's gaze. Something had been attached to the falcon's legs: metal blades that stuck out like extra claws. As the falcon shifted on the cabinet Sherlock could see the varnished wood splintering as the metal bit into it.

Abruptly, the bird dropped towards Sherlock, propelled by a single flap of its outstretched wings. Its legs were held out stiffly beneath it, the metal claws spread wide. Sherlock jumped back, but his feet got tangled and he fell. It was as if he was toppling backwards in slow motion. He saw the falcon zooming over him, claws reaching for his eyes. It seemed as though he could see each individual feather covering its underside. Air blew across his face as the bird flapped its wings and soared past. Time stretched out, leaving him wondering if he had paused in mid-fall, suspended in mid-air, but the sudden impact as his shoulders hit the floor knocked the breath from his body in an explosive *whoosh!* and sent stars spinning through his head.

He rolled over, squeezing into the corner where the wooden base of a glass case met the floor, and scrabbled forward, expecting at any second to feel the bird's claws bite into the flesh of his neck. The muscles in his back spasmed in pain. From the corner of his eye he caught sight of a blur of brown feathers, and he jerked sideways, but when nothing moved he looked more closely and saw that it was a stuffed kestrel behind the glass. He was so close that he could see the stitches around its neck and the dust on its black glass eyes.

Cautiously, he raised his head and looked up.

There was no sign of the falcon.

Sherlock stood and glanced around, eyes scanning every shadowed corner, every darkened recess. Nothing. The falcon had gone.

Somewhere in the distance he heard a flapping of wings, but the sound echoed from the bare walls of the room and he couldn't tell where it was coming from.

Sherlock pressed his back against the glass of the cabinet. He could feel its coolness through his jacket and shirt.

What was his best course of action? He could go forward, but he would be heading into unfamiliar territory. Perhaps he should retreat, back to the entrance hall. He could wait there for Amyus Crowe, or follow him into the section for amphibians and reptiles.

That thought led to another one: Amyus Crowe fighting for his life with a crocodile, or some kind of large lizard like the ones that he, Matty and Virginia had encountered in America, just as Sherlock was fighting with a bird in the stuffed birds section. The thought was patently stupid— there was no reason to think that the stuffed animals were coming to life and leaving their cases—but that started his mind racing. What was a live falcon doing in a museum? What was a falcon even doing in *London*? And why were its claws covered with razor-sharp metal sheathes?

All the questions had the same answer—the bird obviously belonged to someone, the person with the whistle, and that person was using it to injure or kill Sherlock. Maybe they had followed him and Amyus Crowe to the museum or, more likely, they were using the museum as a base of operations and had spotted the two of them entering.

As if in confirmation of his hypothesis, a short whistle cut through the heavy silence again— three blasts, a signal to the falcon. Immediately Sherlock heard wings flapping. A shadow flickered against the ceiling, cast by the sun shining through a skylight and reflecting off the glass of a display case, and interrupted by the bird flying past.

And then silence again.

Sherlock moved as quietly as he could towards the door he had entered through. His gaze flickered in all directions, trying to work out which one an attack was going to come from.

Dust tickled his nostrils. He felt a sneeze coming on. He pinched the top of his nose hard, squeezing until the urge subsided. The last thing he wanted to do was attract the falcon's attention.

Glancing around, he realized that he wasn't sure where he was. He didn't recognize the birds in the cases. He thought they were eagles, but their feathers were mainly white and they had ruffs round their necks.

Sherlock hadn't come past these exhibits on his way in. There must have been another path that he had missed.

Go on or go back?

He decided to go on. If he was lucky then he would find another exit.

If he was unlucky, the falcon would find him. Or

its owner would.

He scanned the cases around him as he moved. The one immediately to his left contained a brown bird of prey with a sharp beak. He passed by, gaze moving on, but something in the back of his mind was trying to raise a warning flag. He thought it was just the similarity between the bird in the case and the falcon that had almost clawed his eyes out, but then the bird in the case turned its head to look at him, and he realized that it wasn't in the case at all, that the case was empty—he was looking *through* the case and the bird was perched on a ledge behind it.

The falcon sprang up, propelling itself with mighty sweeps of its wings. For a moment it hung in the air, poised above the empty case, and then it plunged towards Sherlock.

He raised his arms defensively, forearms crossed in front of his face. The bird hit him in a flurry of claws and wings. Its metal-shod claws scrabbled for a grip on his arms, but only succeeded in ripping the sleeves of his jacket. Its wings battered him around his ears: strong blows, like those of a boxer. One of the claws succeeded in cutting through the cloth of his jacket and shirt: he felt a red-hot line being drawn along the flesh of his left arm, and a flood of wetness after it, soaking into the material. He had automatically closed his eyes when the bird struck, but now, opening them, he found that its head was only inches away from his own. The falcon was drawing back, stabilising itself with its claws, preparing to strike with its sharp-edged beak at Sherlock's right eye. Enraged and panicked at the same time, he lashed out with his right hand. His knuckles connected with the bird's chest, knocking it away. It flapped its wings and took off, but instead of retreating it headed straight back at Sherlock.

Shielding his face with one arm, he struck out with the other. If he had hit it he would probably have broken the bird's wing, but it was too fast for him. The falcon swerved in mid-air, avoiding his clenched fist. He watched as it flew away, down an aisle between display cases, dipping towards the floor as it glided on outstretched wings and then rising in a rapid arc as it flapped them to clear a case ahead of it.

Sherlock bent over for a few seconds, hands on knees and breath rasping in his throat. He could feel the blood pulsing through the arteries of his neck and thudding in his temples.

Still bent over, he felt a prickling sensation on the back of his neck. He straightened up abruptly and stared around. He could see many eyes watching him, but they were all glass. He probed the shadowy spaces around the high ceiling for some sign of the bird. He couldn't see it anywhere. But it could see him. He sensed it.

Whoever owned the bird would probably expect Sherlock to retreat again, towards the exit he had been heading for before. So he moved forward, in the direction the falcon had gone. That, at least, had the benefit of being unexpected.

He got to the large display case behind which the bird had disappeared. It contained a flock of smaller birds, posed on wires with wings outstretched, as if in flight. The aisle split at that point, going left and right. He chose right at random, and headed past a section of seagulls. At the far end the aisle turned right. He stopped there, and peered around the corner.

Ahead was an open area which terminated in a large wooden door, which presumably led to the next room. Floor-to-ceiling windows to either side let bright sunlight spill in. Standing in the centre of the room, silhouetted by the light from the far window, was a man. He was facing away from the door. Sherlock couldn't make out any features, just a general impression of a massive figure with wide shoulders. He was holding a walking stick in one hand, supporting his weight, while the other arm was stretched out straight to support the weight of the falcon. It was obviously disturbed: its head was jerking from side to side and it seemed to be moving its weight from foot to foot. The man was talking to it in a calm voice, and gradually the bird relaxed until it was standing motionless and alert.

The man's head turned, looking left and right. The bird copied him. Sherlock pulled his own head back so that he couldn't be seen.

What to do?

He couldn't get to the door ahead of him. The man was in the way. He had to go back, to the door he'd come through.

A thought struck him. He slipped his shoes off and stuck them in his pockets. In his socks he would make less noise on the hard wooden floor. He moved backwards, then turned and ran off down the aisle. He'd lost track of the exact route, but this was a museum, not a maze. As long as he headed in the proper direction, he should be all right.

He turned left, then right. Birds everywhere, staring at him with cold eyes. Maybe he'd seen them before, maybe he hadn't. They were all blurring together.

An empty glass case! This was where he had seen the falcon before, *through* the glass, as it had perched on a ledge on the wall. He thought he knew the way from here. Just two more turns . . .

Something struck him between his shoulder blades, knocking him over. Claws bit into the muscles of his back, tearing through the cloth of his jacket and shirt as if they were tissue paper. At any second he expected to feel the falcon's beak strike at the nape of his neck, and his skin crawled at the thought. He rolled over, trying to trap the bird beneath him, but it was too quick for him. Releasing its grip it hopped a few feet down the corridor and then took off. The harsh beat of its wings left a couple of feathers floating in the air.

Sherlock climbed shakily to his feet. He couldn't take much more of this.

He heard the big man, the bird's owner, whistle again.

At the far end of the aisle the falcon suddenly headed straight up, then paused and seemed to turn over in mid-air with a complicated flick of its wings.

And then it was heading back down the aisle towards him like a feathered bullet.

Sherlock reached out with his left hand to steady himself on the empty case beside him. The glass door shifted slightly under his fingers. It was unlocked. Whoever was responsible for fitting the exhibits had left it open while they went off to fetch whatever stuffed bird and background landscape materials they required.

The falcon had covered half the distance now. It was dipping towards the floor, but another massive beat of its wings accelerated its speed and kept its height up.

It was aiming for his throat.

Sherlock grasped the middle of the door frame. No time to calculate the right moment; he had to do this on instinct.

When the bird was six feet away he yanked on the door frame.

The glass door pulled open, right into the path of the falcon. The bird smashed into the glass, *through* the glass, and fell to the floor, stunned, amid a rain of glass fragments. Sherlock watched as it shook its head and tried to get up. He couldn't see any blood, and its wings appeared to be undamaged, but it wasn't in any condition to continue the fight. The rabbit had suddenly turned round and bitten it.

Sherlock glanced up, along the aisle. At the far end stood the massive man with the walking stick. He was still just a black shadow, with the light behind him, but Sherlock could feel the man's gaze drilling into his forehead, the way he had earlier felt the falcon's gaze drilling into the back of his head.

He raised a hand in a wave that was significantly more relaxed than he felt, then turned and headed for the door he'd previously come through. He didn't care that it was locked. He'd fought off a killer falcon; a locked door should be child's play.

The door was indeed still locked, but when he got to it someone was hammering on it and calling out. Moments later there was the sound of a key turning, and the door sprang open. A man in the uniform of a security guard almost fell in.

'What's going on?' he demanded. 'Who locked

this door?'

'You tell me,' Sherlock said. 'You're the one with the key.'

The guard's gaze moved over Sherlock's torn, bloodied clothes. 'What was going on in here?' he asked. 'I heard breaking glass.'

Sherlock was on the verge of telling the man everything, but he bit back the words. It would sound like he'd made the story up to disguise an act of vandalism. Who would believe that a live falcon would attack him? He'd be caught up in explanations and recriminations for hours, and he had to get to Amyus Crowe to tell him what had happened.

'One of the cabinet doors opened as I was walking past,' Sherlock said wearily. 'The glass smashed. I got cut. Who do I report this to?'

'Report it to?' the guard parroted.

'Yes. I was injured. Who do I see for compensation?'

The guard stood back, nonplussed. 'I suppose you see the manager,' he said, considerably more calm than moments before.

'Where can I find him?'

'In his office. Just between the baboons and the hooved ungulates.'

'Thank you.' And with all the dignity he could muster, Sherlock left.

He strode back through the various galleries, heading for the main entrance. He had to find Amyus Crowe and tell him what had happened. Assuming, of course, that Crowe hadn't fallen foul of some other form of attack.

He found Crowe in a small tea shop that was located on the other side of the main staircase.

He was perched on a white-painted wrought iron chair, sipping from a china cup that looked like something from a doll's house in his massive hands. Fake tree branches had been built out of the wall in plaster and covered with fabric leaves, and stuffed parrots and birds of paradise had been artfully placed amongst them. Their brilliant green, red, blue and yellow plumage shone like jewels. The tea shop was almost empty, apart from a man sitting by himself in a corner, reading a newspaper, and two elderly women nattering by a window. A young man wearing black trousers and a striped waistcoat moved among the tables, wiping barely perceptible crumbs from the tablecloths.

'You look as if you could sink a slice of Battenberg cake,' Crowe observed mildly, taking in Sherlock's appearance with a swift up-and-down glance. 'And maybe ah could stretch to a lemonade as well.'

'Don't you want to know what happened?' Sherlock groaned, slumping into a chair on the other side of the table.

'Ah can tell most of the story just by lookin' at you,' Crowe rejoined. 'You were attacked, an' by some kind of animal, far as ah can tell. You got the better of it, but you took some damage. What was it?' He paused. 'No, don't tell me.' He frowned. 'A bird? An eagle? No, too small. A falcon, ah guess, by the size of the tears in your clothes.'

'I was in the birds of prey section, and I was attacked by a bird of prey.'

'Not a stuffed one, ah presume.'

'A *real* one,' Sherlock snapped tetchily.

'Of course,' Crowe rumbled amiably. 'Ah was just joshin' with you.'

117

Sherlock took a closer look at his mentor. Crowe's usually immaculate white suit looked creased around the lapels, as if someone had caught hold of them and tugged, and a button was missing from the left cuff. His hair was disarrayed, as if he had been caught in a sudden wind. 'You don't look too hot yourself,' Sherlock said. 'What happened?'

Crowe grimaced. 'Ah was wonderin' if you'd spot anythin'. Ah found a door that led to some offices, an' ah was checkin' behind the scenes. Ah had a story ready prepared—ah was goin' to say that ah was lookin' for a restroom—but rather than ask me some pointed questions about my presence someone tried to cosh me from behind. Fortunately ah saw their shadow as they were swingin' at me, an' ah managed to duck just in time. There was somethin' of a scuffle, durin' which ah got swung into a door frame, but my attacker must have decided that once the element of surprise had gone ah wasn't goin' to be a pushover, so he retreated while ah was tryin' to gather my wits.' He snorted. 'Apart from the fact that my attacker was male, large and rather well versed in usin' a cosh, ah couldn't tell you much about him.'

'So we were both attacked,' Sherlock said. 'That implies we're on the right track.'

'Ah wasn't sure if the attack on me was connected to our investigation, or whether it was just a simple muggin' gone wrong, but in conjunction with the attack on you, we have to assume that we've been rumbled.'

Sherlock looked around. 'Do you think we're being watched now?'

Crowe nodded. 'Wouldn't surprise me.' He

glanced around the room, at the man who was reading a newspaper, the two gossiping women and the waiter in the striped waistcoat. 'Prob'ly not by any of the patrons of this fine establishment, though. Not sure about the chap in the fancy clothes who takes the orders.'

'The thing is, I didn't find anything out,' Sherlock said. 'Nothing of interest, anyway.'

'You may be surprised,' Crowe said. 'Knowin' you as ah do, ah like to think that you picked up some small details along the way that might help us.'

'Did *you* find anything out? Before you were attacked?'

Crowe shrugged. 'Ah had a good look around, includin' some areas that maybe the public aren't supposed to be allowed in, but ah have to admit that ah've come up blank. If there's anythin' goin' on here then ah missed the signs.'

'Do we know enough to report this to the police?' Sherlock asked. 'We can't investigate this place ourselves. Not now the Paradol Chamber know we're here.'

Crowe nodded. 'Both of us have been attacked. That's good enough reason to get the police involved, an' if we're lucky they'll find somethin' incriminatin' while they're searchin' the place for our attackers.' He slammed his hand decisively on the table, making his teacup rattle against the saucer. 'We might just have them!'

He sprang to his feet. 'You're goin' to have to miss out on that Battenberg cake,' he announced. 'Let's go back to Bow Street Police Station an' make a formal complaint.'

119

CHAPTER EIGHT

'Mr Crowe,' Sherlock asked, 'what's happened to my brother. What's happened to Mycroft?'

It was the morning after their adventure at the museum, and they were sitting at a breakfast table at the Sarbonnier Hotel, where Sherlock had stayed the last time he had visited London. Crowe had got up and left before Sherlock woke up, but as Sherlock came down for breakfast he was just re-entering the hotel.

'The good news is that he's been released on bail,' Crowe replied.

'What does that mean?'

'It means that someone—in this case, the Diogenes Club—has stumped up some cash which has been deposited with the court. The court decides on the amount that needs to be deposited, an' they make that decision based on how big a sum would dissuade a suspect from abscondin'. If your brother disappears before the trial—if there is a trial—then that money is forfeit.' He laughed. 'After all, if it only took five shillings to get out on bail, every criminal with a bit of cash would be out within half an hour, and most of them would go straight on the run.'

'How much did it cost to get Mycroft out on bail?'

'Ah believe the sum mentioned was five thousand pounds.'

Sherlock winced. 'So where is Mycroft now?'

'He's in discussions with his solicitor, over a large breakfast at the Diogenes Club. Ah sent him a telegram telling him that you were safe, and that we would be here at the Sarbonnier. He may join us later.'

'How did the Diogenes Club come up with the cash?' Sherlock asked.

'They apparently have a fund which members pay into which enables them to get legal advice and assistance.' Crowe's expression turned broody. 'Strangely, ah don't see his employers helpin' out much. They're maintainin' a strict silence over the whole affair. Ah suppose they don't want to be seen to be interferin', bein' part of the Government an' therefore linked to the police force.'

Sherlock considered for a moment. 'But that man we found—the one who attacked me under Waterloo Station. He admitted that Mycroft was set up. Someone else committed the murder.'

'That's a fact, but it'll take the police a while to collect the evidence which clears your brother. The important thing is that the Diogenes Club's solicitor can point them in the right direction.' Crowe frowned. 'What concerns me now is that the people who framed Mr Holmes are still out there, an' we don't know what their motives are or what they might try next.'

'You think they might try to frame him for *another* murder?'

Crowe shrugged. 'Can't rule it out, but having been cleared of one—assumin' he is—it's unlikely that another one will stick. There's a saying we used to have, back durin' the War Between the States: once is happenstance; twice is enemy action. Even the police will recognize that. No, ah think we need to be prepared for somethin' else to occur. Some other plot.'

'So what do we do? How do we protect Mycroft?'

Crowe gazed at Sherlock for a while. His blue eyes were deceptively mild, but Sherlock knew they saw through everything. 'You're very loyal to your brother, ain't you? Some kids your age would just let their elders get on with their lives, but not you. You want to protect him.'

Sherlock turned away so that Crowe couldn't see the gleam of tears. 'Father is in India,' he said eventually, 'and mother is ill. And our sister . . . well, she's not in a position to help anyone. Mycroft is all I have, and I'm all he has. We have to look out for each other.' He smiled, despite himself. 'And you've probably noticed that he's not the most active or agile of people. He needs help just to get from one side of the city to the other.' He laughed. 'I heard once that he'd been invited to a meal at somebody's house, out in the countryside. Normally he wouldn't accept social invitations, but the owner of the house had an exceptional wine cellar and their cook was renowned for the quality of her desserts, so he made a special effort. He got a hansom cab to the station, then got a train for an hour, then managed to find a cart at the other end to take him the five miles to the house. The final bit of the journey was a walk up a short hill to the front door, but he took one look at the climb and then just turned around and asked the cart driver to take him back to the station. He's that kind of person. He's phenomenally intelligent, but not practical at all.'

'And you love him.'

'He's my brother. Of course I love him.' Uncomfortable at the discussion of close personal feelings, Sherlock glanced at Crowe and asked: 'Do you have a brother?'

Crowe's face seemed to set into a hard mask. 'Let's not go there,' he said, his voice sounding like two stones grating together.

There was silence for a while, as they ate their breakfast. Eventually Crowe looked around, and indicated a young waiter who was serving breakfast to a family nearby. 'Let's see how much you've remembered of what ah've taught you recently. What can you tell me about him?'

Sherlock considered. 'I remember him from last time we were here.' He looked the man up and down. 'His uniform is slightly too short for him, and the trousers have been repaired several times. He has obviously been wearing it for a while without replacing it. Either his salary is low or he is spending it on other things. Although his shoes are new, and well polished, which contradicts the evidence of his uniform.' Sherlock looked more closely at the man's face and hair. 'He is wearing Macassar hair oil.' He sniffed. 'Yes, I can smell traces of jasmine, orange and coconut. Macassar oil is not cheap: I presume, therefore, that he spends the majority of his salary on things that make him look attractive to women—hair oil, shoes and, I would guess, the clothes that he wears when he is not at work. That suggests he isn't married.' He shrugged. 'That's about it.'

'What if ah told you that he has three convictions for pickpocketin',' Crowe said, 'and has spent time in prison. Ah was told this by the doorman. The manager of the hotel took him on, as the lad is the son of his sister.'

Sherlock glanced more carefully at the waiter.

123

'He *is* spending a lot of time near the father,' he pointed out. 'Perhaps he is looking for an opportunity to steal something from his pocket.'

As Sherlock watched, the waiter dropped a knife. With a murmured apology to the family, he bent to pick it up.

'Watch!' Sherlock said urgently. 'I think he did that deliberately. He's going to slip a hand inside the father's jacket pocket as everyone is distracted by the knife!'

'Actually,' Crowe admitted, 'he has no convictions for pickpocketin' at all. Ah made that up. He sings in a choir in Westminister Abbey, although he *is* the manager's nephew.'

Confused, Sherlock glanced back at the tableau at the table. What had moments ago looked like suspicious activity now looked perfectly innocent, as the waiter straightened up holding the knife.

'Is that true?' he asked.

'No,' Crowe said. 'Ah made that up as well. Actually he stabbed a man in a fight in a public house last year, but the case was dropped due to a distinct lack of witnesses willing to testify against him.'

The same tableau—table, family sitting down, waiter standing over them, now took on a distinctly different look to Sherlock. The waiter now seemed to be holding the knife in a threatening way, over the father's neck.

'That's not true either, is it?' he asked in irritation.

'No,' Crowe conceded. 'Ah actually don't know anythin' about the waiter apart from what little can be observed from his clothes, his hair and his hands. Ah know nothing about his history.

My point was that we all see something different depending on the labels we place on things, and those labels are based on what we know—or what we *think* we know. The trained mind will reject convenient labels and proceed using actual and deduced facts. The trained mind will also take advantage of the way other people make assumptions in order to guide them in particular directions, and to make them do particular things.'

Sherlock was about to question Crowe further on this interesting revelation that one person could manipulate another's thinking just by the words they chose to use, when a familiar voice hailed them from across the restaurant.

'Sherlock, Mr Crowe—might I join you?'

'Mycroft!' Sherlock cried.

His brother ambled across the restaurant to the table where they sat. He was looking as immaculately groomed as ever—perfectly pressed suit and waistcoat, hat brushed to within an inch of its life—but his skin was sallow and his eyes were the eyes of a man who had recently seen things that he wished to forget.

'Mr Holmes,' Crowe said, rising, 'please, take a seat. Can ah get you a pot of coffee, or perhaps some tea?'

'Tea would be excellent,' Mycroft said, placing himself on a chair that looked entirely unsuited to take his weight. 'Breakfast would be ideal.'

'I thought you'd already had breakfast with your solicitor,' Sherlock pointed out.

Mycroft gazed solemnly at him. 'If a law has been passed forbidding the consumption of more than one breakfast during the course of a morning then I am entirely unaware of it,' he said. 'In point of fact, my previous breakfast hardly qualifies for the term. The toast was damp, the bacon limp and the black pudding too crisp. The marmalade I will not even mention. I absent myself from the Diogenes for one day and the place starts falling apart. All that meal did was make me hungry for a *real* breakfast, which I trust is available here.'

Crowe signalled to the waiter to bring another plate of breakfast and a pot of tea. Mycroft followed his gaze and stared at the waiter for a moment. 'Norway?' he asked Crowe.

'Finland,' Crowe answered.

'Yes, of course.' Mycroft shook his head. 'My short time in custody has thrown my logical skills somewhat out of balance.'

Crowe caught Sherlock's eye. 'Ah know ah said ah didn't know anything about him,' he said, 'but that was also a lie. His family are from Finland— you can tell by the haircut.'

'Why lie *again*?' Sherlock protested.

'It's a strange fact in life,' Crowe said, 'that if an Englishman catches another man out in a lie, or even two or three lies, he assumes that the man will then tell him the truth. Something to do with a misplaced sense of British fair play, ah suspect. In reality, if a man has lied once then he is likely to lie repeatedly and often.'

Mycroft turned his gaze towards Sherlock. 'I understand there was some . . . unpleasantness,' he said. 'Something to do with a bird of prey. Are you all right?'

'I'm fine. What about you?'

Mycroft shrugged. 'At least I can now say that I have seen how the other half lives, although I do not feel edified by the experience. My solicitor expects to have the charges withdrawn by this afternoon.'

'Any idea why you were targeted in the first place?' Crowe asked.

'There are relatively few possibilities,' Mycroft replied. 'It is possible that someone was taking their revenge upon me for something, but I cannot think who or what. A more likely possibility is that someone wanted me distracted from events that were about to occur, or from something that was going to cross my desk and upon which I might have initiated action.' He glanced across at Sherlock. 'You will be aware that I work for the Foreign Office. The Government has many specialists in various fields, but I consider myself a generalist. Facts and speculations of all kinds cross my desk, and I look for patterns—for connections between apparently separate things. On such connections foreign policy is frequently made.'

'Anything in particular strike you?' Crowe asked.

'I really should not discuss Government business outside the Whitehall enclave,' Mycroft murmured. 'Ah, here is my breakfast.'

The waiter placed the plate in front of him and whipped the metal cover off. Mycroft's face broke into a smile as he regarded the array of food. 'Splendid,' he said. 'A perfect arrangement, perfectly prepared. My compliments to the chef.' As the waiter moved away, he continued: 'Yes, as I was saying, I really should not be discussing Government business outside Whitehall, especially with a man whose allegiances are to another nation entirely, but I believe, based on my long acquaintance with you, that you can be trusted to keep a secret, Mr Crowe.' He speared a mushroom with his fork and bit into it. 'Ah, perfect.' He closed his eyes and chewed. 'Yes,' he said, opening them again, 'where was I? There are several international incidents which may pertain to this issue at the moment, but the one I believe has the highest likelihood concerns the recent sale of a large piece of land to your own country, Mr Crowe.'

Crowe raised an eyebrow. 'Not caught up with that particular news item, Mr Holmes.'

'I am not surprised: it did not make for many headlines. Let me summarize: sometime last year, a vast expanse of land was sold to the American government for the sum of seven million, two hundred thousand dollars, to be paid in gold. Strange how "expanse" and "expense" are only one letter apart. The tract was so large, I have worked out, that the price comes to about two cents an acre, which seems like something of a bargain to me. The land itself lies in the northwest of the North American continent, bordered by Canada to the east, the Arctic Ocean to the north and the Pacific Ocean to the west and south.'

'Who owned the land previously?' Sherlock asked.

'A very pertinent question. Russia, whose Empire is located just across the Bering Strait— which is what that part of the Pacific Ocean is called—was the previous owner, although there were and are a number of indigenous tribes.'

'What is this place called?'

'The Russians called it Alyeska,' Mycroft replied, 'but the American government have apparently settled on the Department of Alaska as a name.'

'So we've got a land sale,' Crowe said. 'Happens

in America all the time. Ah own quite a parcel of land myself in Albuquerque, which some acquaintances are managing for me while ah'm away. What's the big deal?'

Mycroft sighed. 'The "big deal", as you call it, is that the sale may not have been entirely legitimate.'

There was silence around the table for a few moments as the other two took in the importance of what Mycroft had just said.

'How can that be?' Sherlock asked eventually. 'Surely the Russian and American governments have legal advisors who check over the details in the contracts?'

'It's not so much the validity of the contract, more that no payment has yet been made, which renders the actual sale legally dubious.'

'The question,' Crowe said thoughtfully, 'would be—does anybody else want Alaska? If not, the point is moot, and the Russians will just have to whistle for their money.'

Mycroft transferred a piece of black pudding on a fragment of fried bread into his mouth. For a minute or so he ate contentedly in silence, with a blissful smile on his face.

'This is where it all becomes rather sensitive, and rather personal,' he said eventually. 'I have, for some time, had a "man" in Moscow. I say that he is *my* man because although his salary and expenses are paid for by the Foreign Office, he reports directly to me and to nobody else.'

'I presume that you mean he's there pretending to be one thing while actually doing something else?' Crowe asked.

'He is there as a journalist, and rather a good one, but in addition he provides me with intelligence on what the Tsar and his court are up to.' Mycroft sighed, and pushed his plate away. 'Going through my recent communications this morning—the ones that came in while I have been indisposed at Bow Street Police Station—I found two pertaining to this man. The first was from him, telling me that he had solid information that the Spanish Ambassador to the Court of Tsar Alexander II had made a counter-offer in excess of ten million US dollars for Alaska, to be paid immediately—in gold—on signature of a treaty. The second communication was from one of the British diplomatic staff in Moscow. They informed me that my man, my agent, had disappeared.' He lifted his teacup to his lips, then lowered it again. 'The Tsar has a secret police force as well as his normal police force. They are known as the Third Section of His Imperial Majesty's Own Chancellery—not a very catchy title, as titles go, but very Russian. The man in charge is Count Pyotr Andreyevich Shuvalov. I met him in France, a few years back. We got on well. No matter— Department One of the Third Section deals with political crimes, Department Three with foreigners. I very much suspect that my man has fallen foul of one of those Departments and has been taken in the night.'

'Tsar,' Sherlock said to break the ensuing silence. 'Is that like a king or emperor?'

'In a sense,' Mycroft responded, heaving himself out of his own dark thoughts. 'Although it is, in another sense, untranslatable. It derives, oddly, from the Latin "Caesar".' He shook his head. 'The Russians are strangely formal when it comes to titles and so forth, even more so than

130

we are in England. The most recent diplomatic correspondence I have seen from the Tsar's court started off, as I recall—' he closed his eyes '– "We, Alexander the Second, by the grace of God, Emperor and Autocrat of all the Russias, of Moscow, Kiev, Vladimir, Novgorod, Tsar of Kazan, Tsar of Astrakhan, Tsar of Poland, Tsar of Siberia, Tsar of Tauric Chersonesos, Tsar of Georgia, Lord of Pskov, and Grand Duke of Smolensk, Lithuania, Volhynia, Podolia, and Finland, Prince of Estonia, Livonia, Courland and Semigalia, Samogitia, Belostok, Karelia, Tver, Yugra, Perm, Vyatka, Bulgaria and other territories; Lord and Grand Duke of Nizhni Novgorod, Sovereign of Chernigov, Ryazan, Polotsk, Rostov, Yaroslavl, Beloozero, Udoria, Obdoria, Kondia, Vitebsk, Mstislavl, and all northern territories; Sovereign of Iveria, Kartalinia, and the Kabardinian lands and Armenian territories - hereditary Lord and Ruler of the Circassians and Mountain Princes and others; Lord of Turkestan, Heir of Norway, Duke of Schleswig-Holstein, Stormarn, Dithmarschen, Oldenburg, and so forth, and so forth, and so forth".' He opened his eyes again and took a deep breath. 'The salutation was longer than the rest of the letter. You will not be surprised that most diplomats do not relish being sent to Moscow. They have to memorize all this.'

'You memorized it,' Sherlock pointed out.

'Yes,' Mycroft said, surprised, 'but I am Mycroft Holmes.'

'Let's cut to the chase,' Crowe interrupted. 'What's the outcome if the sale of Alaska to the USA falls through and Spain get it? Why should we care?'

'It destabilizes the region,' Mycroft said simply. 'Canada is a new and fragile country. France already has a strong influence in the Quebec region and Great Britain still retains control of British Columbia. If Spain were to gain control of Alaska then we would replicate in another continent all the problems that we once experienced here in Europe. Think of the wars that occurred between France, England and Spain in the sixteenth and seventeenth centuries. The last thing we want is for that to happen again. You want to know what will happen if Spain is allowed to gain control of Alaska, Mr Crowe? The answer is war—and a war that will pull America apart as it tries to work out with whom to ally itself!'

Crowe nodded his massive head slowly. 'Ah can see that,' he said. 'Cram several countries together that way an' you'll get trouble. It's like having three or four families livin' together in a small house. Bound to be arguments.'

'Stability is in our best interests,' Mycroft observed. 'And by *our*, I mean yours and mine. America's and Great Britain's. As should be apparent, Great Britain has been divesting itself of various colonies over the past decade. Our colonies in Canada have become a country in their own right, and I would expect British Columbia to be handed across to join them in the near future. We are trying our best to build stability into the region. Having the Spaniards, the French or anyone else interfering would set up ripples that could affect the political and geographical landscape for hundreds of years.'

'All this,' Crowe said, 'is kind of outside my remit. Ah'm not a politician, and have no intention

132

of ever becoming one.'

'Best not,' Mycroft murmured. 'I have seen you negotiate. Fists are not generally thought of as weapons of diplomacy.'

'Oh, I don' know,' Crowe said quietly. 'Didn't Clausewicz say that war is a continuation of political relations?'

'Yes,' Mycroft said testily, 'but he was German.'

'So what does all this mean to us?' Crowe asked. 'You think that the people who framed you for murder are agents of Spain?'

'Possible, but unlikely.' Mycroft shook his head. 'Why would the Spanish court wish to hide the fact that they had made a counter-offer, unless the negotiations were at a particularly delicate stage? I cannot see them committing murder on that basis. The Russians themselves might have done it—but again, why should they wish to hide the fact that negotiations are going on?' He thought for a moment, his fingers stroking his chin. 'Unless the Tsar did not want the American government to know that he was talking to the Spaniards, on the basis that the US House of Representatives might suddenly approve the release of the seven million dollars in gold and thus scupper his plans to get more money from someone else. The whole thing rests on the fact that the original deal is at best ambiguous until payment has actually been made.'

'There is another possibility,' Crowe rumbled.

'Yes,' Mycroft confirmed, 'there is. Elements in your own government might be trying to avoid any word of the possible ambiguity of the land deal until they can actually complete it—transfer the gold to the Tsar.'

Crowe shrugged. 'Ah'm not goin' to defend my

government. They've made some pretty strange decisions over the years.'

'Or,' Sherlock said, feeling that he ought to say something, 'it might be someone else.'

'A third party?' Crowe asked.

'Fourth,' Mycroft clarified, 'after the Russians, the Americans and the Spanish.'

'Fifth,' Sherlock pointed out. 'You're involved too, which means so is Great Britain.'

'I can see why diplomacy gets so complicated,' Crowe said, smiling. 'But this is all irrelevant to us, surely? You've realized what's goin' on, and you're goin' to do somethin' diplomatic. There's no likelihood of any more action against you, or Sherlock, or even me. Whoever tried to frame you in the first place will have to assume that you've gone back to your desk, seen the reports an' drawn the right conclusions.'

Mycroft shook his head slowly. 'It's not that simple. For a start, my superiors are not inclined to take my word on something this big. They will make their own checks, which could take months or years. And I have lost my main source of information in Russia.' His face took on a brooding quality. I owe it to him to find out what has happened. If he is in the cells of the Third Section then I can at least try to get him out. If he is dead then I can try and bring his murderers to justice— or what passes for justice in the Tsar's court.'

'You have more people in Moscow, surely?' Crowe asked. 'They can do this.'

'I have nobody in Moscow that I trust. I will have to go myself, once the charges against me are withdrawn.'

CHAPTER NINE

A shocked silence descended around the table.

'You're going to go to *Moscow*?' Sherlock asked, stunned. 'In *Russia*?'

'I'm afraid I am,' Mycroft replied.

'But you get vertigo if you go north of Oxford Street!'

Mycroft smiled, but it was one of those smiles where humour was a thin veneer over a deeper pain. 'The fact that I do not *wish* to go to Russia is immaterial. I *should* go. I *have* to go. My own personal comfort is quite irrelevant.'

'I don't understand,' Sherlock protested.

'I do.' Amyus Crowe nodded softly. 'How can you expect subordinates to trust you, to follow your instructions, if they think you will abandon them the first time they get into trouble?'

'That is exactly it. My people across the world must know that I am not just a fair-weather superior. When storms come, as inevitably they will, I will be standing in the rain with them.' He shuddered. 'Uncomfortable as it may be.'

'And you're curious,' Sherlock ventured.

'Curious?'

'You want to know the truth. You want to know who actually tried to have you framed for murder, and what the situation is with this land sale.'

Mycroft shrugged. 'I do confess a certain desire to uncover the actual state of affairs. I dislike uncertainty. It is like having a nagging toothache.'

Across the restaurant, the family that Sherlock had been watching earlier were leaving their table.

135

He stared at them for a moment. The mother was checking that her children were correctly buttoned up and neat while the father looked on. Were they heading off to see the sights of London, or visiting family? Perhaps they were just stopping off in London on their way to somewhere else, and were going straight to one of the main stations to catch a train. Whatever their plans, he felt jealous. He couldn't remember a time when his own family had been like that—normal, ordinary. What with his father off on army business most of the time and his mother confined to bed, there had never been a time when they had all sat around a table and just been . . . a family.

'So I won't be seeing you for a while, just as I won't be seeing Father,' he whispered.

'Unless you come with me.'

For the second time in as many minutes, Sherlock was shocked into silence. 'Me?' he squeaked eventually. 'Go with you? To Russia?'

Mycroft was eyeing the remains of the breakfast on his plate longingly. 'Perhaps you could explain it to him,' he murmured to Crowe. 'I think I may have finished too soon.'

'Ah'm not sure ah understand it myself.' Crowe's expression was severe. 'Perhaps you could explain it to both of us.'

'Oh, very well. Sherlock has already become involved in this affair. If I head off to Russia then the best way to distract me, to get me back, or even to stop me going in the first place, would be to threaten him. If he were kidnapped, and let us say a fragment of his ear, or his little finger, were sent to me in a parcel, then I would be rendered incapable of further investigation. I need to

136

establish Sherlock's safety—ergo I need Sherlock with me.'

Sherlock put a hand to his ear. He didn't like the sound of having it cut off and posted to Mycroft as a warning.

'You are hardly a man of action,' Crowe pointed out. 'Are you sure you could fight off any attackers?'

'I will enlist assistance,' Mycroft said waspishly. 'I intended taking one of my other agents with me, for protection. And protective coloration. The three of us will travel together.'

'What does that mean—"protective coloration"?' Sherlock asked, still trying to fight his way past the immense thought that Mycroft wanted him to go to Russia. He wasn't sure which thought was the most immense—going to Russia, or travelling with Mycroft.

'It means that we will be travelling incognito—in disguise, if you wish to put it that way. A relatively senior Foreign Office official cannot just wander into Russia unannounced, not without causing an international incident. No, we must use noms de plume—fake names. We must have fake histories. We must be part of a large whole, a bigger picture, so that nobody will pay us too much attention.'

'And you've already decided on what this larger whole will be,' Crowe said.

'Indeed. I worked out the plan while in the carriage from the Diogenes Club to this hotel.'

'You took a hansom?' Sherlock protested. 'It's barely ten minutes' walk! Two minutes in a cab!'

'Exactly. Just enough time for a little think. If I had been walking I would have been so concerned with dodging other pedestrians, horses and whatever else that I would not have had any time for thinking at all.'

'So what's the plan?' Crowe asked.

Mycroft speared a fragment of sausage with his fork. 'I was asked, some weeks ago, to give permission for a British theatrical troupe to travel to Moscow to give a series of performances to the great Russian families—Shakespeare, Marlowe, Ben Jonson, that sort of thing. I gave them my permission because their visit had been requested through the Russian Embassy, and because it will improve artistic relationships between our two countries—or, at least, it will if the performances were as good as reports have made them out to be. I heard last week that the trip might need to be cancelled, as the company's General Manager has been taken ill with a heart complaint and been admitted to hospital, and that their principal violinist in the pit orchestra has been arrested for drunken and disorderly behaviour. It occurs to me that the duties of a General Manager cannot be that onerous, consisting mainly of making sure that everybody gets to where they are meant to be and that all bills are paid on time.'

'And the violinist?' Crowe asked. 'How are you goin' to recruit one of those?'

'One of my agents is a passable violinist,' Mycroft said. He seemed to be focusing on his plate very carefully. 'I will engage him to assist us.'

'And what about me?' Sherlock asked.

'General factotum and backstage assistant. There are, I understand, never enough people backstage when on tour.'

'But . . .' Sherlock's mind was racing far ahead of his thoughts. 'But when? How?'

138

Mycroft popped the chunk of sausage into his mouth and chewed. 'As to the "when",' he said eventually, 'I would suggest that we leave as soon as arrangements can be made with the theatrical company. They will, I think, be very grateful that the Foreign Office has gone so far to assist them with their tour as to actually provide them with replacements for their missing people. Their travel arrangements are already made. As I recall, they were planning to leave within the next few days, and were on the verge of sending a letter to their hosts informing them of their cancellation. Let us hope that they have not sent the letter yet, otherwise I will need to come up with another strategy. As to the "how?", the intention is that we sail to France and take the train from there across the continent to Moscow. The journey will take, I estimate, four to five days.' He reached for a slice of toast and proceeded to butter it. 'I will inform our aunt and uncle that you and I will be travelling on the continent for a few weeks. They will understand, I am sure. Travel does broaden the mind. I will go and make the arrangements, while I suggest that you, Sherlock, wander down to Charing Cross Road and look for some books on Russian history and culture. They are very different from us—certainly more different than the Americans.' He nodded towards Crowe.

'But let me furnish you with some facts which may help,' he continued. 'Russia is the largest country in the world. If you were to measure its surface area on a globe you would find that it occupies almost one seventh of the available land, but much of that land is perpetually frozen grassland—tundra, as they call it. Our best estimate is that the Tsar rules over some sixty-five million subjects, which is a number that quite boggles the mind, especially when you consider that those people belong to one hundred and sixty separate races or tribes speaking one hundred and ten different languages or dialects and adhering to thirty-five distinct religions. Russia is, for all practical purposes, a world in and of itself. *That* is the place to which we are going.'

'But . . .' Sherlock started, '. . . but I don't even speak Russian!'

'That will not be a problem,' Mycroft said reassuringly. 'I am informed that most of the well-off households, including all of the Tsar's court, speak French as a matter of course. I speak fluent French, and I believe yours has improved over the past few months since your time in that country. We should be able to get by.'

Sherlock glanced at Amyus Crowe. 'But what about Mr Crowe? I don't think he speaks French at all.'

'Yes, his English is slightly suspect as well,' Mycroft murmured. He gazed across at Sherlock, and his eyes were heavy with an emotion Sherlock did not immediately understand, but recognized after a few seconds as pity. 'I am afraid that Mr Crowe will not be accompanying us. This is a trip for you, me and the violinist I intend recruiting.'

'But why?'

'As you pointed out, Mr Crowe does not speak French, or indeed Russian. He possesses no skills that a travelling theatrical company could make use of. He would either have to bring the lovely Virginia, taking our party up to five, or organize someone to look after her for perhaps several

140

weeks. And he stands out in a crowd, which, if we are meant to be travelling incognito, is a problem.'

'Don't worry,' Crowe said. 'I wasn't expectin' to go on this little trip. You go, an' have fun.'

Sherlock felt his stomach clench. 'But I *want* you to go with us.'

'The problem with life,' Mycroft observed, 'is that it rarely gives us what we want, or even what we need. I've heard it said that the Lord does not give us anything that we cannot cope with. In my experience this is not true, and merely serves as a mechanism for helping religious people accept the unacceptable. Life is harsh, and we cannot even hope to survive it.'

'Ah see the lessons continue,' Crowe said quietly.

Mycroft glanced at him. 'The boy has to learn sometime.'

Crowe took a breath, obviously keen to change the subject. 'What about the museum? Is there goin' to be any further investigation there?'

'I have notified the police as to its role in this case, and I have also initiated some more . . . covert . . . investigations through certain arms of the Government, but I strongly suspect that we will find nothing there. Either they were using it as a convenient meeting point, in which case all they have to do is walk out of the front door and we have lost them, or they had an office of some kind there, in which case they will immediately have cleared it out as soon as you and Sherlock blundered in. Either way, it will not furnish us with any clues. This is a very professional group we are dealing with.'

'You don't think the entire museum is a front for

whoever framed you?' Sherlock asked.

'I sincerely doubt it. The museum is a charitable organization, above reproach. No, I suspect that either the villains met there, or one of the staff was a member of their organization. It will prove to be a dead end.' He popped the last fragment of buttered toast in his mouth, crunched on it for a few moments, and sighed contentedly. 'Now I feel I can start the day properly.' He pulled a watch from his waistcoat pocket and consulted it. 'Another hour or so until luncheon. That should give me enough time to initiate preparations for our journey. Sherlock, Mr Crowe—I suggest we meet at the Diogenes at about one p.m.' Levering himself out of the chair with some difficulty, he added, 'Perhaps someone would be kind enough to secure a cab for me.'

While Crowe and Mycroft talked on the pavement, Sherlock walked off. His head was buzzing with possibilities, and he wanted some time by himself to sort them out.

'Oh, Sherlock!'

He turned around again. Mycroft was flapping a hand at him.

'What is it?' he asked, returning to where the two men stood.

'You may need some money.' He handed across three coins. 'Here're three guineas. Keep them safe, and buy yourself some cold weather clothing, if you see any.'

Sherlock walked alone, up through Piccadilly Circus, through Leicester Square and across to the bottom of Charing Cross Road. The streets were thronged with people on the pavements, and horses, carts and cabs of various descriptions in the road. If this was just a few hundred people, and it felt like he was being crushed, then what would a country of sixty-five *million* people be like? And if there were sixty-five million people in Russia alone, then how many people were there in the world as a whole? The scale of things made him dizzy!

Bookshops, junk shops and pawnbrokers lined the street on either side, and he spent a good hour browsing through the boxes of stuff that were located outside the various emporia, and the shelves and cabinets inside. He let his mind wander, not trying to force it in any particular direction.

He came across a handful of books about the Russian Empire, selected the two most factual and bought them. He also found himself interested in a box of door locks, padlocks and keys, which the owner of the shop warned him were unsorted. There was no guarantee that any of the keys would fit any of the locks; the owner was selling them as seen. Sherlock wondered whether by having numerous padlocks in his possession, to fiddle with and experiment on at his leisure, he might learn how to pick a lock. It was a skill that might prove useful in future. In fact, it would already have proved itself useful in the past couple of months.

In the end he abandoned the box of locks and walked away. He could always go back for them later.

Further up Charing Cross Road he crossed Cambridge Circus, and then went on to the beginning of Tottenham Court Road. Still more shops, although the street was at least wider here, giving more room for the horses and cabs to pass. He checked out a pawnshop in desultory fashion, knowing that it was nearly time to turn round and head back if he was going to be at the Diogenes Club on time. His eye was caught by a violin case resting on a shelf at the back.

He carefully took the case down and blew the dust from it. He opened the lid, and drew a sharp breath when he saw the violin inside. It was old— old and beautiful. The veneer was a deep red, crazed with a tight spider's web of cracks, and the f-holes on top seemed slightly offset to him, but there was something about the instrument that spoke to him. Called to him. He hefted it in his right hand, holding it by the neck and taking its weight on the heel of his palm. The balance seemed better than Rufus Stone's violin, which he had held and played on the SS *Scotia*, on the way to New York. He let the violin's curved body rest on his forearm and plucked at the strings. Sounds filled the shop, plangent and long-lasting. The tuning was awful, but there was something about the tone, some complexity, that thrilled him. It wasn't a pure sound, by any means, but it was warm and expressive. He ran his finger along the edge between the top and the side of the violin. It felt like velvet.

'You have a good eye,' a dry-as-dust voice said from the back of the shop.

Sherlock turned. A section of shelving was in the way, and he walked around it to see a man so old and frail that a strong wind might have blown him away. He was sitting behind a desk piled high with books and other objects. He wore a black skullcap, and he peered at Sherlock through a set of glasses that were perched on the bridge of his nose and secured from falling to the ground by a chain that hung around his neck.

'I beg your pardon?'

The man moved out of the shadowy nook in which he had been sitting and into a dusty beam of sunlight. 'That violin I brought with me from Krakow, many years ago. My father won it in a game of cards, would you believe? It has travelled with us across most of Europe, and now I have to sell it in order that I buy food and firewood, and yet still I want to keep it.'

'It's a lovely instrument.'

'It *is* lovely, just as my wife is lovely, and it plays like a dream, or so I am told by those who know. Me, I play the piano, and sometimes the accordion, but only when I drink too much.'

Sherlock looked in the case. 'Does it have a bow?'

'For you, I have a bow,' the man said. He dug around on the desk, moving some books. 'There are some who say that the bow is as important as the instrument. Me, I'm not so sure. The instrument is a work of art, but the bow is just horsehair. Maybe the type of horse is important, I don't know. Ah!' He pulled a bow from a hidden recess and handed it across to Sherlock. 'Go ahead, try!'

Sherlock thought back to the lessons he'd had from Rufus Stone. He'd not practised since getting back from America, because he didn't have a violin, but he'd missed the discipline of repetitive scales and the way his mind could be calmed from its perpetual churning by the simplicity of music.

He quickly tuned the violin, plucking the strings repeatedly and turning the pegs at the end of the neck until the notes were correct. He raised it to his shoulder and nestled his chin against it. It felt natural. It felt as if it was meant to be there.

Placing the bow against the strings, he played a sustained note on each one in turn: G, D, A, E. The notes sounded like a voice, singing in heaven. He tried some scales, and was surprised at how quickly his fingers seemed to remember what to do.

When he lowered the violin, he was amazed to see tears in the old man's eyes.

'It has been a long time since she was played,' he said. 'I was worried that the passing of years and the passing of miles had dulled her tone, but she sounds more beautiful than ever—which is more than can be said for my lovely wife, who sings like a crow.'

'How is it,' Sherlock asked, 'that different violins can sound . . . so different? I mean, a cart is a cart is a cart. They each have four wheels and they move when they are pulled. It's difficult to choose between them. But violins—they all look the same, more or less, but they don't *sound* the same.'

The old man shrugged. 'You ask three fiddlers, you get four different answers. Some say it's to do with the wood that they're made from. Denser wood is better, they say. Some say that wood that was towed behind boats passing through the Adriatic Sea outside Venice gives a sweeter tone. Others say it's nothing to do with the wood, but all to do with the varnish, and whatever secret ingredients the violin makers put into it. Me, I believe that it has to do with love. An instrument made for money will sound—' he rocked his hand back and forth expressively, '– acceptable, but an instrument made out of the sheer love of making instruments—that will sound beautiful.'

'Do you know who made this one?'

'I do not. It came into my family unheralded and unadvertised. But there is a lot of love in its construction, along with the wood and the glue and the varnish—you can tell that much.'

'How . . .' Sherlock swallowed. 'How much does it cost?'

'Seventy shillings,' the old man said promptly. 'But as you appreciate a decent instrument, I will sell it for sixty-five.'

'I can give you forty-five shillings,' Sherlock said nervously, knowing that he had three pounds and three shillings in his pocket. That was sixty-three shillings, but he wanted to make sure that he had some money left, just in case something unexpected happened.

The old man cocked his head to one side. 'Did I mention the food and the firewood I need to buy for my family?'

'You did. Forty-five shillings,' Sherlock repeated firmly.

'You are a boy whose heart has turned to stone. Fifty-seven, and no lower.'

'Fifty,' Sherlock said. He realized that he was breathing fast.

The old man sighed. 'Maybe I leave the firewood for another day, and tonight we eat cold meat and cold soup. Fifty-five.'

'Agreed.'

They shook hands solemnly, and Sherlock put the violin back in the case. He handed three one-guinea coins across. The old man handed back five shillings in change. 'You take care of her,' he said, 'and if you manage to find out anything more about her, come back and tell me. I would be interested.'

'I will.'

The door to the shop opened, and a shadow fell across the floor. A section of shelving blocked the back of the shop from the front, so neither Sherlock nor the old man could see who had entered, but before the old man could call out Sherlock heard a voice say: ''E came in 'ere! I swear 'e did!'

'You should've come straight in an' nabbed 'im,' another, deeper voice said, sounding like bricks grating together. 'Not waited for me.'

'What if I'd got the wrong one?'

'Then some other family would be grieving tonight.'

CHAPTER TEN

The old man's hand closed on Sherlock's shoulder. 'There is a door at the back,' he whispered. 'It leads into an alley. Go, with my blessing.'

'Maybe 'e's in the back,' the first voice said.

Sherlock nodded a quick 'thanks' as the old man shuffled forward to the edge of the shelving. 'You are looking for books, maybe? On boxing, judging by the look of your ears. Or maybe some gloves to protect those knuckles of yours?'

'We're lookin' for a boy who came in 'ere,' the deeper, rougher voice said.

'Boys I do not allow in the shop,' the old man replied. 'They steal. Thieves they are, all of them.'

'But I saw one come in . . .'

The voices faded away as Sherlock moved through

148

the cramped storage area behind the shop and found a door that led out into a rubbish-strewn alleyway running perpendicular to the road on the other side. He glanced both ways. There was nobody about. He sprinted, as quickly as he could, back towards the Charing Cross Road, with his heart pounding in his chest and the violin case banging against his legs as he went.

Well, that answered at least one question. Whoever it was who had framed Mycroft was still interested in them.

Sticking to the crowds, and always aware of the people around him, Sherlock made his way through London to the Sarbonnier Hotel. When he got there, lungs burning with the effort of running so hard, he found Mycroft in conversation with a big man who appeared all the bigger thanks to the bulky coat he wore. His shoulders, Sherlock thought, were so wide that they made him look like a sideboard. His abundant red hair didn't end with his scalp: it continued down in flourishing sideburns, an extravagant moustache and a vast, spade-shaped beard.

'Ah, this is Mister Kyte,' Mycroft said, interrupting their conversation. 'He is the Actor-Manager of Kyte's Theatrical Company. Mister Kyte, this is my . . . protégé . . . Scott Eckersley.' He stared warningly at Sherlock, but Sherlock had already picked up the fact that he, and—presumably—Mycroft, were using false names.

'Pleased to meet you, sir,' Sherlock said, shaking the man's hand. The backs of Mr Kyte's hands were covered with reddish-brown hairs, and the palms prickled against Sherlock's, as if hairs were growing there as well.

149

'And you, sonny, and you.' Mr Kyte's voice was a deep wheeze. 'Mr Sigerson here tells me that you're a dab hand with ropes and scenery.'

'I am that, sir,' Sherlock said brightly. Inside, he was wondering what the man was talking about. He stared at Mr Kyte's face. There was something strange about it: Sherlock could see a series of small cuts around his eyes, nose and cheeks. How had they got there?

'Good stuff. Good stuff indeed. Well, come on down to the theatre later and meet the cast and crew.' He turned to Mycroft—or Mr Sigerson, as Sherlock now had to think of him. 'Thank you again for joining our motley team. I'm sure it'll be an adventure to tell the grandchildren about!'

'Indeed,' Mycroft said. 'It is not likely that I will end up with grandchildren, but I shall make copious notes just in case.'

Mr Kyte left, and Sherlock turned to Mycroft. 'Mister Sigerson? The son of Siger? Couldn't you have come up with a better name than that?'

'I was thinking on my feet,' Mycroft said. 'Not the most comfortable position for me to be in.' He gazed at the violin case under Sherlock's arm. 'What is that?'

'It's . . . a violin. In a case.'

'Yes, I can see that. The question was rhetorical. You *have* covered rhetoric during your Greek lessons at school, haven't you? The question it was meant to spark in your mind was: why have you gone and bought a violin when you should have been buying warm clothing, as I told you?'

Sherlock thought quickly. 'There were two men looking for me,' he said. 'I went into a shop. They followed me in. I had to get out through the

150

back of the shop. I bought the violin on impulse, because—'

'Because you needed something to change your profile, to make yourself look different,' Mycroft said. Sherlock could tell from his voice that he was dubious about Sherlock's story. 'This is a worrying development: it means that they are still looking for you, and by extension Mr Crowe and me as well. This makes it even more imperative that we leave London, indeed the country, as soon as is practicable.'

As Mycroft spoke, Sherlock started to feel uneasy. He hadn't actually *lied* to Mycroft, but he had moved around the sequence in which events happened in order to make it look as though he had a reason for buying the violin other than the fact that he had fallen in love with the instrument.

'Well, I suppose we can always burn the violin for warmth, should the need arise,' Mycroft continued. 'How much did it cost you?' He raised a hand. 'No, don't tell me. I would rather remain happily in ignorance. Go and put that . . . thing . . . in your room, and then join me for lunch.'

'But you only just finished breakfast.'

'Sherlock, if I want to be scolded then I will return to my lodgings and talk to my landlady.'

Sherlock scooted upstairs to the room that Amyus Crowe had booked for him and left his new violin on the bed. As he came out, he noticed that the door to the room next to his, the room Crowe had booked for himself, was open. He looked inside, expecting to see Crowe, but a maid was making up the bed. Crowe's bag had gone.

'Excuse me—what happened to the man who rented this room?'

151

'He's checked out, sir,' the maid said, turning round and curtseying.

'Checked out?'

'Yes, sir—unexpected, like.'

'Oh. Thanks.'

He rushed downstairs to tell Mycroft, but Crowe was standing in the hotel lobby with his coat on and his bag at his feet.

'Ah, Sherlock, ah was hopin' ah'd see you.'

'You're *leaving*?'

'There ain't anythin' for me to do here. Your brother is takin' you off my hands. Ah should get back an' look after Ginny.'

'But . . .' Sherlock trailed off, knowing that Crowe was right.

'Exactly. Ain't no point fightin' against the facts. Ah ain't needed on this trip. That's all right—ah'm a grown man. Ah can take it.'

'I wish you *were* coming.'

Crowe's face was grim. 'So do ah. There's somethin' awry 'bout this whole business. Ah think your brother's normally infallible mind has been affected by gettin' locked up like a common criminal, an' by the fact that things are gettin' close to home. Ah can't help feelin' that he's made a miscalculation somewhere, but ah can't quite put my finger on it. Ah do believe that this little expedition to Russia is a mistake, but ah can't convince him to call it off. We had an exchange of words about it earlier. He's set on goin'. Ah think the disappearance of his man in Moscow has discomfited him more than he will admit.' He shook his head. 'It's never easy, losin' one of your team. It's happened to me, more than once. Even so, ah don't see why he needs to drag you along with him.'

'Give my . . . my regards to Virginia.'

'Ah will, right enough.' Crowe stuck out his hand. Sherlock shook it solemnly, his fingers vanishing inside Crowe's massive fist. 'Take care, an' take care of Mycroft. He's goin' to be out of his element.'

A hotel porter rushed over to take Crowe's bag, but he waved the man away. 'When ah'm too old to pick a bag up, that's when ah'll ask for help,' he said. He picked the bag up and threw it over his shoulder. 'Come and visit us when you get back. Tell us everythin' that happened.'

'I will.'

Sherlock watched as Crowe walked out of the hotel door without glancing back. He felt as if a chunk of himself had just been carved away. He felt vulnerable, alone.

Eventually he walked through into the restaurant, where Mycroft was sitting at a table with a whole turbot on his plate. He was meticulously filleting the fish with his knife and fork.

'If I were the Good Lord,' he said conversationally as Sherlock sat disconsolately at the table, 'I would have ensured that fish that were edible were also easy to eat. It seems like a failure in design that something that tastes so good creates such difficulty in removing the bones. Either we are meant to eat it or we are not; there should be no middle ground.' He glanced up. 'Has Mr Crowe left?'

'Yes, he has.'

'Good.' Mycroft lifted a slice of fish on his knife and carefully transferred it to his fork. 'He disapproves of my plan to take you to Russia.'

'He said you argued.'

'We did. He was very forceful in his opinions. He is very protective of you, you know.'

'We've been through a lot together, over the past year or so.'

'Indeed.' Mycroft popped the fragment of fish into his mouth and chewed for a moment with his eyes closed. 'Beautifully cooked. The black butter sauce is exquisite. I shall have to remember this place. It is not *so* far from my office that I could not take my luncheon here on a regular basis.'

'Mycroft, are you *sure* we should travel to Russia in disguise?'

'I have considered the matter thoroughly, and I see no other option.' He checked his watch. 'The third member of our expedition should be joining us in a moment. I sent him a telegram earlier.' He glanced briefly at Sherlock. 'There is something I should warn you about. I said that this man was one of my agents, and that he was a violinist.'

'Yes?'

'What I did not say was that you already know him.'

Sherlock heard the words, but he didn't understand them. 'I *know* him? But I don't know *any* of your agents. I've never met any of them—except perhaps Mr Crowe, but I don't think he counts as one of your agents.'

'He certainly does not.' Mycroft's expression was of a man who was preparing himself to convey bad news. 'Sherlock,' he said, as he lifted his gaze to look past his brother, 'I believe you are acquainted with Rufus Stone.'

Eight words. Eight simple words that seemed to drop like stones into the deep well of Sherlock's

154

mind. He could feel the ripples bouncing around his mind long after Mycroft had finished speaking. He turned his head so that he could see what Mycroft was looking at, but the logical, analytical part of his mind already knew. The other part—the emotional part that still belonged to a fourteen-year-old boy—was hoping that it wasn't true, that whoever was standing behind him was a complete stranger.

But it wasn't, and that emotional fourteen-year-old part of his mind shrivelled up just a little bit more than it already had.

Rufus Stone was standing behind him. Rufus Stone, with his unkempt brown hair and his stubble-flecked chin and his green velvet jacket. He wore a gold ring in his ear. He looked uncomfortable, as if he desperately wanted to be somewhere—anywhere—else. Sherlock certainly did.

'Sit down,' Mycroft said. 'You are making the place look untidy. Don't mind the waiters; I don't think they get many Gypsy violinists in here. The experience will do them good.'

'Hello, Sherlock,' Stone said as he sat down.

'You work for my brother?' Sherlock asked. 'Why didn't you ever tell me?'

'Because I told him not to,' Mycroft replied. 'When we decided that you and Amyus Crowe were to travel to America a few months ago, I was worried that Mr Crowe would find himself dragged off on side-business, or suddenly discover that he loved his homeland so much that he couldn't return to England. I arranged for Mr Stone to get a ticket on the same ship, to keep an eye on you. In New York he was to shadow you and keep you safe.' He snorted. 'That, of course, did not turn out as well as

155

I had anticipated, thanks to your actions in following young Matthew Arnatt's captors on to a train bound for who-knows-where.'

'You work for my *brother*!' Sherlock repeated. The thought was like an obstacle in the centre of his mind that was too big to climb over.

'I need hardly add,' Mycroft continued, 'that teaching you the violin was *not* in his instructions.'

'No, that was my choice,' Stone said. 'And my pleasure.'

'But what do you *do* for Mycroft?' Sherlock asked.

Rufus Stone shrugged. 'Mostly I travel, free as a bird and just as poor. I can move unchecked and unhindered through a lot of the Central European countries. Nobody bothers an itinerant violinist like me. I pick up rumours, and I hear things in conversations in taverns and the like, and I report them back to Mr Holmes here.'

'One can often judge more about the state of a nation's economy by what the farmers are saying over a glass of ale than one can by reading the newspapers,' Mycroft said. 'I have a large number of people, all over the world, whose only task is to reap big bushels of what the general public are saying, winnow it down and send me the resulting kernels of truth.'

'And moving to Farnham?' Sherlock's hands were shaking, and he had to hold them together beneath the table to stop anyone else from seeing. He felt *betrayed*. 'Whose idea was that?'

Stone looked across at Mycroft. When Sherlock's brother remained silent, Stone said: 'When I came back to England, Mr Holmes asked me to stay in the country for a while, see what I could learn about the state of the nation. I suggested that I should start in Hampshire.' He paused, awkwardly. 'I wanted to see how your violin playing was coming along.'

'I bought a new violin,' Sherlock said. His voice sounded small, even to him.

'I'd like to see it.'

Mycroft coughed. 'Mr Stone will be accompanying us to Russia. He has travelled in that country before, and of course we need a violin player in order to complete the theatrical company roster.' He paused for a moment, and then continued in a softer voice, 'Sherlock, believe me, I would never have done this for any reason other than for your own good, and I would not have let you find out that I had done it if it had not been entirely necessary.'

'That doesn't make it all right,' Sherlock said. He stood up. 'I'm going out.'

'Be at the King's Theatre in Whitechapel at four o'clock this afternoon,' Mycroft instructed him. 'We are to meet our travelling companions.'

Sherlock walked away without answering. Behind him, he could hear Mycroft saying: 'No, let him go. He will come to understand, in time, that what I did was entirely logical and for his own protection.'

He walked out of the hotel and into the street. It was beginning to rain, and he felt the cold prickle of raindrops on his face, but he didn't seem to care. Everything around him was grey and uninteresting. Meaningless.

He turned left and started to walk, not really caring where he was going. He clamped down hard on his thoughts, not letting any consideration of his brother, or Rufus Stone, or the trip to America that now turned out to be largely fiction, to get started. He just walked; walked and observed. Like some kind of mobile calculating machine, he took in the facts around him and let his mind join them together. The man wearing the red-spotted neckerchief over in that doorway—he had caught an illness, probably in India, and would be dead within a week, judging by the state of his skin. The watch that the gentleman in the top hat was consulting was not his own: he had most likely stolen it from someone, and the theft had only occurred in the past few days. The beggar on the corner in the trolley with the wheels, the one who was wearing a sign round his neck claiming that his legs were paralysed, actually walked several miles a day, judging by the recent wear to his shoes. All of this Sherlock deduced from the things he observed, and none of it mattered to him. None of it mattered at all.

He lost track of time as he walked, but when he checked his watch and found that it was nearly four o'clock, he realized that he was already near Whitechapel. His mind had steered him in the right direction without him realizing.

The theatre was tucked away in a side street off a main thoroughfare. Its frontage was red brick and white portico columns; four steps led up to the main doors. Sherlock trudged up them and through into the lobby. There was nobody present—the shutters were closed over the ticket booth—but Sherlock could almost sense the essence of the crowds that presumably crossed the foyer on a regular basis: a trace of cigarette smoke, eau de toilette and perfume that had been absorbed by the ornate plaster of the walls and ceiling.

Stairs led up on either side of the lobby, presumably to the circle seats, but on the far side was a pair of doors which he presumed led directly to the stalls. A door to one side of the ticket booth probably led to the backstage areas: the dressing rooms, the green room and the stage itself.

Sherlock stood for a moment, breathing in the aromas of the theatre, listening to the sighs and groans as the building flexed, letting his gaze skip across the old posters which were framed behind glass on the walls. There was something almost *alive* about this place. He'd been in a lot of buildings which were public spaces, but this was the only one he'd ever known which felt as if it had absorbed something good from the people who had passed through its doors. Deepdene School for Boys had reeked of desperation, and the Diogenes Club felt prickly and irritable, but the King's Theatre felt like a home he'd never been in before.

He walked to the main doors into the auditorium and pushed them open.

The space inside was smaller than he had expected. Rows of seats curved away to either side of him and sloped away in front, all of them covered in tired green velvet. The underside of the circle seating loomed like a low, dark cloud above him. It was supported by iron columns that had been wrought into artistic shapes and painted brown and red and green, like slender trees with leaves and flowers on them. Curtain-backed boxes were attached to the walls on either side, containing small numbers of secluded seats for anyone who had the money to pay for them. That was the way the tickets were arranged, Sherlock knew: the stalls were the cheapest, the circle seats the next most expensive and the boxes most expensive of all, although 'expense' was probably a relative term as far as this isolated little theatre went. Aisles cut through the stalls seating, leading down towards the stage.

On the stage was a group of people, including his brother. Mycroft was resplendent in overcoat, top hat and cane. For a moment, gazing at him, Sherlock could see him as a person, not as his brother. He had a natural authority to him; he radiated importance and power.

Rufus Stone was standing just behind and to one side of Mycroft. The red-haired, bear-like man Sherlock had seen earlier—Mr Kyte—was standing next to Mycroft, still wearing his massive coat, and on his other side was a group of people that Sherlock presumed to be actors and backstage staff. The actors were, in the main, wearing costumes of a bygone age: ornate velvet dresses for the women, lace shirts and puffed breeches for the men.

'Ah, Scott,' Mycroft said. His voice boomed through the auditorium. 'Come and join us.'

Sherlock made his way down one of the aisles. The way to the stage was blocked by a fenced-off area that Sherlock supposed would contain a small orchestra for musical productions. He glanced left and right. Five steps led up from the floor of the stalls to the stage on either side. Arbitrarily, he chose to go to the right.

When he got up on the stage, he was surprised to see that it sloped slightly. It was about a foot lower at the front than it was at the back. He supposed that tilting the stage in that way gave the audience a better view of what was going on, especially the people in the cheap seats, some of whom would actually be looking up at the actors. The edge of the stage was lined with gas lamps behind reflectors and there was a trapdoor in the centre.

He crossed the stage to where Mycroft was

standing, watched by everyone else.

'I have already introduced Rufus Stone, who will be playing violin in the pit,' Mycroft said grandly. 'Allow me, then, to introduce my protégé, Master Scott Eckersley. With the kind permission of Mister Kyte, Scott will be joining the company as general factotum.' He turned to Sherlock. 'Scott, allow me to introduce you to the cast and crew.' He indicated a tall man with long blond hair brushed back from a wide brow. He was in costume. 'This is Mr Thomas Malvin. He is the company's leading man.'

Malvin nodded at Sherlock, barely even looking at him.

'And this,' Mycroft continued, nodding towards a beautiful pale woman with green eyes and raven-black hair who smiled at Sherlock, 'is Miss Aiofe Dimmock. She plays the romantic female leads opposite Mr Malvin.'

Sherlock smiled back. Aiofe must have been at least ten years older than him, but there was something about her smile and her green eyes that made his heart skip a beat.

Tearing his eyes away from Aiofe Dimmock, Sherlock followed Mycroft's waving hand. 'Mr William Furness and Mrs Diane Loran provide invaluable supporting roles to the two main actors,' he said.

William Furness was a portly man with a fringe of dyed black hair running around the back of his scalp, from ear to ear. His nose was swollen and knobbly, and his cheeks had the red-veined appearance of the heavy drinker. Presumably the veins would be covered by make-up when he was actually giving a performance, but there wasn't much that could disguise that cauliflower-like nose apart from distance. He raised two fingers to his forehead in mock-salute. Mrs Loran was a matronly woman with her hair tied up into a bun. She looked as if she would be more at home in a kitchen than on stage. She smiled warmly at Sherlock. If he had been closer he suspected she might have given him a hug.

'Along with Mr Kyte,' Mycroft said, 'who often appears on stage with Mr Malvin and Miss Dimmock as well as running the company, these four are the main performers. The others you see here serve to fill in crowd scenes and come on in minor parts when they are not shifting scenery backstage. From left to right we have Rhydian, Judah, Pauly and Henry.'

Sherlock nodded to the four boys of about his own age who were standing behind the main actors. Rhydian was thin and dark, with a pointed chin and heavy eyebrows. Judah was also thin, but his hair was so pale and fine that it was almost white, seeming to float around his head, and his eyes had a pinkish look to them. Pauly and Henry were twins: both muscular, both brown-eyed. The only difference between them was that Pauly (Sherlock assumed it was Pauly, as he was the one nearest to Mycroft) had lost the little finger of his left hand in an accident at some stage.

Someone coughed in the wings. Looking into the shadows, Sherlock could just about make out a tall man whose mouth was overhung by a thick black moustache. He seemed almost to be leaning backwards, hands in his pockets, as he stared at the people on stage. His eyes glinted in the darkness.

'Ah yes, I almost forgot,' Mycroft said. 'Although the rest of the pit orchestra will be joining us later, this is Mr Eves. He is the conductor and musical arranger.'

'Mr Eves,' Sherlock acknowledged.

'Master…Eckersley,' the conductor acknowledged. His voice was dry, laconic. 'A pleasure to meet you, I am sure.'

'Mr Kyte, ladies, gentlemen,' Mycroft—or, rather, Mr Sigerson, as Sherlock supposed he should be known from now on—proclaimed, 'thank you for taking us into your company, into your confidence and, I hope, into your hearts. Mr Kyte has seen my references, and knows that I can be trusted to serve you responsibly, as I have served other theatrical companies in the past. I undertake for my part to serve you as General Manager to the best of my abilities, and to take you ever onward and ever upward. To that end, the first order of business is to ensure that the incipient trip to Moscow goes without incident. My aim is to ensure that all business affairs are concluded swiftly and painlessly, so that you may concentrate on your artistic endeavours. Put your trust in me, and I will not let you down.'

A smattering of applause followed these words.

'And with that,' Mr Kyte rumbled, 'I suggest we get back to rehearsals. Five minutes, everybody, and then I want everyone on stage. Remember—we leave for Moscow in three days!'

CHAPTER ELEVEN

The next week passed like a feverish dream. After a few days in London, settling in with the theatrical company while Mycroft arranged the final details of their transport, Sherlock had boarded a train at Charing Cross Station with the rest of them. If it had been Waterloo then he might have been more nervous, remembering the chase in the tunnels beneath, but Charing Cross was a smaller place with no bad associations for him. The train had taken them through the familiar English countryside down to Dover, where they had transferred on to a boat that took them across the English Channel to France. At Dunkerque they had boarded another train, and in three days they would be in Moscow. Three days to cross Europe! Incredible!

The accommodation was fairly basic. The seats were barely padded, and there were no beds. Instead, the troupe pretty much just slept where they sat, stretched out where possible across the seats.

The musicians, to whom Sherlock had not been introduced, sat together and seemed to sleep or play draughts on small folding tables all the time. Only Mycroft and Mr Kyte had their own separate berths, as befitting their status as General Manager and Actor-Manager of Kyte's Theatrical Company. They spent most of their time alone.

Sherlock spent much of the time glued to the window, watching the land flash past. Names that he'd only ever seen in atlases were suddenly coming to life in front of him: countries such as Belgium and Prussia; towns and cities including Brussels, Koln, Berlin, Warsaw and Minsk . . .

He was staring out of the window, watching wide swathes of fir trees slip past, when Mrs Loran sat down beside him.

'You seem lonely,' she said. 'I thought you might fancy a chat.'

'I'm fine. I'm just . . . fascinated by the way some things change as we travel, like languages and food, and yet other things, like plants and animals, stay more or less the same. There's always birds and cats, for instance.'

'And sausages,' she pointed out. 'I don't believe there's a country in the world that doesn't have sausages.' She gazed at him sympathetically for a while. 'Your mentor, Mr Sigerson, doesn't seem to have had much time for you on this journey,' she said eventually.

'He's been busy,' Sherlock replied, feeling that he ought to defend Mycroft.

'Nevertheless, I would have thought that, having taken you under his wing, he would have been keen to look after you, not leave you on your own.' She cocked her head to one side. 'He doesn't seem very interested in your welfare.'

'He's got a lot of things to think about.' Feeling sensitive, Sherlock tried to change the subject. 'Have you been acting for long?'

She gazed past him, out of the window. 'Oh, sometimes I feel as if I have been acting all of my life,' she murmured.

The landscape changed as they moved further and further west. The little bit of France that Sherlock had seen, and the broad swathe of Belgium that they had travelled through, were a mixture of dark green forests and light green fields. But as they travelled through Prussia and into Russia itself the land became more and more waterlogged and the temperature plummeted until the smaller ponds were frozen and there was snow on the ground. The people seemed shorter and darker, or perhaps the low cloud that sat

165

perpetually over the land was having an effect on his senses.

At one point, Sherlock walked along the carriage corridor to see how Mycroft was doing. His brother was sitting in his compartment, propped up by pillows, looking decidedly unwell. He was surrounded by open books, and appeared to be making notes in a small notebook. He looked up as Sherlock knocked and pushed the door open.

'Yes?'

'I wanted to see if you were all right.'

'No, I am not. The infernal rattling of this train is upsetting my digestive system. I am attempting to distract myself with books, but they are of limited help.'

'Is there anything I can do?'

'Just leave me alone to suffer in peace,' Mycroft snapped. 'I do not feel up to conversation at the moment.'

Sherlock backed out and closed the door. He stood for a few moments outside his brother's compartment, unsure what to do. He couldn't remember feeling as lonely and as useless as this since the first time he'd walked into his aunt and uncle's house in Farnham.

He turned to walk away, but something caught his eye. It was just outside the door to Mr Kyte's compartment, lying by the door frame: a small brown object about the size and shape of his thumb with a thin piece of cord or string attached. He bent to pick it up. As his fingers and thumb closed on it, and it gave slightly under the pressure, he realized with a shock that it was a mouse. A dead mouse. The thing that he had thought was a piece of string dangling from it was its tail.

A dead mouse? He supposed that trains must have mice, just like houses. He looked around for somewhere to put it, but the door to My Kyte's compartment opened a crack, and the burly, red-bearded man stared out at Sherlock through the gap. 'Yes?' he wheezed. 'What is it?'

'Nothing,' Sherlock said. 'I was just . . . visiting Mr Sigerson.' He slipped the dead mouse into his pocket. For some reason he didn't quite understand, he didn't want to mention it to Mr Kyte.

'If you're bored,' Kyte breathed, 'go and talk to the boys. You'll need to work with them on the backdrops and the props. Get to know them.'

He closed the door in Sherlock's face.

Actually, after three days in London, learning how to raise backdrops and move props on stage, Sherlock had got to know the four younger members of the company pretty well. To pass the time on the train, Sherlock finally gave in to their requests to join them in a game of cards. Within the space of a day they had taught him the rules of whist, backgammon and baccarat, and with his mathematically oriented mind—not to mention the retentive memory that seemed to be the genetic heritage of the Holmes family—Sherlock soon caught on to the subtleties of the games.

He became fascinated with the way that the twins handled the cards. They manipulated the pack like expert gamblers, shuffling easily and dealing the cards smoothly and with precision. Eventually, inevitably, he asked them how they did it, and so they showed him, beginning with the various different types of shuffle—the Overhand, the Hindu, the Weave, the Table Riffle and Hand

167

Riffle and the Strip. It was, they told him, all a matter of dexterity and practice. That was what Rufus Stone had said about playing the violin, of course, and so when the games had finished he borrowed the pack and spent the next few hours trying, over and over again, to master the different techniques for shuffling the cards. With his thin fingers and his sheer tenacity, he soon got the hang of it, and for the rest of the games he was shuffling and dealing almost as well as Henry and Pauly.

By the third day, staring out of the window had lost its attractions. Sherlock found himself more and more watching the actors and actresses— Mr Malvin, Mr Furness, Miss Dimmock and Mrs Loran. He tried to use the skills that Amyus Crowe had taught him to determine something about their histories and their characters, but he found himself foxed. Just as he thought he had nailed down a particular deduction about one of them, something came along and changed it. Perhaps it was something to do with their acting training—perhaps what he was seeing was different characters coming out in them without their knowing.

At one point, as the train was clattering across a particularly marshy and boring landscape, Sherlock noticed that Mr Furness—the older, fatter actor with the veined skin and the cauliflower-like nose—had a box on his lap and was sorting through the contents. They seemed to be jars of various sort. He noticed Sherlock watching, and gestured him over.

'Theatrical make-up,' he said. His breath smelt of gin. 'You've seen it before, surely?'

'Not close up,' Sherlock confessed. 'I'm usually

backstage.'

'This kit's been with me for years,' Furness confided. 'I've got face paints made out of beeswax and mutton fat with zinc, lead, lampblack, cochineal, ultramarine, ochre or Prussian blue added to give 'em their colour. Then there's the other stuff: burnt cork and lampblack for the eyelids and eyelashes, burnt paper for making shadows, spirit gum for fastening wigs down, or crêpe hair for moustaches and beards. Use them properly and you can change the shape of your whole face, at least as seen from a distance.'

Seeing Sherlock's disbelieving look, he continued: 'See, if you highlight the protruding bones of the face, like the nose and the cheekbones, with a lighter colour, your features become exaggerated. If you put some dark shadowing in the bits that dip in, it adds depth. Changing the highlights and shadows, you can make sagging jowls, forehead wrinkles, eye pouches and prominent veins. And when all else fails . . .' He produced a metal tin from the box. 'Nose putty!'

'Nose putty?' Sherlock asked in disbelief.

'Changes the shape of your nose, your chin—any bit that doesn't move much. Nose putty doesn't flex, see, so if you put it on your cheeks then it'll crack, but you wouldn't believe how much a different shaped nose and chin can change your appearance. Your best friend wouldn't recognize you!'

Eventually, after Sherlock had lost track of the hours and the days, and the journey had become a timeless haze, the train pulled into Moscow Kursk Station.

A tall man in a black frock coat, black fur-trimmed overcoat and black top hat stood just the other side of the ticket barrier. He wore a small, trimmed beard and moustache. His skin was pale, like porcelain. He seemed to be watching for someone, and as soon as he caught sight of the party he smiled and raised a hand.

Mr Kyte was first through the barrier. He extended a hand, but the man stepped forward and embraced him warmly. Mycroft, who was just behind Mr Kyte, stepped backwards quickly.

The bearded man spoke to Mr Kyte and Mycroft for a few moments, then turned to the rest of the party. 'My name is Morodov,' he said in accented French; 'Piotr Ilyich Morodov. It is my pleasure and my duty to represent Prince Yusupov, who is sponsoring your visit to this our motherland, our beloved homeland. Please be assured that not one detail has been left unchecked to ensure that your visit is enjoyable as well as artistically productive. Now, please follow me. I will take you to the Slavyansky Bazaar Hotel, where I have secured rooms for you.'

He snapped his fingers and porters, dressed in crudely stitched and badly fitting green serge uniforms, leaped to take the various bags and suitcases that the party had brought with them. He led the way outside, where several carriages were drawn up waiting for them.

The weather was cold and the ground was snowy, but instead of the brown slush that built up in England when it snowed and carts and carriages mixed the snow up with mud and straw, this snow was white and deep. It crunched under their feet as the party left the station and found the three

170

carriages that would take them to their hotel.

Along with the rest of the party, Sherlock stared in amazement at the various means of transport that thronged the street outside the station. He was used to the flat farm carts of Farnham and the hansom cabs and broughams of London, but these were something completely different. They were more like the gymnasium equipment he'd used at Deepdene School for Boys than anything a person would willingly ride in: long, narrow planks on which passengers sat astride, as if they were on a horse instead of being pulled by one, with sides that sloped outward to a footboard, the whole thing set on four sprung wheels with a driver sitting at the front of the line of passengers. They looked uncomfortable for men, and entirely unsuitable for women in their dresses.

The group watched as the porters loaded their bags and suitcases on to the backs of the carriages, then climbed aboard. The journey through the streets of Moscow was short, but Sherlock was fascinated by the impressiveness and the age of the buildings. Everything seemed to be built on a larger scale than in England—a scale that dwarfed the locals, who scurried around in the shadow of the buildings, hunched up against the cold, like mice running along skirting boards. And the colours! He was used to buildings that were the colour of the stone, or brick, or wood that they had been constructed from, but here in Moscow every second building seemed to have been painted. Some were pink, some blue, some green, and a lot of them were yellow for reasons that escaped Sherlock. Maybe Russia had a surplus of yellow paint.

When they had arrived at the hotel, and Piotr

Ilyich Morodov had signed them all in, said his goodbyes and left, Mycroft and Mr Kyte gathered the troupe together in the lounge.

'I have prepared itinerary sheets,' Mycroft announced, 'which detail the events that will be taking place over the next few days.' He raised the back of his hand to his lips and coughed. 'I will hand these sheets out in a moment, but let me summarize the details for you. Firstly, we are here in Moscow at the invitation of Prince Yusupov. The Prince is a well-known patron of the arts, and has long nurtured a desire to see a British theatrical company act on stage. The Prince has put at our disposal for the next three days the Maly Theatre. The Theatre is undoubtedly the foremost theatre in Moscow, which means that by definition it is the foremost theatre in Russia.'

'What is the seating capacity?' Mr Malvin, the leading actor, asked. He projected his voice as if he were already on stage. 'I am a respected actor. I do not appear in front of a mere handful of people.'

'The primary stage has a capacity of nine hundred and fifty people; the secondary stage a capacity of seven hundred and fifty.'

'And which stage are we on?' Miss Aiofe Dimmock, the leading lady, interrupted.

'We are performing on the secondary stage,' Mycroft replied smoothly, 'but only because the stage area itself is smaller and more suited to our rather more intimate performances.'

Mr Kyte stepped forward. 'I would not wish to have your delicate and nuanced acting to be swamped in a vast auditorium,' he explained.

Miss Dimmock nodded, and stepped back demurely. 'Very thoughtful,' she said. 'Thank you.'

'I will need to examine the auditorium in advance,' Malvin said loudly. 'It would be impossible for me to act on a stage on which I have never trod before. I will need to assess the acoustics and determine for myself how to project my voice to the most far-flung corners so that everyone might hear.'

'Of course. Let me come to that in a moment.' Mycroft paused, gazing at the company members. 'We are engaged, as you know, for three performances, spread over three separate nights. For the first night, Prince Yusupov has sent out invitations to the crème de la crème of Russian society. This, I am assured, is the social event of the season.'

'Will the Tsar be there?' Mrs Loran piped up from beside Sherlock. 'Oh, I do hope he is!' She glanced at Sherlock, and said conspiratorially, 'When I was a little girl all I ever wanted was to marry a prince. It's too late now, but I can still dream.'

'Alas, the Tsar is detained by affairs of state.' Mycroft spread his hands in apology. 'But rest assured that the audience will consist of a panoply of titled heads—Princes and Princesses, Counts and Countesses, Barons and Baronesses, Dukes and Duchesses. The Russian aristocracy is extensive, and most of them will be present on that first night, as will the British Ambassador to the Court of the Tsar and his good lady.'

'Oh, how marvellous!' Mrs Loran exclaimed, clapping her hands together. She leaned towards Sherlock. 'Perhaps one of them might take pity on a middle-aged lady and make an honest woman of me,' she whispered. He smiled back. He suspected that Mrs Loran would be more than a match for any Russian nobleman.

Mycroft turned his attention to the rest of the company. 'On each of the three nights you will, I understand, be performing a selection of scenes from the great British playwrights—William Shakespeare, of course, Ben Jonson, Christopher Marlowe and John Webster. Mr Kyte—' he turned to the big man who stood behind him, 'I understand that you will be introducing the scenes and placing them in context for the audience.'

'That is my intent,' Mr Kyte rumbled. 'I will be speaking in French, although the performances will be in English.'

'Excellent.' Mycroft turned to the younger members of the company—the dark haired Rhydian, the pale Judah and the twins Henry and Pauly. 'In terms of scenery and props, I am assured that the theatre has a number of backdrops that can be used to represent everything from the battlements of Elsinore Castle to the Forest of Arden, along with a large amount of furniture and other things that might prove useful. I suggest that first thing in the morning we all go to the theatre, and while the actors are performing whatever vocal exercises they need in order to check the acoustical properties of the auditorium, you lads sort through everything with the aid of Mr Kyte. Work out what you want to use, and the regular staff at the theatre will get it all set up for you in the afternoon and familiarize you with the means of raising and lowering the backdrops.'

'It's all ropes,' Henry said. 'In the end, it's all just ropes and pulling.'

'Tomorrow afternoon, while the theatre staff are

174

organizing the backdrops, there will I understand be a full rehearsal in which everyone will take part.' He switched his gaze to the tall, moustached Mr Eves and the gaggle of musicians who stood behind him. Rufus Stone was there as well. He appeared to have bonded quite happily with the other musicians. 'That rehearsal will include the various musical numbers which are a part of the performance, and so all musicians will be required to attend.'

Mr Eves nodded, 'We will, ah, be there. Worry not.'

Mycroft nodded. 'I am sure you will.' He let his gaze roam around the members of the company. 'On the second night the audience will consist of the artistic, rather than the titled, Moscow community. On the third night, tickets have gone on sale to the general population of Moscow. I think we can safely assume that you will be performing in front of a representative selection of the upper middle class of this fair city.' He paused, and clasped his hands in front of his rather prominent stomach. 'Remember that you are artistic ambassadors for your country.' He clapped his hands. 'Now, to dinner, and then to bed. We meet for breakfast tomorrow at eight o'clock, and then to the theatre!'

The various members of the company headed for the hotel restaurant. The matronly Mrs Loran paused beside Sherlock and reached out to ruffle his hair. 'Do you want to join me in the hotel lounge after dinner, Scott?' she asked. 'I was hoping you could help me with my lines by reading the other parts in the script.'

Sherlock's initial reaction was to say yes. He was

growing to like Mrs Loran more and more. Before he answered, he glanced over at Mycroft. His brother had obviously heard Mrs Loran's question, and he shook his head briefly.

'I wish I could,' he said, 'but I need to go to bed early and get a good night's sleep.'

'Perhaps tomorrow, after breakfast, then,' she said, smiling, and walked off.

Mycroft beckoned to Sherlock and Rufus Stone to join him.

'I apologize for spoiling your evening,' he said to Sherlock, 'but the more time we spend socializing with these people the more likely it is that we will let something slip, and they will realize that we are not what we seem. Our best course of action is to be polite but reserved.' His glance moved to Stone, and then back to Sherlock. 'The journey has been tiring,' he said quietly, 'and I see no reason to exert ourselves this evening. Get some rest. Tomorrow, when the remainder of the company head for the theatre, Sherlock will accompany me to the apartment of my agent here in Moscow. I wish to establish what exactly has happened to him.' He glanced at Stone. 'You, I am afraid, should go to the theatre with the rest of them. As principal violinist, your absence would be noted.'

'You might need me,' Stone said, 'if there's trouble.'

'If there's trouble, I suspect that nothing will help,' Mycroft said soberly. 'We are in a foreign country in which the free expression of any thought that runs counter to the Tsar's is ruthlessly suppressed by both his official and his secret police forces. But we do what we must.'

'Then why take Sherlock?' Stone pressed. 'If it's

176

that dangerous, he should come to the theatre with me.'

Mycroft shook his large head. 'I accept the logic of your thoughts, but I may need Sherlock's sharp eyes, sharp wits and athletic skills. It may be necessary to gain access to the apartment through a window, in which case I am entirely unsuited to the task. Once inside, he may spot some clue that I miss. At the very least, he can keep watch for the police while I am inside. And if something happens to me, he may be able to return and warn you.'

Stone nodded reluctantly. 'Very well. If that's all . . . ?' Receiving Mycroft's nod, he walked away, towards the restaurant.

Mycroft gazed critically at Sherlock. 'There is something on your mind, I perceive.'

Sherlock shrugged. 'It's not important.'

'It *is* important. You are displeased with me because I did not tell you that I was employing Rufus Stone, and you are displeased with Rufus Stone because he did not tell you that he was working for me. You believe that you have been let down by both of us—that you cannot trust us.'

Sherlock steadfastly looked away, refusing to meet Mycroft's eyes.

'Sherlock, like it or not, I have a responsibility to look after you. Setting Rufus Stone to watch over you when I could not was a part of that.'

'I thought . . .' Sherlock started, surprising himself, 'I thought he was my *friend.*'

'People can be several things at once,' Mycroft cautioned. 'I am your brother, but I am also an official of the British Government. Amyus Crowe is a bounty hunter, but he is also your tutor. Mr Stone is a violinist, and he is also an occasional agent of mine. That does not, by the way, preclude him from being your friend as well.' He placed a hand on Sherlock's shoulder and squeezed gently. 'If it comes as any consolation, on his return from America Mr Stone told me that he had come to regard you with something approaching brotherly affection. He enjoyed your company. He asked me if I considered this a problem. I told him that I did not. I would rather he was looking out for your welfare because he wanted to, than because I had told him to.'

Something that had been wound up tightly inside Sherlock's chest for several days seemed to loosen slightly. Not completely, but slightly.

'Now,' Mycroft said, 'let us sample the delights of Russian gastronomy. I am led to believe that Russian chefs are almost as good as French ones.'

They walked into the restaurant, which had a high, arched ceiling. Its walls were lined with paintings showing soldiers in brightly coloured uniforms—blue, green and red—riding horses and slashing at each other with sabres.

Mycroft noticed the direction of Sherlock's gaze. 'Ah, the Crimean War,' he said. 'Fought with Britain, France and Turkey on one side and Russia on the other. A curious and rather pointless conflict. And here we are, barely a dozen years later, having dinner in the capital city of our enemies. Diplomacy makes strange bedfellows.' He paused, and a shudder ran through his large body. 'Sherlock, I think this will be the last time I leave England. It may well be the last time that I leave London. Travel may broaden the mind, but so do newspapers and books of reference, and they can be experienced from the comfort of an armchair and in the presence of a bottle of fine brandy. I shall, in future, allow things to come to me, rather than me going to them.'

'You must badly want to know what happened to your agent, for you to be here,' Sherlock said quietly.

The maître d'hôtel looked up from his book of reservations as they approached. 'A table for you, gentlemen?' he asked in perfect French.

'If you please,' Mycroft replied. As the maître d' led them across the restaurant, Mycroft said quietly: 'His name is Wormersley: Robert Wormersley. We were at Oxford together. We shared digs, and we would talk long into the night about our hopes and dreams for the future. When we left Oxford we went our separate ways: while I went into the Foreign Office, he travelled the world adventuring and writing well thought out pieces of travel journalism, but we would still write letters to each other. Eventually our orbits intersected again, and he became my most trusted agent abroad.' He paused. 'We were friends, Sherlock. We were the best of friends. Acquaintances are ten a penny, but one does not get the chance to make friends like that very often in one's life. When they come along, they should be cherished. *That* is why I need to be here. I owe it to him.'

'I understand,' Sherlock said as they sat down. 'Or, at least, I think I do.'

'Of course you do. You went all the way to New York to rescue young Matthew Arnatt. Now,' he said, taking the menu from the maître d', 'what do you wish to eat this evening? I understand the seafood in this city is particularly fine.'

The meal was excellent—good enough to please

even Mycroft—and Sherlock's brother allowed him to have a glass of wine with the meal. They talked of inconsequentialities—the different types of grape that could be used to make wine, the way brandy, sherry and port were made either by distilling or by fortifying wine, and the fact that sparkling wine was first made by Benedictine monks in the sixteenth century.

Sherlock sensed his feelings towards his brother easing as the meal went on. He still felt angry that Mycroft—and Rufus Stone—had gone behind his back, but he realized that part of that anger was directed against himself for not working it out.

He resolved to learn a lesson, though: never take anything on face value ever again.

At the end of the meal, while Mycroft was relaxing with a glass of brandy and a cigar, Sherlock said, 'I'm going to bed. I'll see you tomorrow.'

Mycroft nodded. 'Sleep well. Tomorrow will be a difficult day.' He frowned. 'I have a feeling I am missing something obvious. It is not a comfortable feeling. If I was back in London, safe in the Diogenes Club, I am certain I would work it out in an instant, but here, with all these distractions . . . ?' He sighed. 'Perhaps a good night's sleep in a comfortable bed will help. Goodnight, Sherlock.'

Sherlock's room was small, and on an upper floor, but it didn't matter. It was more comfortable than his room back at Holmes Manor, and he was asleep within moments of undressing. If he dreamed at all then he did not remember what his dreams were.

The next morning was bright and crisp. Snow still lay on the ground, but the sun shone from a clear blue sky. Sherlock washed and dressed and then headed down to the same restaurant where he and Mycroft had eaten dinner.

Mycroft was sitting with Mr Kyte. He nodded at Sherlock as he entered the restaurant, then went back to his conversation.

Sherlock looked around. Mr Malvin and Miss Dimmock were eating together, while Mrs Loran was sitting by herself. She caught Sherlock's eye and smiled at him. He smiled back. He liked her: she seemed to be treating Sherlock more and more like a surrogate son. He wondered about the missing and unmentioned Mr Loran. Had he died, or run off with another woman, or was he waiting at home for her?

The four stagehands—Rhydian, Judah, Pauly and Henry—were sharing a table and bickering. The musicians were scattered across three different tables, segregated by instruments: strings on one, brass on another and woodwind on a third. The conductor, Mr Eves, was sitting alone.

Despite the fact that he was in the string section, Rufus Stone was also sitting by himself. He waved as Sherlock caught sight of him, and indicated the spare chair at his table. For a long moment Sherlock debated whether to find a table by himself, but in the end he walked across and joined Stone.

'Sleep well?' Stone asked.

'Not too badly,' Sherlock replied.

'The hotel is very impressive. Speaking as a man who is more used to hay as his quilt and the night sky as his ceiling, the bed was far too comfortable for my liking. When I woke up I found I was marooned in the centre of a mattress that was so soft it would have given a marshmallow a run for

181

its money. It took me five minutes of exertion to struggle to the edge. I swear that if I'd slept for a half hour longer I would have sunk without trace.'

Sherlock didn't reply.

There was silence for a few moments, then Stone continued quietly: 'You said back in England that you had bought yourself a violin.'

'Yes, I did.' Sherlock felt as if he should add something, but he couldn't think what to say.

'I presume that your purchase of such an instrument indicates that you still wish to wrestle the muse of music to the ground?'

Sherlock shrugged.

'Sherlock,' Stone said, 'I understand your feelings. I wish things were otherwise. Life being the way it is, bad things happen more often than good. The trick is to see the sunshine behind the dark clouds.' He paused. 'Sherlock, if you believe only one thing that I say, believe this: I enjoy your company, and if your brother were to tell me tomorrow that my services are no longer required then I would still wish to continue to teach you.'

Sherlock felt an unaccustomed tightness in his throat. He looked away, then back at Stone. 'I'd like that,' he said hesitantly.

'Of course,' Stone said, 'that will have to wait until this particular mission is over. If I am not careful, playing down to the level of these fiddlers and blowers will seriously compromise my skills.' He looked around, then lowered his voice. 'I have a bad feeling about all this,' he said. 'I can't quite work out why, but something is wrong here. Something is very wrong.' He glanced at Sherlock. 'Be careful this morning. Be very careful.'

182

CHAPTER TWELVE

After breakfast, Sherlock watched from the hotel lobby as the rest of the theatre party, minus Mycroft, left in horse-drawn cabs for the Maly Theatre. Once they had vanished around a corner, Mycroft said: 'Come on then. Let us go.'

He hailed a cab—a proper cab, not one of the thin boards on which people sat astride—and gave a junction of two streets as the address. Leaning over to Sherlock, he said, 'We can walk the last hundred yards or so. Uncomfortable, but necessary. I always make it a rule not to reveal my ultimate destination to people I do not know, if I can help it. Half the cab drivers in this city are in the pay of the Third Section.'

When they arrived, Mycroft handed the driver a coin and waited until he had driven away before he indicated to Sherlock that they were going to cross the road and walk back a little way.

The building that Mycroft stopped outside was three storeys high, and made of a reddish-brown stone. A main entrance was situated in the centre of the ground floor, three steps up from the pavement.

Mycroft and Sherlock entered through the doors. Stairs led up from the lobby. As if he'd been there a thousand times before, Mycroft walked straight across to the stairs and put his hand on the banister. He turned to Sherlock. 'They say that in the Winter Palace, here in Moscow, the Tsar has a small room that ascends from one floor to another, moved by some kind of steam-driven screw mechanism. The time when all buildings have such rooms cannot come too quickly for me.' Puffing, he started to climb the stairs. Sherlock followed, smiling.

The first-floor landing gave on to a long, dark corridor that ran the length of the building. Sherlock could smell vague odours of food: boiled ham, boiled cabbage, bread. Mycroft walked confidently down the corridor until he came to a particular door. Glancing in both directions, checking that nobody was watching, he pushed against it.

The door moved.

'The wood around the lock is splintered,' Mycroft said. 'This is decidedly *not* good.'

He opened the door and entered the hallway, pulling Sherlock after him. With a movement that was surprisingly quick for such a large man, he moved sideways, to the wall, and pushed Sherlock in the other direction. Sherlock realized that Mycroft was trying to minimize the time they were silhouetted in the doorway, just in case there was somebody in the apartment with a gun. Good thinking.

They waited for a few moments, listening. There was no sound from inside. Eventually Mycroft moved forward, down the hall to a half-open door.

The room inside was a mess. It was, or had been, a living area, but the chairs were smashed and the tables knocked over. Paintings on the walls were disarranged. Shards of pottery and glass lay on the floor: the detritus of smashed decorative figurines, teacups and wine glasses. There was nobody there, living or dead.

Mycroft's eyes scanned the room quickly. He

184

turned and walked back into the hall to check the other rooms. Looking over his shoulder, Sherlock could see that one was a bedroom, the other a bathroom. They were empty of people as well, but they had been comprehensively wrecked in the same way as the main room.

'Someone was searching for something,' Mycroft murmured, standing in the entrance hall and looking around.

'They didn't find it,' Sherlock said.

'You are correct, but how did you come to that conclusion?'

'Because if they had, there would have been areas where nothing was smashed or overturned—the areas that they would have got around to if they hadn't found what they were looking for.'

'Unless . . . ?' Mycroft prompted.

Sherlock thought for a moment. 'Unless whatever it was they were looking for was actually in the last place they looked.'

'Or, more likely . . . ?'

'Or they weren't sure how many things they were looking for, so they had to search everywhere.'

Sherlock's brother nodded. 'Correct. What else can you deduce from the state of this place?'

'Whoever searched it didn't care if anybody knew they had searched, otherwise they would have made an effort to be tidier.'

'You are again correct.' Mycroft's face was bleak. 'I fear for Robert Wormersley's life. Either he was here at the time, in which case he has been taken away by whoever smashed the door down and ransacked the apartment, or he was absent, in which case he would have turned tail and run as soon as he saw the damaged door. Either way, his

185

fate is still uncertain.'

'He wasn't here at the time,' Sherlock said with certainty.

'And you deduce that how?'

Sherlock indicated the front door. 'The door was locked, but not bolted. You can see the bolts still intact on the back of the door. If your friend was in the apartment and had locked the door then he would certainly have bolted it as well. The fact that it was locked but *not* bolted indicates that he had left, and locked the door behind him.'

'Good work,' Mycroft said approvingly.

Sherlock moved back into the main room and looked it over again. There was something about it that bothered him, but he wasn't quite sure what it was. Something out of place. Or something in place where everything else was out of place. It nagged at him like something caught between his teeth.

'I'm not seeing something,' he said. 'Or I'm seeing something but not understanding it.'

'It will come to you,' Mycroft said, 'if you let it. Let your mind mull the problem over while you think about something else.' He looked around. 'I fear there is nothing else to see here. We should leave.'

Outside, in the street, Mycroft hailed a passing carriage. Sherlock tugged his sleeve. 'I think I can remember the way back to the hotel. I was taking note of the streets as we came here. Is it all right if I walk back? I want to see some of the city.'

'Very well,' Mycroft said. He passed Sherlock a handful of money. 'The principal currency in Russia is the rouble. The rouble is divided into exactly one hundred kopeks.' He clapped Sherlock on the shoulder. 'Now, you go and take a look around. I believe I will return to the hotel and think about our next move.'

As Mycroft's carriage vanished round a corner, Sherlock began to walk. Moscow looked, sounded and, more importantly, smelt different from the places he was used to. The snow, for instance, muffled a lot of the noise, so that the clamour he'd been used to in London was largely absent. Moscow seemed like a quiet city. Although, he considered, it might also have been quiet through fear of the Tsar's secret police and what they might do to people who said the wrong things.

The route was fixed firmly in his mind, and as Sherlock walked he found himself admiring the solid, impressive architecture of the city. As he got closer to their hotel he found himself turning into an open square so large that it almost seemed to bend with the curvature of the Earth. Ahead of him a cathedral rose up like some fantastic creation made out of strawberry ice cream and spun sugar. He had never seen anything like it in his life. It seemed to be a series of towers of different heights and apparently different diameters, each one randomly topped with a pointed spire or an onion-shaped dome which was painted or tiled in different colours: red, green, blue, yellow and white, all intermixed in various combinations of chequerboard patterns or swirls. Each spire or dome was topped with a large crucifix. As Sherlock walked slowly around the cathedral, staring all the time, he noticed that it kept changing its appearance. There was no obvious symmetry about it. Whichever angle he examined it from, it was a different shape. Like many things he'd seen in Russia since they had arrived, it looked like a collision between a complete accident and a deliberate creation.

On his right, just across a moat of partly frozen water, he could see the tall, red-brick walls of what he thought was the Kremlin—the palace and grounds where Tsar Alexander II lived, and from where he ruled over his immense domain. In between the cathedral and the Kremlin walls, and extending off to Sherlock's right, was Red Square.

Several straight, wide thoroughfares led away from Red Square. Sherlock chose the one that he thought would lead to the Slavyansky Bazaar Hotel and began to walk down it. A sign attached to a nearby wall told him that this was Neglinnaya Street. As well as being lined with shops on both sides it had a long row of stalls running down the middle. The shops seemed to be mainly selling fur coats, hats, boots or pastries of various sorts. Each shop had a brightly painted sign outside showing in pictorial form exactly what was on sale. The stalls were more plebeian, dealing as they did in all sorts of knick-knacks from knives to tobacco, from bags to old clothes, buttons and fragments of cloth. A few stalls were selling religious items: crosses, paintings on wooden plaques of saints and the like. Russia, it appeared to Sherlock, was a much more openly religious society than England.

Tea sellers wandered along the street between the shops and the stalls, pushing handcarts on which heated urns of tea were precariously balanced. They also sold snacks: strings hung around their necks from which rings of bread dangled like huge beads.

At each junction Sherlock noticed wooden booths occupied by men in grey uniforms and black helmets. They had swords strapped to their sides. The ones that weren't actually asleep at their post just looked bored and cold.

Checking his watch, Sherlock decided that it was time he headed back. As he drew level with a side street, he stopped. Someone walking close behind him collided with him. He turned, already apologizing, but the man pushed past him with a muffled curse. At the same time he noticed an animated conversation happening at one of the wooden booths. A man in a heavy coat and a hat with fur earflaps was talking to the policeman in the booth, gesturing wildly with both hands. Sherlock was about to turn away when the man in the furs turned and pointed towards him. The policeman stared darkly at Sherlock.

A shiver ran through Sherlock's body.

The man in furs appeared to be saying that something had been taken from him. He was gesturing to a pocket on his coat, sliding his hand in and out as if miming the fact that he had been pickpocketed. He pointed at Sherlock again. Sherlock glanced over his shoulder to see if anyone else was around, anyone that the man could have been pointing at, but there was nobody within ten yards.

Sherlock spread his arms wide in a gesture of innocence, gazing at the policeman and hoping the man would just wave him away, but instead the policeman gestured imperiously to him to approach the booth.

Sherlock switched his gaze to the man who had made the complaint. Just for a second, he smiled. It was the smile of a man who had pulled off a particularly cunning trick and was waiting to see the inevitable outcome. When he noticed that Sherlock was watching him the smile vanished from his face like a picture wiped from a blackboard.

Struck by a sudden and very unwelcome thought, Sherlock plunged his hand into his jacket pocket. His fingers closed on an object that hadn't been there before: something square, something made of leather.

A wallet.

Suddenly it was all crystal clear to him. The whole thing was a set-up! The man who had barged into Sherlock's back and walked off must have slipped the wallet into his pocket. The other man—the one talking to the policeman—hadn't been robbed at all, but the moment he had seen the wallet slipped into Sherlock's pocket he had gone across to the policeman and made his complaint, singling Sherlock out as the thief. And when Sherlock's pockets were checked a wallet would be found in them, and the man who had made the complaint would undoubtedly recognize it as his, whether it was or not. He would be thrown into prison, and the evidence was completely against him.

This was a nightmare!

The policeman gestured again, more sternly this time. Sherlock's heart started to race. He could feel sweat gathering damply at his armpits and down the centre of his back, sticking his shirt to his skin. Arrested in a foreign country for theft? He would be lucky if he ever saw daylight again, and that was even assuming that he got a fair trial. Given the clever way the whole thing had been set up, the chances were that every possible way out had been anticipated. They—whoever *they* were—might have paid off the judge, the jury, everyone. And that was assuming they even had judges and juries in Russia. He had no idea how the justice system worked. He had a feeling, based on things he had read in the newspapers back home, that Tsarist Russia worked on the basis of secret police and people vanishing off the streets and never being seen again.

He could run, but they must have anticipated that as well. He glanced around, trying to work out who in the surrounding throng of shoppers was part of this conspiracy.

To his left, a man in a black coat and fur hat turned his head away when Sherlock's gaze passed across him. To his right, a teenage boy with a smallpox-scarred face glared sullenly at him, and a woman with her hands inside a fur muffler suddenly took an interest in the tobacconist's stall she was standing by.

Three people at least. Three people who would stop him if he tried to run.

He desperately scanned his immediate vicinity again, hoping against hope that he would see a means of escape, but there wasn't one. He wasn't close enough to any of the stalls to snatch something up and use it as a weapon, and he was pretty sure that nobody near him would come to his aid if he yelled for help.

The policeman was striding across to where Sherlock stood. His sword was by his side but he was swinging a long stick in his right hand. The scowl on his face suggested that whatever Sherlock did he was intending to use the stick within the next few minutes.

A sudden gust of wind bought a smell of spiced tea to Sherlock's nostrils. He turned his head. The

191

tea seller was moving through the crowd a few steps away.

Without thinking, Sherlock took two steps and shoved the man in the small of the back.

The tea seller sprawled forward, pushing his cart away as he fell. The cart rolled on for a few feet and then hit a loose cobblestone. One wheel jolted upward and the cart tipped over. The silvery urn toppled over. The top flew off as it hit the cobbled street and a flood of brown tea spilt everywhere, immediately turning the snow to brown slush. People jumped out of the way of the steaming liquid. Some of them got splashed, and they cried out as it scalded their legs.

While the three watchers and the policeman were distracted, Sherlock slipped away through the crowd. As he moved he tried to make himself smaller, and to make sure that there was always a group of people between him and the people who wanted him, but there were five of them at least and he couldn't block all of the possible sight lines as he moved.

A shout went up behind him. It was the policeman! He had seen Sherlock, and he pushed his way roughly through the crowd in pursuit. People stumbled and fell as he lashed out at them with his wooden stick.

Sherlock broke into a run, heading back the way he had come. If he could just lose them for a couple of minutes he could get back to the hotel and warn Mycroft.

A shrill whistle ripped through the air. Sherlock glanced back over his shoulder. The policeman was still in pursuit.

The cobbles shifted unevenly beneath Sherlock's

feet, and he nearly fell over. Catching himself, he looked ahead. There was a wooden booth on the corner ahead of him, and the policeman inside had already emerged and was looking in his direction. He must have heard the whistle.

Ahead was blocked, and so was behind. Sherlock swerved to the right, looking for a doorway or an alleyway through which he might escape. All he saw were shops and brightly painted signs. The colours began to blur as he ran. He could feel his heart pounding in his chest.

Suddenly an opportunity presented itself: a set of steps leading down to a basement area. Desperately praying that it wasn't a dead end, that whatever door was down there wasn't locked, Sherlock ran for the steps. He grabbed the railing at the top, swung round and flung himself down into the bricked basement area.

There was a door down there, but it was boarded shut, big planks nailed across it. No way out.

He turned to head back up the stairs, but a sudden whistle deafened him. The policeman was only a few feet away. Maybe he hadn't seen where Sherlock had gone, but if Sherlock poked his head up above the level of the pavement then he would be noticed.

A second whistle, further away, and a third. Was the whole of Moscow chasing him?

Approaching footsteps. Just a few seconds and he would be seen.

He looked desperately back towards the blocked door, hoping that there might be a gap between the boards large enough for him to crawl through. Then he noticed an iron manhole cover set into the ground. He threw himself to his knees and tried to pull it up. The manhole cover was heavy and slick with ice, and his fingers were slippery with sweat. He managed to raise it by an inch or so, but it fell back with a loud, dull *clang*. Desperately he scrabbled at it again. This time, when he managed to prise it up, he slipped his fingers beneath it. If it fell again it might break them.

With his last reserves of strength he pulled the cover up and slid it to one side. A smell of dank earth and sewage rose up, making him choke. The meagre light from the clouded sky illuminated the first few rungs of an iron ladder.

He had no choice. Swinging his legs over the edge, he started to descend. When his face was level with the ground he grabbed the edge of the cover and pulled it back across. There was a handhold underneath, and he managed to pull it all the way across so that it settled into its previous position.

From above, he hoped, it would look as if the manhole cover had never been removed.

His intention had been to stay there in the darkness for as long as necessary, clinging to the iron ladder, but it was not to be. The rungs were mossy and wet, and his fingers had no strength left in them. Just as he heard a set of boots hit the manhole cover and stop, his fingers suddenly spasmed and let go of the rung. He fell into darkness, trying not to cry out.

CHAPTER THIRTEEN

Sherlock braced himself for a bone-shattering landing on brick or stone, but he fell into water. Ice-cold, running water.

It was barely three feet deep. His back touched the bottom and he thrashed his way to the surface, choking and spluttering. He braced himself against the flow, one foot in front of the other.

Darkness surrounded him. He stood up. The cold sapped the warmth and the strength from him. He tried to touch the sides of whatever sewer or drain he had fallen into, but there was nothing. The sound of the water was odd as well: it didn't echo the way it should have done in a brick-lined tunnel.

As his eyes got used to the darkness he realized that there *was* light down there after all. The manhole cover above him was perforated with tiny holes, through which narrow shafts of sunlight shone downward. Further ahead, and behind, there were similar patches of illumination. Wherever it was that he had found himself, at least he would be able to navigate.

He could see that he was in a fast-flowing stream of water. On either side, about ten feet away, instead of the curved brick walls he would have expected of a sewer or a drain there was a bank of stones and muddy earth that sloped away from him, home to the occasional anaemic weed and tufts of ghostly white grass. At the top of the slopes, a few feet of brickwork supported a brick ceiling that stretched away in front and behind.

Moss dangled in long fronds from the brick

ceiling. They looked to Sherlock like the tentacles of some bizarre creature that was blindly feeling for its prey.

A sudden grating noise made him flinch. Directly above him, the manhole cover was being opened. A pillar of bright light shone down on to the muddy water in which he stood. Quickly he splashed a few paces in the direction that the water was flowing so that he couldn't be spotted.

'Where is he?' a whispery voice asked from above. It was speaking in French, but Sherlock detected a strong accent. The man was probably Russian by birth. 'Did he go down there?'

'I can't see him,' another, gruffer voice, replied in the same language but without the accent. 'What is this thing—some kind of sewer?'

'Don't you know anything?' the first voice whispered. 'This is the old River Neglinnaya. It flows into the Moscow River 'bout a mile downstream. It was covered over fifty years ago or more when they rebuilt the city.'

Sherlock looked around. A river rather than a sewer? It made sense. Somewhere upstream it must have been out in the open, but here, for fifty years, it had been locked in darkness.

The Moscow River was just a mile or so downstream. He could make it!

'He must've gone down here,' the gruff voice said. 'There's nowhere else he could have gone. But did he go upstream or downstream?'

'Downstream,' the other man whispered. 'He'll follow the flow of the water. No point fighting it, after all.' He paused, thinking. 'You go down there and follow him. Kill him if you can; let the body rot in the water.'

'Why didn't we just grab him in the street?' the gruff voice asked. 'Why go through all that palaver with pretending that he was a thief?'

'Grabbing him in the street would have attracted attention,' the whispery voice replied. 'Someone might have interfered. There're police all over the city. Instructions were to get him out of the way. Having him arrested was the best option, but now he's out of sight we can make sure he's out of the way—forever. Now go down there after him.'

'Are you joking? That water must be near freezing!'

'You got a better idea?'

'Yeah—*you* go!'

The man with the whispery voice snorted. 'You want to talk to the policeman, you go ahead. He's not going to listen to you the way he would listen to me—a native-born Russian! And besides, we've already established that it was my wallet the kid took. How's it going to look if I suddenly vanish and you take over?'

'All right.' The man with the gruff voice sounded cowed. 'What are *you* goin' to do?'

'I'll get this idiot policeman to organize a search above ground, along the line of the Neglinnaya. We'll meet you at the Moscow River outlet.'

Sherlock's mind raced. He had to get moving, and he had to start out now, before the thug with the gruff voice started down the ladder!

He moved away, trying not to make any splashes as he moved. The cold water sloshed around his legs, infiltrating his shoes and making his socks squish as he walked. He could smell a rancid odour: it may not have been a sewer that he was wading through, but he had a feeling some people

197

were using it as one.

Behind him he heard noises as the gruff-voiced man slowly lowered himself down the ladder. He must have slipped as well, because there was a sudden shout, echoing off the brick ceiling, and moments later a splash. A wave of water washed past Sherlock, pushing him onward. Inwardly he cheered. Maybe he'd got lucky; maybe the man had drowned! Then he heard a voice spluttering in the darkness, and his momentary good spirits subsided. He was going to have to do this the hard way.

Sensing, rather than seeing, the river bank to either side, Sherlock wondered whether he could climb up it and get out of the water, but he quickly rejected the idea. From what he had seen the banks were steep and muddy. Chances were he would just slide down and into the water, and he'd lose a few minutes of precious time. No: attractive as the option sounded, he had to keep moving through the water. The cold, smelly water.

He realized that he was nearing another manhole cover in the brick ceiling. The weak sunshine trickling through the metal disc would illuminate his shoulders and the top of his head if he wasn't careful, giving away his position. He moved to one side, closer to the right-hand bank.

In the weak light that filtered down like solid rain Sherlock could see the rungs of a ladder that descended from the manhole. It was supported at the top, and was probably set into the bed of the river. The rungs and the uprights looked corroded: rusty and damp. For a second Sherlock debated whether to climb the ladder and try to shift the manhole cover from beneath, but he quickly pushed the idea away. Too much could go wrong. His pursuer would see him the moment he stepped into the shaft of light and would just pull him off the ladder. Even if by some fluke he got to the top he might not be able to shift the heavy cover, or if he did he might just emerge into the midst of the search party in the street above. No—like it or not, he had to keep going.

Sherlock's fingers trailed in the water as he pushed his way through the resisting river. Something brushed against his hand and he jerked it away with a muffled cry. In his mind he imagined it was a rat, swimming through the polluted waters, but maybe it was just a piece of rubbish that had been thrown away through a grating, or a hole in the street. Maybe. But his heart was still hammering like a steam engine and his hands were shaking.

The river bed beneath his feet was uneven and muddy. His feet kept on getting stuck and he had to strain to pull them free. God alone knew what state his shoes were going to be in by the time he got out—*if* he ever got out. There were plants down there in the water as well, weeds that kept tangling around his ankles and slowing him down even more. He had to jerk his feet forward so that he could break the weeds free of their roots. He imagined his shoes encrusted with mud and trailing handfuls of weeds behind them as they moved.

The sounds behind him were more regular now: an even *slosh . . . slosh . . . slosh* as his pursuer moved forward. His breath rasped and wheezed, rasped and wheezed, over and over like a dying machine.

199

Sherlock strained his eyes against the darkness, hoping he might be able to make out the shape of the outlet ahead of him. He was expecting it to be an arch, or a circular opening, that gave out on to the Moscow River, which he imagined to be a wide stretch of water, probably with bridges over it. He couldn't see anything, however. The darkness ahead of him was intense and unbroken.

What if the opening was below water level, and above the surface there was nothing but a blank brick wall to mark the point where one river poured into another? What if there was a grille separating the two? What if he couldn't get through, and had to turn round and try to get past the man who was following him, the man who had orders to kill him? The thoughts rolled round and round his head like marbles, never getting anywhere but colliding and sending shock waves through his brain.

He had to get a grip. He had to concentrate if he was going to survive this.

Something touched his face. He flinched, nearly crying out in terror, but managed to stifle the sound by jamming the back of his hand across his mouth and biting down hard. Whatever it was had felt slimy and cold. He waved his hand around in front of his face. Something wet wrapped itself round his wrist, and he realized with relief that it was just one of the mossy tendrils that he'd seen previously, hanging down from the ceiling. He pulled his hand away and the tendril tore out of the brickwork with a sucking noise.

As he moved off, Sherlock realized that he had lost all sensation in his toes.

All the time, behind him, *slosh* . . . *slosh* . . . *slosh* . . . and the wheezing sound of his pursuer breathing heavily. When he glanced over his shoulder, all he could see was darkness. At any second he might feel a hand close over his shoulder, pulling him backwards, pushing him beneath the surface of the Neglinnaya River where he would drown in absolute blackness and his body would never be found.

A thought suddenly occurred to him, and he hesitated.

Maybe he could climb the bank here and wait for his pursuer to go by. As he passed beneath the next manhole cover, he edged across to the side of the river again, where the bank rose up, so that he wouldn't be seen. He reached up and grabbed a clump of pale grass that he could use to pull himself up.

Out of the shadows, something stepped forward and growled.

It walked on four short legs and its head was triangular, with a pointed muzzle and a skull that flared backwards to two large ears. Its eyes were small and dark, hardly eyes at all, but its lips were pulled back as far as they would go and its mouth seemed overly full of teeth like shards of broken glass. The brown and black hair that covered its body was matted and patchy.

Behind it, three other similar creatures moved forward. Sherlock realized they were dogs, but they were nothing like any dogs he'd ever come across before. They must live down here, he realized, in the dark, generation upon generation, descended from some strays that had found their way into the buried river and living on rats and maybe fish. With nothing to see, their eyes had closed up and ceased to function, but their ears had grown large to replace them. Sherlock suspected that, to them, sound was everything.

For a moment his mind snapped back to the tunnels beneath Waterloo Station and the feral children there. He felt a rush of pity for them, something that he had been too busy to feel when he was trying to escape them. They had been forced to live like wild animals, but at least the dogs here in Moscow had the claws and the teeth to survive. The children had nothing, apart from their intelligence, and Sherlock had a feeling they were fast losing that.

The lead dog wrinkled its nose. It looked like it might be trying to sniff the air, but the smell of decay that rose up like a gas from the river would have made that almost impossible. Its ears twitched as it vainly tried to work out where Sherlock had gone. He was right in front of it, hand extended, but if he didn't move then it couldn't hear him.

That, at least, was the theory.

Sherlock's hand was so cold that he had to clench his fist to keep from shivering, but the numbness was too much to bear and his fingers suddenly twitched. The sound of skin moving against skin, just a whisper to Sherlock, must have been like an explosion to the dogs. The lead one jumped forward. Sherlock pulled his hand away, and the dog's teeth snapped shut on nothing. Its head jerked back and it began to bark. The other three dogs joined it. The sound echoed and re-echoed through the tunnel.

Sherlock backed off, but the noise he made splashing through the water made his position easy to fix for the dogs.

The lead dog took a few steps and leaped towards Sherlock, jaws agape.

An arm looped round Sherlock's neck and clenched hard, twisting him around in the water. His pursuer just had time to gloat 'Gotcha!' before the lead dog hit him like a cannonball, fastening its jaws on his arm. It wasn't the target the dog had wanted, but it wasn't fussy. It bit down, hard.

Sherlock's pursuer screamed: a high-pitched sound for a man with such a gruff voice. His grip on Sherlock's throat loosened and Sherlock tore himself free.

In the light that drizzled down from the manhole cover, Sherlock could see his pursuer thrashing back and forth in the water, trying to dislodge the dog. Two of the three others on the bank also leaped. One of them hit the water and dived for the man's leg, while the other landed on his chest and fastened its jaws around his throat. He fell backwards into the scummy river, arms thrashing wildly.

Sherlock backed away quietly through the water as the remaining wild dog dived in and vanished. For a second he thought about climbing out on to the bank, but there might be more dogs there in hiding. Reluctantly, he pressed on through the water.

Behind him he could hear splashing and grunting, and then just splashing, and then nothing.

Far ahead he could make out a glimmer of light, like an oil lamp hanging in a doorway on a dark night. He pressed forward, water churning in front of him as he hurried along. The light grew brighter, hurting his eyes. It took the form of an arch —an arch through which he could see the grey-blue waters of a greater river crossing the one through which he was wading.

His eyes had grown accustomed to the daylight by the time he reached the arch. It wasn't barred and there was no grille across the entrance. The Neglinnaya River just poured into the Moscow River from an opening in the banks that ended about a foot above the surface, causing the Neglinnaya to form a small waterfall.

Sherlock edged forward. Holding on to the brickwork with one hand, he leaned out and looked sideways, along the banks of the Moscow River.

It ran between stone walls. If there was any soil, any sand, any ground at all there then it was hidden beneath the surface of the water. Looking up, Sherlock could see that the top of the opening through which the Neglinnaya poured was perhaps six feet below the level of the streets. An iron ladder, flakes of red rust breaking through black paint, led up from just beside the opening. The trouble was, Sherlock knew, that if he went up that ladder he might just end up in the arms of the policeman and the man who had accused him of stealing his wallet.

He looked along the line of the river again, and noticed something that he had missed before: a line where the stones were set back by a foot or so. It seemed to happen every six feet in height: probably an attempt by the architect to ensure that the space above the river got wider the higher it went, maybe to avoid flooding. Whatever the reason, it meant that Sherlock had a way out. All he had to do was edge his way along that line of stones like a man walking a tightrope.

It took him half an hour of careful manoeuvring,

during which he almost fell three times into the waters of the Moscow River as it flowed beneath him. He started off wet and cold and ended up dry and frozen, although he wasn't sure whether that was because the wind channelled by the stone-clad riverbanks had dried him or because the water soaking his clothes had frozen into ice. When he finally found another rusted iron ladder to take him up to the surface he was fortunate enough to see a brazier just a few yards away, full of burning coals. A local Russian man was roasting chestnuts over the coals. For a few kopeks he let Sherlock warm himself beside the brazier.

After half an hour, and two bags of roasted chestnuts, Sherlock felt human enough to head back to the hotel. He was fairly sure that he was safe doing so: nobody had come in that direction along the riverbank looking for him, and as far as he could tell the thugs had discovered him by accident, the way the ones in London had. He waved a grateful thanks to the chestnut vendor and walked off. His legs were sore, he had a headache and his clothes were stiff in a way they hadn't been earlier, but at least he was relatively warm and dry.

The walk back only took twenty minutes, and by the time he got to within sight of the main doors of the Slavyansky Bazaar Hotel he was sweating with the exertion. The cold Moscow wind pulled the heat from the dampness on his forehead and froze it within moments.

Some kind of altercation was going on at the front of the hotel. A black horse-drawn carriage with no obvious markings or crests had drawn up outside. Instead of being at the sides, the

205

doors were at the back. The driver was wearing nondescript grey clothes and a fur hat, as were the two men who were emerging from the hotel and walking towards the carriage, but the difference between them was that the two men emerging from the hotel were pulling a third man with them. This man was dressed in a well-cut black suit and waistcoat.

It was Mycroft.

He was protesting loudly, and struggling, but Sherlock couldn't hear what he was saying.

The driver climbed down from his perch and helped the two men push Mycroft into the back of the carriage. The two men climbed in with him and shut the door. It looked as if the driver threw a bolt, locking the door from the outside.

He climbed back and flicked his whip over the horses' heads. They trotted off, pulling the carriage away from Sherlock.

Sherlock felt his spirits plummet. All he'd been through in the past couple of hours, in the past weeks—it had all led to this: standing alone on the street of a foreign city with his brother being taken away by the secret police. Sherlock tried to find some thread of a plan, some small seed that could be grown into a way of getting Mycroft back, but there was nothing. He literally had no idea what to do next.

CHAPTER FOURTEEN

'If you value your life and your freedom, don't look!'

Sherlock glanced round. A man was standing beside him, threadbare coat drawn tightly up to his neck and fur hat pulled down low over his eyes. Sherlock couldn't even see his mouth.

'Why not?'

'Because the Third Section are invisible. They come and they take people, and nobody sees. Nobody sees because nobody is looking.'

'What are they going to do with him?'

'If he is lucky,' the man said, 'then perhaps a quick execution. If he is unlucky, then it is the *knout* or the *pleti*.'

'What are they?' Sherlock asked, horrified.

The man shuddered. 'They are like whips, only worse. Much worse.'

Sherlock suddenly realized that the man was speaking in French, not Russian. 'Who are you?'

'My name is Robert Wormersley.'

'You're Mycroft's—' he was going to say 'agent', but switched the word at the last moment, '–*friend*.'

'Indeed.' Wormersley's face was bright and alert beneath the fur hat as he scanned Sherlock's face. 'And you're his brother. His only brother. You have the same eyes. He used to talk about you.'

Sherlock's gaze was drawn back to where the carriage was pulling around a corner. 'He's gone. What do we do?'

'I'll tell you what we *don't* do—we don't go back into that hotel. We don't go back into that hotel

207

because they'll have left someone behind to wait for you.' Wormersley looked around. 'There is a decent cafe not too far away. Let's get some hot liquid inside you—you look like you could use it, and I certainly need somewhere to sit down and rest for a while. We can work out a battle plan there.'

'All right.' Sherlock was so tired that he just wanted all this to go away. He wanted someone else to take charge. 'Let's go.'

The cafe was ten minutes' walk away. It was located in the basement of an office building, down an outside flight of iron stairs. At the bottom was a tiny patio area and a glass frontage behind which was the cafe.

Wormersley led the way in and directed Sherlock towards a rough table. He went across to the tiny counter and bought two cups of tea, poured from a large urn.

Sherlock looked around at the other patrons. There were men, women and children sitting in pairs or alone, all wearing too many clothes. Most of the men were reading, either newspapers or books. Nobody was looking in their direction.

Sherlock focused on one man in particular, wrapped up in a heavy overcoat and eating some kind of pancake. His face was lumpy, like a potato, and flushed. Sherlock had never seen him before, but there was something about him that was familiar.

'*Pirozkhi*,' Wormersley said, putting the plate on the table between them. 'Russian pastries: some meat, some vegetable, all spiced.' He removed his coat and hat and put them on a spare chair. He was a thin man, in his twenties, Sherlock estimated, with sparse blond hair, large sideburns, a thin curve of moustache that looked like it had been drawn on with a fine-nibbed pen and a neat little goatee beard.

Sherlock took a grateful sip of the black tea. He glanced again at the man at the next table, trying to work out why he looked familiar, but the man was a complete stranger. Sherlock realized that his hand was shaking. He was under a lot of stress. 'Mycroft thought you might have been arrested,' he said.

'And he came all the way to Russia to check? *Mycroft* came all the way to Russia to check?' Wormersley smiled. 'I should be honoured.'

'So what happened?' Sherlock put his cup down and took a bite from one of the pastries. The savoury filling was hot—minced beef and mushrooms. Steam burned his lips.

'I came back one day to find the Third Section turning my place over. I knew they were the Third Section because of the cheap suits. I turned and walked away before they realized I was there. I've been moving around ever since, going from one bad hotel to the next, never staying too long in one place. I tried to get word out to Mycroft, but all the telegraph offices are under the control of the Tsar's officials.' He shook his head. 'Who'd have thought it—old Mycroft, levering himself out of his comfy armchair in London and coming all the way here, just to see if I was all right.'

'It's more than just you,' Sherlock said. Quickly he told Wormersley what had happened in London and in Moscow.

Wormersley leaned back in his chair and sipped his tea. 'Interesting,' he said. 'Interesting and bizarre.'

'It's like having a partial set of broken china fragments,' Sherlock said. 'I have no idea what kind of object they would make if you put them together.' Catching the words as he was saying them, he wondered why the simile of a broken china object had come suddenly to mind.

'It all depends on why Mycroft was arrested,' Wormersley mused. 'Is he here under his own name or an assumed name?'

'He's here as Mr Sigerson,' Sherlock replied. 'He's part of a theatrical company who are putting on a performance at the invitation of a Russian Prince. Yusupov, I think his name was.'

Wormersley nodded. 'Good cover. Did he go to my apartment?'

'We both did.'

'That's probably why he was arrested. They were watching the apartment, and arrested Mycroft on the basis that he might know where I was hiding.'

'That doesn't make any sense.' The tea and the pastries were helping Sherlock's brain to break out of its paralysis. 'If that was true, they would have arrested him—arrested both of us—at the apartment instead of waiting until we got back to the hotel. And it doesn't explain why they tried to frame me for pickpocketing.' He paused for a moment, trying to collect his thoughts and then examine them in the way that Amyus Crowe had taught him. Regard them as traces left in soil and vegetation by some animal—which way did the animal go and how big was it?

And how many animals were there?

He drew a sudden breath in realization. 'It's almost as if there are two separate organizations at work—one secretive, that works by framing people

210

for stuff they didn't do, and one that arrests people in the open and throws them into carriages. One unofficial and one official.'

Wormersley nodded cautiously. 'I'm with you so far. Go on.'

'The official organization—the Third Section, I suppose—had no reason that I know of to arrest Mr Sigerson, the innocent manager of a theatrical company. On the other hand, if they knew that Mr Sigerson was actually Mycroft Holmes, a British Government official, in Moscow on an undercover mission, then they would have every reason to detain him.'

'Indeed they would, but who would tell them?' Wormersley nodded. 'This shadowy, secretive second organization of yours, presumably. But why would *they* want Mycroft arrested?'

'To get him out of the way?' Sherlock thought for a moment. 'No, that doesn't make any sense. There are easier ways to get someone out of the way. No, they must have *wanted* him to be arrested.' He paused for a moment, grasping at thoughts. 'They must have *wanted* him to be arrested by the Third Section—which is under the control of a man Mycroft said he knew: Count Pyotr Andreyevich Shuvalov. They met in France a few years ago.'

Wormersley gestured to Sherlock to keep his voice down. 'Best not to mention that name in public,' he cautioned. 'The Third Section has ears everywhere. Even mentioning their name is enough to attract their attention.'

Sherlock was too excited to stop. It was as if he was looking at a set of jigsaw pieces and mentally moving them around until he could work out what the picture was. Or, his brain said again, like a collection of china fragments which he was reassembling in his mind into a porcelain figure. It was clear to him now that this second organization—the secretive one—actually *wanted* Mycroft to be arrested because they knew that Count Shuvalov would question him in person. His brother was an important diplomat, and Shuvalov knew him. It was unlikely, Sherlock thought, that Shuvalov would trust the interrogation of an important diplomat to an underling, and he probably wouldn't want anybody else to be there in case any diplomatic secrets were revealed. It would be a polite chat between two men who were acquainted at some stage in the past—held in Shuvalov's office, because that was where he would feel most comfortable, most at home. And because Mycroft was an important man, and deserved some measure of respect.

The truth came crashing in on Sherlock suddenly, so obvious, so monumental that he was momentarily breathless with surprise that he hadn't already seen it. This had all been arranged from the start! Everything that had happened in London was designed to get Mycroft to Moscow! Framing him for murder in the Diogenes Club wasn't an attempt to stop him from seeing those reports in his office—it was a way of making *sure* that he would see them. If he thought those reports were important enough that someone would frame him for murder to stop him reading them, then he would definitely pay them serious attention once he got back to his office! They were the lure at the end of a fishing line that reached all the way to Moscow!

Wormersley was staring at Sherlock intently, but Sherlock's thoughts were whirling too quickly for him to speak. The china pieces were coming together in his mind now. The details were getting clearer by the moment.

The theatrical company itself was a sham, Sherlock realized in shock. It had to be. It was another report on Mycroft's desk—he'd assumed it was a coincidence, but it hadn't been. This secret organization, whoever they were, wanted him in Moscow so that he could be arrested, and so they gave him a *reason* to go to Moscow and a way of *getting* to Moscow, all packaged up and ready to go!

Sherlock's head was filled with the faces of the theatrical company—Mr Kyte, Mr Malvin, Miss Dimmock, Mrs Loran, not to mention the conductor, Mr Eves and his musicians. And what about the stagehands—Pauly, Henry, Judah and Rhydian? Were they *all* part of the charade? Were they *all* acting, even the ones who weren't actors? The scale of this undertaking was fantastic!

Looking at it now, it was all so obvious. This secret organization was counting on Mycroft being confused after his arrest in London and grabbing the first good opportunity to get to Moscow that came along. But Sherlock had been there as well, and so was Amyus Crowe, and so the organization had to get the two of them out of the way. That explained the attack in the museum. The organization was reacting quickly to unexpected events, which was why their plans had seemed so difficult to understand.

He was breathing fast now, feeling the excitement of knowing he was *right* flooding through his body and tingling every nerve.

213

It was all designed, every bit of it, to get Mycroft alone with Count Pyotr Andreyevich Shuvalov, the head of the Third Section, in Shuvalov's office. It all led to that moment. But why? Thinking back over everything that had happened, the answer was blindingly obvious to Sherlock. They wanted to kill Count Shuvalov, and they wanted Mycroft to be blamed. That was their modus operandi— they framed people for things they didn't do. They framed Mycroft for a murder, and then they framed Sherlock for pickpocketing.

Sherlock's gaze came up to meet Wormersley's. 'And you are part of it, aren't you?' The words came suddenly to his lips, but he knew them to be true. His mind, a split second behind, had all the proof laid out.

Wormersley gazed admiringly at Sherlock. 'You really are your brother's brother. Bravo!'

Silence fell across the cafe. It was as if all the other customers paused for a moment in their conversations or their eating and drinking, letting the moment run on.

Wormersley nodded. His thin lips twisted into a smile. 'Of course I am part of it. I'm not surprised that you realized, not surprised at all, given who your brother is, but I *am* interested to know what it was that gave me away.'

'Two things,' Sherlock replied. He tried to keep his voice calm. 'There's your beard, of course. You said you've been on the run for a week or more, going from bad hotel to bad hotel, but your beard and moustache are neatly trimmed. I would have thought you'd have more important things on your mind than personal grooming.'

Wormersley ran a hand across his chin. 'A good

214

point. I can never resist the urge to look my best. And the other thing?'

'Your apartment. It was supposed to have been searched, but the wreckage was too organized.' This, Sherlock realized, was what his mind had kept trying to direct his attention to when it was thinking about fragments of smashed figurines. 'If someone had really gone through the apartment pulling everything to bits then the fragments would be scattered randomly, but all the smaller broken ornaments were on top of the smashed furniture. Someone went through the apartment methodically, breaking the bigger stuff first, then the smaller stuff. That's not a search—that's setting a scene.'

Wormsley nodded. 'I will remember that for next time. Excellent observational skills, Mr Holmes. Excellent indeed.'

Sherlock looked around. 'We're in public, you know? You can hardly drag me out of here, kicking and screaming, without anyone reacting.'

'Oh, I think you underestimate the Russian ability to look away and not get involved.' He laughed abruptly. 'But just in case you wish to give it a try . . .'

He looked around the tiny cafe, and suddenly snapped his fingers.

Everyone in the cafe turned to look at him. There was no surprise on their faces. There was the look that soldiers give their commanding officer: patience while awaiting orders.

Sherlock stared at the two women across by the far wall. One was young, with brown hair pulled back beneath a headscarf, while the other was middle-aged and wore a fur hat. Miss Dimmock

215

and Mrs Loran? He couldn't tell, not for sure, not until the younger woman smiled at him and suddenly he could see the fine line of her jaw beneath her make-up.

The men—could they be Mr Malvin, Mr Furness, Mr Eves and the various musicians whose names Sherlock had never caught? The pit orchestra conductor, if it was him, had shaved his moustache off—or, more likely, removed his false moustache—but one of the men was tall enough to be him.

The man with the blotchy, potato-like face winked at Sherlock. He reached up and pulled at his puffy skin. Bits of it came away, like putty, and he peeled them off until his real face was revealed beneath: his red-veined cheeks and cauliflower-like nose. It was Mr Furness. 'That's a relief,' he said. 'Itches like hell! Theatrical putty, remember?'

Now that he was looking at their faces, he could see that the four children were actually Judah, Pauly, Henry and Rhydian, all bundled up against the cold, with dirt rubbed into their faces, false teeth in front of their own, pads in their cheeks to push them out and subtle make-up altering the lines of their faces. Pauly nodded at Sherlock; Henry just shrugged nonchalantly, as if this was an everyday occurrence.

Although he had worked out most of what was going on in a massive rush of deduction, Sherlock hadn't anticipated this.

'So what happens now?' he asked.

'Now,' Wormersley said, 'we just sit here, drink our tea and eat our pastries. The owner of the cafe won't disturb us: he is being paid enough to keep out of the way. We stay here until Count Pyotr

Andreyevich Shuvalov is dead and your brother has been arrested for the murder.'

'But what does that accomplish?' Sherlock asked. 'Why go to such lengths to get Mycroft here in Moscow, and in the right place? Why not just kill Count Shuvalov yourself?'

Wormersley shrugged. 'You have no idea how well-protected he is. He is never seen out in public, and when he travels he is always accompanied by bodyguards who have been with him for twenty years or more. They are fanatically loyal. When he travels he sends out several carriages in different directions, any of which might contain him. He is an important man, second only to the Tsar. No, believe me, we have tried. Many times. The only solution was to create a situation where we knew he would be alone in a place and at a time we knew about.'

'But what's he ever done to you?'

'He knows about us. He knows, and he disapproves. He wants to stop us.'

'And who *are* you?'

'We are the Paradol Chamber,' a voice said behind Sherlock.

The words sent a chill of fear through Sherlock.

He turned his head. Mrs Loran, the woman who had always been so kind to him, had crossed from her table to theirs. She was still smiling her sympathetic smile, bundled up in clothes that made her look like a Russian grandmother, but there was a hard glint in her eyes that Sherlock had not noticed before.

'What *is* the Paradol Chamber?' Sherlock's voice was unsteady with fear and disappointment that, once again, an adult he liked and trusted had let him down.

'An organization,' she said. 'A club. A group of like-minded individuals. A state of mind. Perhaps even a nation without territory. All of these things and more. We are the people who see the way the world is going and who have decided that we don't like it. We are the people who have decided to change the course of history.'

'So the whole thing about the sale of Alaska to America, and the possibility that the Americans might default on the payments and the Spanish might step in and buy it? That was all false?'

She laughed. 'No, it was all true. True, but largely irrelevant. Bait in a trap. The best lies are the ones that are mostly true. We just took advantage of a real political situation and set it up as bait for your brother. That, and the disappearance of Mr Wormersley here.'

'And what about Mycroft? Why him?'

'He was a convenient choice—a man who, although young, has become identified as being at the heart of the British Government. It will be difficult for your Prime Minister to claim that Mycroft Holmes was some kind of hot-headed idealist. I can't imagine anyone further from hot-headedness or idealism than Mycroft Holmes. No, when Mycroft is identified as Count Shuvalov's assassin then every government of the world will know that Great Britain has committed an act of state-sanctioned political murder. Britain will be a pariah nation. Nobody will listen to you any more. Your influence over world affairs will fade away.'

'And that's important to you? As important as getting rid of Count Shuvalov?'

'We are the Paradol Chamber,' Mrs Loran said

218

simply. 'When we do something, there is never just one reason. Each action that we take serves many different ends. It's neater that way.'

Sherlock gazed critically back at Wormersley. 'But why *you*? What dragged *you* into this whole thing?'

Wormersley glanced up at Mrs Loran as if seeking her permission to speak. She nodded.

'I've travelled a great deal,' Wormersley said, 'and everywhere I have been I have seen people abusing each other, enslaving each other and hurting each other, all in the name of politics or religion.' The distant expression on Wormersley's face suggested that he was remembering other times and other places. 'The world is descending into chaos. Somebody needs to step forward and take charge.' He smiled, and the smile was dreamy and dangerous at the same time. 'Imagine it, Sherlock—a *world* government! Not since the time of Alexander the Great has that been possible, and the world is much bigger now! I doubt that it will happen in my lifetime, but I can help make it possible—working for the Paradol Chamber.'

'More prosaically,' Mrs Loran said, 'Wormersley was in prison in Japan. The Japanese don't like outsiders. He would have been tortured and executed. We got a message to him, telling him that we would get him out if he would work for us.'

Sherlock frowned. 'But there's one thing I don't understand. Mycroft and Count Shuvalov will end up in Shuvalov's office, alone. What happens then? How does Shuvalov die, and how does Mycroft get blamed? You can't pull the ice knife trick again, surely? The count isn't going to stab himself.'

'The ice knife was a useful trick, and a good

rehearsal for some future assassination, but you're right—we can't use it again here. No, we have a different, plan, a better one.'

'What is it?' Sherlock asked.

'We'll leave that as a surprise, shall we?' she said.

Sherlock shook his head. 'Are all your plans this complicated? I know Mycroft got here, and was arrested, and is probably on the verge of being questioned by Count Shuvalov, but any number of things could have gone wrong at any stage. Mycroft might not have been released by the police, or he might have decided not to come, or he might have decided to make it an official visit under his own name, or Shuvalov might have decided to let someone else question Mycroft, or he might have questioned Mycroft in a cell—any of the links in the chain might have broken. The chances of this all coming right were astronomically low.'

'Don't think of it as a chain,' Wormersley explained. 'Think of it more as—oh, I don't know—a fishing net. Each knot is a decision, but there are many ways of getting from one side of the net to the other. For instance, if Mycroft hadn't been released by the police then we would have found legal advice for him, paid for by a well-known benefactor. We would have dropped clues—clues that would lead the police to evidence that would help to clear Mycroft's name, although not too easily. We were surprised when you and the big American got involved, but it saved us some trouble.' He shrugged. 'Although we had to try and get both of you out of the way at the museum, and then adjust our travel plans when it was clear that Mycroft wouldn't travel without you. If Mycroft hadn't taken the bait and headed to Moscow then we would have raised the stakes. Perhaps I would have sent him a personal message begging for help. One way or another—and many ways were planned—Mycroft would have come to Moscow, and once he was in Moscow we could slip word to the Third Section and have him picked up. Genius, they say, is an infinite capacity for detail, and the Paradol Chamber does have a number of certified geniuses working to further its aims. And so, inevitably, it all comes down to a single point, at three o'clock this afternoon, when Shuvalov will have Mycroft Holmes bought to his office, and will die.'

'But how do you *know* it will happen at three o'clock?' Sherlock asked helplessly. He considered himself intelligent, but he was in awe of the incredible patience and planning that the Paradol Chamber displayed.

'We have access to his diary,' Mrs Loran said quietly. 'A minor secretary who has been bribed. He never sees Shuvalov, never gets close enough to assassinate him, but he knows Shuvalov's movements. Shuvalov has a half-hour slot between three and three thirty this afternoon. Before that he is at a briefing in the Kremlin; after that he has an audience with the Tsar. If it happens today, it happens at three o'clock. If not today, then we know where the gaps in his schedule are for the rest of the week.'

'And what happens to me?'

Wormersley looked at Mrs Loran again.

'Oh, you know too much,' she said quietly. 'That's why Wormersley intercepted you at the hotel and bought you here—we needed to determine what you knew and what you might work out from that. The answer was that you know too much, and you *are* as clever as your brother. Baron Maupertuis told us, but we had to check. We can't let you live. You'll be taken out into the Russian countryside and disposed of. The bears and the wolves will clear up the traces for us.'

A shiver ran through Sherlock's body. Gazing around, he couldn't see any way out. He was surrounded by the agents of the Paradol Chamber. If he tried to run for it, they would be on him in seconds.

And Mycroft? Poor Mycroft, about to be framed for a murder he wouldn't have committed—again. Only this time there would be nobody to prove his innocence.

It might lead to war—war between Russia and England. A diplomatic incident of this magnitude could shift the axis of history. But wasn't that just what the Paradol Chamber wanted?

'Take him away,' Mrs Loran said over her shoulder to Mr Furness. 'Make sure that his body is never discovered.'

Mr Malvin came up behind Mrs Loran. He was holding a wooden box. Sherlock noticed that holes had been drilled in the top, but he couldn't work out why.

'This,' she said to Wormersley, indicating the box with a wave of her hand, 'is for you. Be careful with it. And remember—three o'clock, on the dot.'

She turned to Sherlock. 'Please understand, this is nothing personal. We have no animosity towards you, despite what happened with Baron Maupertuis. You are merely a stone in the road—a stone we need to remove before the cart of history goes past.'

'Come on,' Wormersley said, standing up. 'Let's get you to a place of extreme danger.'

Glass shattered on the stone basement steps outside. Sherlock glanced up just as the patio area exploded into flames.

CHAPTER FIFTEEN

Within seconds the cafe had filled up with greasy black smoke. Wormersley cursed and tried to grab Sherlock's shoulder, but Sherlock pulled away. His chair tipped over backwards, sending him toppling to the floor. Quickly he scrambled away on all fours, underneath a vacant table.

The other patrons of the cafe—the members of the theatrical company he'd travelled with, ate with, trusted—sprang to their feet, shocked by the sudden fire. Tables and chairs crashed to the floor.

'Get him!' Mrs Loran shouted. 'Get the boy!'

Flames were licking up the wooden front of the cafe now. Glass shattered in the heat. A table in the front, near the door, caught fire.

Something caught Sherlock's arm and pulled him away, towards the back of the cafe. He tried to resist, but a voice with an Irish accent said: 'If you only trust one person at one time in your life, lad, trust me now.'

Rufus Stone!

Sherlock let himself be dragged behind the counter by the back wall. One of Wormersley's people—Sherlock thought it was Mr Malvin, but he couldn't be sure—saw them and tried to get to them, but Stone pushed him to the floor.

A small door was half-hidden behind the counter. Stone pulled Sherlock through and shoved the door shut after him.

They were in a storeroom. Heavy bags of flour and crates of tea were piled around the walls. Stone started piling them against the door. Sherlock joined in, eyes stinging from the smoke.

'How are they going to get out?' he shouted.

'Not my problem,' Stone replied. He glanced across at Sherlock and, seeing the expression on his face, added: 'They can use some of the tables at the back as shields, push their way through to the steps. If they're quick they can get up to the road. People outside will be trying to put the fire out too. Don't worry—we're not condemning them to a fiery death, much as I might want to!'

'How did you start the fire?'

'Simple—there was a tea vendor with a cart just down the street. He was using spirits to heat the samovar.'

'The what?'

'The tea urn—it's called a samovar. He had a bottle of spirits. I just borrowed them, splashed them around outside while they were concentrating on you, and threw a lighted scrap of paper down on top. Worked nicely, even if I say so myself.'

Stone led Sherlock to the rear of the storeroom, where a set of stone steps led up into a small yard.

'How did you find me?' Sherlock asked.

'I was heading for the hotel to talk to Mr Holmes. I saw him being arrested, then I saw your path being crossed by a tall, dark stranger. I was intrigued, so I followed you here. Strange how much you can pick up if you're lurking outside an

224

open window.'

'You heard everything?'

Stone's face was grim. 'I did.'

The yard gave out on to a narrow alley that ran between buildings. Stone turned right and walked fast. Sherlock had to break into a near-run to keep up.

'So what do we do?' he asked breathlessly.

'We head for the the British Embassy and throw ourselves on the mercy of the Ambassador, that's what we do.'

'No!' Sherlock stopped dead.

'Come on,' Stone urged. 'We're at risk every moment we stay on the street.'

Sherlock stood where he was: stubborn; defiant, and bone-achingly tired. 'We have to get to my brother,' he said grimly.

'Look, lad, he's far beyond our help now. The best thing we can do is let the diplomatic staff sort things out. That's the kind of thing they live for, frankly: urgent diplomatic crises. That and cocktail parties. If we're lucky, they might be able to get to Count Shuvalov before Wormersley or Mrs Loran do.' He glanced back in the direction of the cafe. 'It depends on whether they managed to get out of there in one piece. We may have scotched their plans already.' He smiled. 'Or scorched them.'

'Their plans may not depend on them being present,' Sherlock pointed out. 'Mr Kyte wasn't in the cafe. There's no way he could have disguised himself. Maybe *he* controls the assassination attempt.'

Stone stared at Sherlock for a moment. 'I recognize that expression. You had that same look in your eye when you were trying to master scales and arpeggios back on the SS *Scotia*. You're a stubborn cuss, aren't you?'

Sherlock shrugged, momentarily embarrassed. 'It's a family trait,' he muttered.

Stone exhaled heavily. 'All right,' he conceded, 'let's at least go to the building where Shuvalov's office is located. We might be able to pass a warning note to the security guards on the door, or something.'

'Do you *know* where his office is?'

'Lubyanka Square.' Stone smiled mirthlessly. 'It's a well-known address in Moscow, although few people who get in ever get out again.' He checked his watch. 'We haven't got much time. If Wormersley's timings were correct, Mycroft will be brought in to see Shuvalov in about twenty minutes.'

Sherlock looked around. 'I don't see any cabs!'

'No time to wait,' Stone said. 'And we can get there faster on foot by cutting through alleyways.'

Stone led the way, running through the alleys and streets as if he'd lived in Moscow all his life. Sherlock sprinted after him. Buildings flashed past: different colours, but similar blocky architecture. People moved out of their way as they ran, not willing to make eye contact. Flocks of starlings and sparrows took flight as the two of them plunged in among them. The air was bitterly cold, and even as Sherlock felt warm sweat trickling down his ribs and spine from the exertion he could also feel his face tingling as the snow crystals in the wind whipped against his skin. He imagined that his cheeks were covered by thousands of tiny cuts left by the crystals. The thought reminded him of Mr Kyte's face, and the small cuts around his eyes, cheeks and nose. What had caused them? he wondered. He supposed he would never know.

His heart pounded in time with his footsteps. He'd run races at school, but they had been short and intense—just a dash for the ribbon. This was a marathon: unending, almost unendurable.

The thudding of his footsteps vibrated up his legs, rattling every bone in his body. Snow was underfoot everywhere. At one point, while racing across a road and dodging the various carriages and wagons, Sherlock's foot hit a patch of ice and skidded backwards. For one terrible moment he thought he was going to fall. His arms windmilled helplessly as his body pitched forward and he tried to keep his balance. The moment seemed to last forever, but finally he bumped into a passing Russian woman, bundled up in layers of clothes, and managed to regain his stability. 'Sorry!' he called back over his shoulder.

He tried to force his legs to move faster. Stone was well ahead of him.

The fluttering of startled starlings and sparrows taking flight around him became mixed up with a fluttering in the corners of Sherlock's eyes. The world seemed to close in on itself as he chased the fleeting shape that was Rufus Stone.

Eventually, Stone began to slow down. It took the length of an entire alleyway for him to come to a stop. Sherlock drew up beside him, lungs burning. He sucked in great breaths of air, bending over with his hands on his knees. It was like breathing fire. Stone was leaning against a nearby wall, coughing.

After a minute or so both of them had recovered enough to talk.

'We're on Lubyanka Square,' Stone puffed. He jerked his head, indicating the building across the road. 'That's the Headquarters of Section Three.'

Sherlock let his gaze run up the building. It was more like a fortress: small, narrow windows with bars in front of the glass, smooth red stonework that nobody could climb, turret-like towers on the corners from which guards would have a good view along the sides of the building and could, presumably, fire at any attacking mob.

Across the road was a handful of wagons, carriages and carts, pulled up against the pavement so that their drivers could rest. Presumably too, so that any important and therefore high-tipping Russians leaving the building could be assured of finding transport straight away.

'Which office belongs to Count Shuvalov?' Sherlock asked hoarsely.

Stone's eyes scanned the various windows. 'I won't point,' he said. 'I don't want to attract any more attention than we've already managed with our little athletic display. Let your gaze fall on the tower to the left, then let it drift along the edge of the roof until you come to an open window that's larger than the rest and set out slightly from the building. That's his office.' He paused to cough again. 'Note the extra bars, and the fact that there's no way to get to it from below, the side or above. No ledges. The glass is darkened so that nobody outside could aim at a target inside, and if you look around you'll notice that it's the tallest building in the vicinity. There's no vantage point for a marksman. Inside is just as bad: reports are that you have to go through six different security checkpoints before you get to the guards outside the door of his office—and they are hand-picked by Shuvalov himself. I really can't see how Wormersley can hope to assassinate the man.'

Sherlock stared up at the office window. He checked his watch. Nearly three o'clock! If the Paradol Chamber were correct—and he suspected they were always correct—Mycroft would be on his way to the office right now!

He glanced around, looking for anything out of the ordinary, anything that might give a hint as to what was going to happen next.

And he noticed something.

'No birds,' he pointed out.

'What?'

'No birds. This city is full of starlings and sparrows, but where are they now? I can't see any.'

Stone glanced around. 'You're right, but I'm not sure what point you're making.'

'What frightens birds away?'

The violinist shrugged. 'Cats?'

'Cats, yes, and other birds. Birds of prey.'

Stone frowned, then his eyes widened in understanding. 'That falcon Mycroft told me about, back in the museum in London! You think *that*'s Wormersley's plan?'

'Look at the office window,' Sherlock urged. 'Nobody could get to it, not from the outside and not from the inside, from what you've said. But a bird could *fly* there.'

'And do what? The bird isn't going to able to stab or shoot Shuvalov, and if it just attacks him with its claws then there's no way Wormersley can make it look like Mycroft's responsible for the attack.'

Sherlock's thoughts were firing off in all

229

directions. 'When that falcon attacked me in the museum, it had something attached to its claws— some kind of sharp blade. Imagine that Mycroft has been taken to Shuvalov's office, through all those security checks. It's just Shuvalov and Mycroft in the office. Wormersley's trained falcon flies in through the open window and makes straight for Shuvalov. It slashes the blade across his throat, cutting deeply, then it flies out again. Shuvalov cries out, perhaps, or maybe Mycroft calls for help. Shuvalov's guards run in. All they see is Shuvalov bleeding to death from a cut throat and Mycroft standing there, in a room where no other person could get in or out!'

'But Mycroft won't have a knife,' Stone pointed out.

'It doesn't matter. All the evidence is against him. They'll assume he just threw the knife, or the razor blade, or whatever, out of the window!'

'I'm not sure . . . What if the window was closed?'

'Then they would probably use a slingshot and stone to smash it so that the falcon would fly inside. In the confusion afterwards they would assume that Mycroft had smashed it trying to escape. This is the Paradol Chamber. They think of everything! It makes sense! I never understood why I was attacked with a *falcon* of all things. Who takes a live falcon to a museum of stuffed birds? They must have been training it there, using the museum as a base of operations.'

A memory flashed up in his mind, and he plunged his hand into his jacket pocket. There, nestling next to the glass bottle from the Diogenes Club, the one from the dead man's jacket, was the small shape of the dead mouse he'd found in the train on the way from Dunkerque to Moscow and forgotten about. It fitted perfectly into his palm. 'And this must have come from its food supply,' he said urgently. 'I found it on the train. Mr Kyte must have been looking after the bird—that's why he spent so much time in his compartment during the journey. He was keeping it calm and fed, making sure it didn't escape.'

'Let's assume you're right.' Stone glanced around. 'Where will they be flying it from?'

'Somewhere close at hand. Possibly a building— if they could get access to the roof or an empty room.' Sherlock looked around urgently. 'Or somewhere on the street, maybe.'

His gazed snagged on a black carriage that was stationary on the other side of the street. It was just like the other carriages that rattled past, but something about it drew Sherlock's attention. Perhaps it was the bulk of the driver, or the unsuccessful way he was trying to hide his bushy red beard beneath a scarf.

'Over there,' he said urgently. 'That carriage.'

Stone followed his gaze. 'That's Mr Kyte.'

'I thought so.'

'Wormersley will be inside. With the falcon, if you're right.' His gaze switched to the building that was home to the Third Section. 'We have to go to the front desk—get them to take a warning note up to Count Shuvalov.'

'No time!' Sherlock said.

Over at the carriage, the window facing the building had been pulled down to leave a gap.

Something appeared in the dark square that was all Sherlock could see of the carriage's inside. An arm—an arm with a brown-feathered bird sitting on it. Maybe it was the bird that had attacked him at the museum in London, maybe it was a different one, but it looked just as lethal.

A low whistle cut through the air: three notes; the same kind of whistle Sherlock had heard at the museum.

'A flat, E, G sharp,' Stone murmured.

The falcon took off, bounding into the air with a thrust of its legs and then pushing down hard with its wings once, twice, three times, hauling itself into the sky. It coasted for a moment, orienting itself, then flapped its wings again, gaining more and more height. The sun glinted cruelly off two curved metal blades attached to its legs, just above the claws.

The man in the carriage—Wormersley?—whistled again, different notes this time, and the falcon adjusted its course, curving slightly to the left and straightening up. The whistles were guiding it to the correct window! Wormersley had probably trained it on a replica of the building, or something painted to look the same, but he wasn't taking any chances. He was aiming the bird right where he wanted it to go.

'We're too late,' Stone said.

'No,' Sherlock said, and there was such certainty in his voice that he even surprised itself. '*No!*'

He clenched his fist, the one that was holding the dead mouse, and drew it back. Balancing himself with his left arm outstretched in front of him, he threw the mouse the way a fielder would throw a cricket ball.

The tiny corpse arced through the air towards the open window. Sherlock whistled, trying to replicate the sound of Wormersley's commands. The falcon's head twisted round to see who else dared signal it. The dead mouse, just beginning its long drop back to the ground, caught its eye. The falcon twisted in mid-air and dived. The mouse was falling under gravity, but the falcon propelled itself forward with two powerful strokes of its wings and then folded them close to its body. It shot through the air, its path converging with that of the mouse.

Its beak opened and then closed, and the mouse was gone, swallowed whole.

More whistles filled the air as Wormersley tried urgently to regain control of the bird, but hunger had won out over training. Falcons had to be kept hungry, Sherlock knew, otherwise they would lose interest in what their handlers wanted them to do. The bird coasted in a broad curve back towards the carriage. Towards the closest thing it had to a nest at the moment: the covered box that Wormersley had been given at the cafe.

In the square of darkness inside the carriage, Sherlock saw Wormersley's face floating like that of a ghost, a mask of twisted frustration.

Sherlock thought of the signals that he'd heard in the museum: the signals that had instructed the falcon to attack. He forced his brain to remember the notes. He could play the violin—to a degree. He could read music. He could surely identify a musical note if he had to.

He whistled loudly, repeating the phrase that he remembered.

Descending towards the carriage, the falcon heard the signal. Instead of readying itself for a landing on its handler's outstretched arm, it spread its claws into two vicious instruments of

233

destruction.

It plunged through the carriage window and into Wormersley's face.

A scream burst from the inside of the carriage, and the whole thing rocked on its wheels as Wormersley struggled with the bird inside. Kyte, sitting on top of the carriage, twisted round to see what was happening. Startled, the horse that was attached to the shafts reared up on its hind legs.

'Come on!' Sherlock shouted to Stone. 'You get Kyte—I'll get Wormersley.'

'But—'

'Come *on*!'

He wasn't going to let the Paradol Chamber get away, not if he could stop them. They had too many deaths on their hands, too much explaining to do. He was going to pull Wormersley out of that carriage with his bare hands and force him to tell Count Shuvalov exactly what he had planned to do.

Aware that Stone was heading past him, aiming for the preoccupied Kyte, Sherlock hurled himself at the nearest carriage door. As he got to it the door burst open towards him, knocking him backwards, into the street. Wormersley jumped out, pulling the falcon off his head as he did so and throwing it towards Sherlock. His face and shirt were streaked with blood, and there were beak marks in his forehead and slashes across his throat.

In a flurry of wings the falcon took flight. Training only went so far: all it wanted now was its freedom.

Wormersley rubbed his sleeve across his face, smearing the blood into a crimson mask from which his eyes blazed angrily.

'You meddling, interfering *brat*!' he screamed.

'That plan was years in the making, and you *ruined* it in moments!'

'Give up,' Sherlock said. He was braced in case Wormersley made a move towards him. 'There's no way out.'

'There's always a way out.' Wormersley reached behind him and pulled something out of the carriage. It looked like a hoop in his hand, a child's toy hoop, but then he shook his hand and it uncoiled to the ground.

It was a whip, but not like anything Sherlock had ever seen before. Not like the one Mr Surd, Baron Maupertuis's manservant, had used against him months ago. No, this one looked like it was made from plaited metal, and attached to its tip was a sharp metal talon.

'You remember I mentioned the Russian *knout*?' Wormersley asked. 'Well, you're about to get *much* better acquainted with it.'

He lashed out suddenly, flicking the whip. The tip whined as it sliced through the air. Sherlock flinched to one side and the hooked metal tip brushed past his ear.

It caught on his jacket as Wormersley pulled it back.

Sherlock's body jerked forward, pulling him off balance. He went sprawling to his hands and knees on the snow-covered ground.

Wormersley moved behind Sherlock and looped the *knout* round his throat. He pulled tight, snapping Sherlock's neck back and cutting off his air supply.

Sherlock's vision went red. He desperately tried to claw air into his chest, but nothing was getting past the steel links of the *knout* as they bit into his flesh. He scrabbled with his fingers, attempting to get them beneath the metal, but Wormersley was pulling so tight that there was no gap.

The red mist across his eyes started to turn black. The world receded into a fuzzy blur of light and noise.

Sherlock lashed backwards with his right foot, but Wormersley had moved his legs out of range, leaning forward to strangle Sherlock. His knuckles dug into the back of Sherlock's neck.

'Die!' he hissed, bringing his head close to Sherlock's left ear. 'Just *die*!'

Trying to find some purchase on the ground, some leverage he could use to push himself upright, Sherlock's hand brushed the outside of his jacket pocket. He felt something hard and curved inside—the spray bottle from the Diogenes Club. The one that had been used to drug Mycroft.

With his vision turning black and his ears filled with the thudding of his pulse, Sherlock used the last of his strength to pull the bottle from his pocket. He fumbled with it, trying to get his thumb on to the spring-loaded button on top. He didn't even know which direction it was pointing, but he held it above his head and pushed the button frantically.

Behind him, Wormersley gasped. His hands went slack. Sherlock fell forward, pulling great gulps of air into his lungs. He turned over on to his back, raising his hands to ward Wormersley off if the man attacked again, but through the fading red mist Sherlock saw Wormersley standing still, staring into nowhere, with a dazed expression on his face.

Sherlock closed his eyes and let his head fall

back against the cobbled road.

Hands grabbed Sherlock and pulled him away. He thought for a moment that it was Mr Kyte, but other hands unwound the metal and leather thong of the *knout* from his neck. Turning his head, he saw that he was surrounded by soldiers in blue and grey uniforms. One soldier was holding him while another was freeing him from the *knout*. A third soldier was taking hold of Wormersley, whose face was almost unrecognizably swollen beneath the blood. A fourth soldier was pulling Rufus Stone from around the other side of the carriage. Stone was bleeding from a gash in his arm, a cut that went all the way through the material of his jacket to the flesh beneath.

There was no sign of Mr Kyte.

The next few minutes were a blur. Sherlock and Rufus Stone were bundled into the grim Lubyanka Square building and half-pushed, half-dragged along dark corridors and up flights of stairs. Sherlock lost track of where they were in the building. Eventually they were taken past uniformed guards and into a series of linked offices.

In the last office, two men were standing waiting for them.

One was also in military uniform, but it was much more ornate than the ones the soldiers were wearing, and he had a cloak thrown over it. He was in his forties, his hair grey and close-cropped, and his moustache curled up at the ends. The other was in his twenties, wearing a black suit and a striped waistcoat.

'Ah, Sherlock,' Mycroft said calmly. 'This is His Excellency Count Pyotr Andreyevich Shuvalov.

Count Shuvalov, allow me to present my brother, Sherlock.'

Shuvalov stared at Sherlock. Finally he glanced back at Mycroft.

'Yes,' he said in excellent English. 'I presume *he* must take after your father's side of the family.'

CHAPTER SIXTEEN

The dining room at the Diogenes Club was as silent as a tomb, which was why Mycroft had arranged for their meal to be served in the Strangers Room. At least there the four of them could have a reasonable conversation.

Mycroft was at the head of the table, with Sherlock to his left and Amyus Crowe to his right. Rufus Stone was seated opposite Mycroft.

Looking around, Sherlock found it difficult to remember that this was the very room where the whole adventure had started. He checked the carpet for bloodstains, remembering the unfortunate man who had been so desperate for his family to have a little money that he had killed himself on the instructions of the Paradol Chamber, just to provoke Mycroft into going to Russia. Either it had been expertly cleaned or the entire carpet had been replaced.

Mycroft and Crowe were discussing what the American government were going to do with Alaska now that they had finally paid for it. Sherlock turned his attention back to his dinner. Silent black-clad waiters delivered bowls of soup to the table.

Crowe stared dubiously at the creamy reddish liquid. 'This surely ain't fit for human consumption?' he asked. 'It looks like somethin' made up out of cow's blood an' milk.'

'It's borscht,' Mycroft replied. 'Russian beetroot soup with *smetana*, or sour cream, stirred in. I thought that we should share a little memento of our adventures with you. Our chef has been very cooperative. Unusually adventurous, in fact. I wasn't sure that he could even attempt anything other than Brown Windsor soup, but he was eager for a challenge.'

'Talking of challenges,' Stone said, 'is there any news of Mr Kyte?' His hand crept up to rest on his right arm, where a dressing concealed a nasty cut. There was an edge to his words that suggested to Sherlock that he felt he had unfinished business with the burly red-headed man.

Mycroft shook his large head sorrowfully. 'Not a word. He seems to have gone to ground. I presume the Paradol Chamber are looking after him somewhere—assuming they have a forgiving nature, of course.'

'What about the rest of Kyte's Theatrical Company?' Sherlock asked.

'As with Mr Kyte, they are missing, presumed hiding.' His face was grave. 'To have been that close to the Paradol Chamber—to have been that close to Mrs Loran, who I now believe is one of their most important members—and not to have realized . . . it galls me, Sherlock. My mind was affected by the accusation of murder and my subsequent, although short, incarceration. I should have realized there was something odd about that

239

entire company. I should have realized that we were being set up from the start.'

'And Wormersley?'

'Now, there I do have an answer. For understandable reasons, Count Shuvalov would not release him to us. He languishes in the cells at Lubyanka Square. Ironic, considering the fact that we went all the way to Moscow because that's where I thought he was to begin with.' He sighed. 'He changed. He was not the man I thought he was. But then, I suppose that travelling the world does that to you, which is why I fully intend to do as little travelling as humanly possible for the rest of my life.'

'Ah'm surprised Shuvalov believed you so readily,' Crowe rumbled, still staring dubiously into the bowl. He stirred the soup experimentally with his spoon.

'That's another irony,' Mycroft said. 'I knew Shuvalov considerably less well than I knew Wormersley, and yet in the end it was that relationship which survived on trust and the other that failed. Shuvalov and I understand each other. We think alike. When he was informed that I had been arrested, he immediately called for me to be brought to him. We drank tea, and we talked in a very civilized manner. He apologized for any harsh behaviour his men had exhibited, and I apologized for arriving in his country without proper notification. That is the way international relations ought to be conducted: politely and with refreshments, not using trained falcons as instruments of assassination.'

'An' he believed the whole crazy story?'

'Once Sherlock told his story, it was obvious that

the evidence backed it up. People had seen the falcon, with its metal claws, fly into the carriage, and they'd seen both the fight between Sherlock and Wormersley and the fight between Mr Stone and Mr Kyte. And Shuvalov had already received reports of my arrest here in London for murder. He has his own agents in London, of course, as I have—or had—in Russia.' He paused, thoughtfully. 'Although his agents probably *don't* work secretly for the Paradol Chamber, which is a point to him in our ongoing game.'

'Game?' Sherlock queried.

'The continual strategic struggle between Russia and Great Britain for control of Central Asia— Afghanistan and India. We call it the Great Game.'

'Father is in India,' Sherlock pointed out. 'He's fighting out there. It's hardly a game, Mycroft.'

Mycroft had the grace to look abashed. 'You're right, dear boy. It is not a game, let alone a great one. Sitting here in London, in a comfortable armchair, it is possible to lose track of that. Perhaps if my time in Russia has taught me one thing, it is that the pieces that we so blithely move on the chessboard are real people, with real feelings. That is a lesson I will remember.' He smiled tentatively. 'But you have reminded me that I still owe you sight of Father's letter, which he sent from India, and which you travelled up from Farnham to see. I have it with me. I will let you read it later.'

Amyus Crowe cleared his throat. 'So what's the plan now?' he asked, obviously seeking to change the subject to something lighter. 'Where do we go from here? For myself, ah'm plannin' to spend some time with my daughter.'

'I intend going back to my lodgings and my job,'

Mycroft said.

'I suppose I'm heading back to Holmes Manor, to my aunt and uncle, and to the wonderful Mrs Eglantine,' Sherlock said morosely. He looked over at Rufus Stone. For a moment his thoughts turned to Farnham, and to the black-clad woman who had been watching him, and who had vanished in an alleyway. At the time he'd assumed it was Mrs Eglantine, but now he wasn't sure. Maybe it had been Miss Aiofe Dimmock checking on Mycroft's brother before the Paradol Chamber swung their complicated plan into action. Or maybe it *had* been Mrs Eglantine. Sherlock decided there and then that when he returned to Holmes Manor he was going to get to the bottom of that particular mystery, and find out the true nature of the hold she had over his family.

'What about you, Mr Stone?' Mycroft asked, breaking into Sherlock's train of thought.

Stone smiled and glanced at Sherlock. A gold tooth towards the back of his mouth twinkled in the candlelight. 'I understand that you have a fine violin,' he said. 'I was hoping you would give me the pleasure of hearing you play it. Twice a week, for an hour a time. Do Tuesdays and Thursdays suit you?'

'Perfectly,' said Sherlock.

HISTORICAL NOTES

The museum in which Sherlock is attacked by a bird of prey is based on my memories of the Passmore Edwards Museum in Stratford, East London. I remember being taken there on school trips back in the early 1970s, and my overriding impression is of the sheer number of stuffed animals scattered around the old Victorian hallways (that, and the very musty smell). I've since discovered that John Passmore Edwards (1823–1911) was a British journalist and newspaper owner whose bequests resulted in the construction of 70 major buildings (primarily hospitals, libraries, schools, convalescence homes and art galleries) as well as 11 drinking fountains and 32 marble busts. A true Victorian philanthropist.

The Necropolis Railway really did exist. Only the Victorians could have thought of having a railway specifically for the dead. To be fair, if the Egyptians had known about railways they probably would have thought of it too, but only the Victorians would have charged different ticket prices for First, Second and Third Class travel for the coffins. I first came across mention of the Necropolis Railway in a book about the things that are hidden beneath London's streets, and have since chased up more details in other similar books. The important ones are:

London Under London: A Subterranean Guide by Richard Trench and Ellis Hillman (John Murray, 1993)

Underground London: Travels Beneath the City Streets by Stephen Smith (Abacus, 2005)

Necropolis: London and Its Dead by Catharine Arnold (Pocket Books, 2005)

The King's Theatre in Whitechapel is based to a large extent on the Theatre Royal, Stratford. When I was at school, I used to do a fair amount of amateur dramatics, and some of the shows we did were put on at the Theatre Royal. It was built in 1888, and I spent a lot of time wandering around the backstage areas soaking up the atmosphere.

Sherlock and Mycroft's sojourn in Russia was, surprisingly, very difficult to research. The majority of history books on the country concentrate on the Russian revolution (1917), the years of the Soviet Union (principally concentrating on Lenin, Trotsky and Stalin), and the time since the Soviet Union fell apart. The mid-nineteenth century is a bit of a blank. Eventually I decided to come at it sideways, through the Crimean War (1853–56), but I did discover late in the day a book which took quotes from Russian writers of around the right time and wove them into a kind of descriptive document. For the record, the books were:

A Brief History of the Crimean War by Alexander Troubetzkoy (Robinson, 2006)

Literary Russia: A Guide by Anna Benn, Rosamund Bartlett (Gerald Duckworth & Co, 2007)

I do admit, with some shame, that Wikipedia provided quite a lot of background detail on the Tsar, his secret police, and the Alaska land deal. Late in the day I discovered some issues of the *London Illustrated News* online, dating from the 1850s. A couple of these had reports from a journalist who had travelled to Moscow, and I shamelessly borrowed some of his descriptions of the city and its inhabitants.

Count Pyotr Andreyevich Shuvalov was a real person, and he really was in charge of the Third Section, which was actually the Tsar's secret police force. Shuvalov did spend some time in France, which is where he would have met Mycroft Holmes. Prince Yusupov was also a real person, and a well-known patron of the arts.

And on a non-historical note, I can echo Sherlock's thoughts in the last chapter and reveal that the next book—which will probably be entitled *Fire Storm*—will tell (among other things) of how Sherlock finally confronts the unpleasant Mrs Eglantine.

Until then . . .